DISHONORABLE

NATASHA KNIGHT

A NOTE FROM NATASHA

It's taken me a long time to write this book. After writing Dominic, my brain was tired and I needed a little rest. Some books do that to you. Actually, at this point, I guess all books do that to me. That's a good thing because I hope what I'm giving you is memorable every single time.

Dishonorable came to me the way most of my stories come—with a very clear image of the hero, in this case, Raphael. Or, more accurately, his eyes.

I knew going in that the story would be set in Italy and that the chapel and the cellar were important pieces, even though at first, I wasn't sure why or what I was going to do with them. But one thing I'm learning is to trust that the story will come as it comes and that in the end, all those pieces I wasn't quite sure about will fall into their place.

Raphael is, in his own words, a *"wrecked monster."*

And to me, he is broken and some parts of him will never heal or stop hurting, but I think that's okay.

I have a favorite quote from The Tale of Despereaux and it goes like this: "Sometimes when a heart breaks, it can grow back crooked." I guess in a way, that's what happened to Raphael. But there's this clichéd saying that love conquers all that I believe with all my heart. And I often think those nicks and cracks we all have only make us better able to feel, better able to love.

So, without taking up more of your time, I want to say thank you for trusting me to take you on this ride along with Raphael and Sofia.

x

Natasha

PROLOGUE 1

SOFIA

July 2016

I shuddered at the sweep of cold air that rushed me when the basilica doors opened. They carried a warning. An omen.

My husband-to-be stood at the head of the aisle dressed in black from head to toe, opposite my bridal white.

Like a funeral.

Like my funeral.

He was striking, even if I hated him. His victorious eyes devoured me whole without ever leaving my own, trapping me, predator and prey. I wondered if his mouth was watering, saliva wet on his tongue, as he imagined my submission, my yielding to him.

I knew what was expected of me tonight. What he and my grandfather had worked into the contract that made me Raphael Amado's property. We must consummate. My virgin blood must stain his sheets. My face burned with shame and fury, and each step reminded me that it was the devil I was about to marry. A monster, hiding beneath the most beautiful mask. And I knew as I walked toward my unchosen, unwanted destiny that I would never forgive my grandfather for his betrayal.

PROLOGUE 2

RAPHAEL

July 2016

She stood like a vestal virgin at the doors, her golden gaze arctic as it swept down the aisle to collide with mine. She masked her thoughts well, but when she lay beneath me tonight, I would own her. I would know her pleasure. Her pain. I would possess every inch of her.

She belonged to me already, even if she couldn't stomach the idea. I wondered if I'd have to make her tonight. If I'd have to pry her legs apart and hold her down to soak my cock in her virgin's blood. I needed to get that thought out of my head, though. It wouldn't be right to stand before God and man with a fucking hard-on.

I watched her as she commenced to walk down the aisle: stunning, striking—and on my twin brother's arm. She'd refused her grandfather. Beautiful, that. He deserved only her hate.

Her thick chestnut hair with its intricate braids had been arranged on top of her head. Even with the lace draping her pale face, I could see her eyes, set and accusing, burning into me, at odds with her soft, full lips and innocent, almost cherublike features.

When she reached me, my brother lifted the veil from her face. The look they exchanged grated on my nerves. They'd become fast friends.

Before handing her over to me, he pierced me with a look of clear disapproval. As if what I was doing was just for me. As if it weren't for him too. As if I didn't deserve everything I took, after what I'd been put through. His look accused me of stealing this virgin bride as if *I* were some sort of monster.

Well, he hadn't walked the last few years in my shoes, so he could go fuck himself.

I shifted my gaze from my brother to Sofia, let it sweep down over her, seeing her in the dress I'd chosen. She only narrowed her shadowed eyes at me for that, but she didn't fight, not when I covered her hand with mine, not when I drew her down to kneel before God. And when time came to promise to love, cherish, and obey—yes, I made sure to include the vow of obedience—Sofia spoke the words that would seal her fate and mine.

I do.

That was all it took, and she was mine.

And when we stood and faced each other as husband and wife, I wrapped my hand around the back of her neck and drew her to me, claiming her mouth with my own, announcing to anyone who had any doubt at all, that I owned this woman.

That she was mine.

And what was mine, no man had better put asunder.

Because I'd fucking kill any bastard who tried.

1

Christmas 2015

The Christmas holiday was my favorite time of year, and this year, because the twenty-fifth fell on a Saturday, St. Sebastian's Preparatory School gave us a full additional week off. This was my last year at the private school. As grueling as the work was and as uptight as the nuns could be, I kind of liked it. The old mansion that housed the girls was beautiful. The boys lived across the vast property in a second, more modern mansion. I loved the grounds, the thick woods that surrounded the remote school, and even the small room I shared with another student.

My grandfather's mansion, although beautiful,

was very different from the school. Driving along the familiar curve of the winding driveway and seeing the large, white stone house come into view was always a bittersweet moment for me. It made me miss my parents, especially my mom. That never seemed to change.

Then I saw my sister, Lina's, face peering out the window. I wished Lina attended the same school as me. She had a gift for piano that I did not, though, so she went to a special music academy near home. She complained her poor fingers were worn-out, but I knew she loved playing.

We came to a stop at the front door, behind an SUV I didn't recognize.

"Who's SUV is that?" I asked Stephen, a man who'd worked for my grandfather ever since Lina and I had moved into his house.

"Raphael Amado. He arrived early this morning, just an hour before I left to pick you up."

My school was about a two-hour drive from Grandfather's house, and every Christmas, my grandfather sent Stephen to pick me up. Only once had my sister been allowed to come with him.

"Raphael Amado?" I didn't recognize the name.

"Business associate."

He climbed out of the car, his glance toward the house more serious than it had been during our drive back.

Before I could ask if everything was okay, the

curtains moved, and Lina disappeared from behind the window. I guessed she was running to the front doors.

"I'll bring your bags, Sofia. Your sister's waiting, so go on in. She was upset she couldn't come with me as it is."

Stephen was always so much kinder than Grandfather. "I hope he's not going to make her study during break."

He opened the trunk and unloaded my two suitcases, looking like his mind was elsewhere. I peered into the SUV and noticed a man sitting behind the steering wheel.

"Your grandfather only wants what's best for you both."

That was at times hard to believe.

Smoke puffed out of the chimneys. The front door flew open, and Lina ran out, stopping just a few steps outside the door. She wore no shoes, and she stood there hugging her arms to herself in the freezing morning air. We were going to have a white Christmas.

"Lina!" I ran up the stairs to meet her, hugging her tight. Her full name was Katalina Guardia, but we'd always called her Lina.

"Finally! This house is completely boring without you."

We pulled back to look at each other. Lina, who

at sixteen was almost two years younger than me, was nearly my height now.

"Damn!" I shook my head, teasing.

"Are you allowed to say that?" She winked.

"You look wonderful. And so tall! You get that from dad." Her smile drooped at the mention. Our parents had died on the day after Christmas eleven years ago. It had been their first trip alone together since having Lina and I, a sort of second honeymoon in Thailand. Their bodies had never been recovered after the tsunami.

"Nah, you still have half an inch on me."

She shrugged her shoulder and pulled me inside.

"It's freezing. Come in."

"Sofia!"

Marjorie came running around the corner. I gave her a huge smile and let her wrap me in her warm, soft hug. "Marjorie. I missed you so much."

"So did I, honey. So did I."

After our parents had died and Grandfather had taken us in, he'd hired several nannies. Marjorie had been the longest lasting of the bunch. When we were younger, she was our full-time, live-in nanny. She essentially raised us. Now she came three days a week. Lina had been three, nearly four, and I'd been five. I knew Lina's memories of our parents were vague, if they existed at all, and as my own images of them had faded, Marjorie had become a source of warmth and compassion in an otherwise cold house.

"Shh, now," Stephen said, following us in and closing the door.

Marjorie straightened and glanced at the study.

"Why do we have to shush?" Surely Grandfather could forgive a few cries of happiness at our reunion. It had been months since I'd seen my sister or Marjorie.

Lina gestured toward the closed study door. "He's in a meeting with Mr. Amado. He's been here three days this week, and Grandfather is very hush-hush about it all."

"Who is he?"

"No idea. I haven't even seen him. He won't introduce me, and I swear he only lets him in and out of that room after making sure the coast is clear and I'm out of sight. Weird."

"That is weird." I turned to Stephen. "I'll just pop in and say hi." Although one didn't just pop in with my grandfather. He wasn't like a normal grandparent. He pretty much kept his distance, and honestly, it always felt like we were more of an obligation, a burden to him. Well, at least I was. He seemed to have slightly more affection for Lina, and I knew their relationship had improved over the last four years.

He shook his head. "I'm sure they'll be out soon. Why don't you and Lina have lunch first?"

"Yes, come on. I've already set the table for the three of us," Marjorie said.

"See, weird," Lina whispered in my ear. "We'll be right there, Marjorie."

Marjorie nodded and headed toward the kitchen, and Stephen disappeared somewhere. Lina led me into the living room where the huge Christmas tree stood ready to be decorated. I smiled a little when I saw the open boxes of ornaments, recognizing them, liking the familiarity of the decorating ritual Lina and I had started together after our parents' death. She was too young to remember, but I had memories of decorating the Christmas tree with our parents in our little house. It was always a bittersweet memory.

Lina took my hand. "Let's have lunch. I want to hear everything. You know, boys, gossip, who's doing who. Although I guess you'll have to tell me that later when we're alone." She waggled her eyebrows.

I rolled my eyes. "There isn't much to tell. The nuns are like freaking police."

"Oh, come on. I'm locked up in here most days with tutors and piano teachers. Make something up if you have to."

"Well, there *is* this one girl..." I started as we headed into the kitchen.

After lunch, Lina started to unpack the ornaments while I went up to my bedroom to change clothes. They'd still made us wear our uniforms this morning, even though most of us were just going home for the holiday. I felt sorry for the few students who spent the holiday at school.

I was at the top of the stairs when I realized I'd forgotten my purse in the foyer. I went back down to grab it, mostly wanting to check my phone for messages, when I heard a low, deep male voice I didn't recognize.

"It's done, old man."

I froze at the bottom of the stairs. *Old man?*

"You cannot do this."

My grandfather's voice was stern, his tone angry, rattled. I'd never heard him like that before. He always spoke quietly, never raised his voice, didn't need to. In his late sixties, he was still a formidable man.

My mother had been his only surviving child, and I remembered well the night I'd met my grandfather. Our parents had never brought us here, and Lina had been a baby when he'd come to our house one evening. I could almost feel the panic that had emanated from my mother. He'd stood in our hallway, too tall, too big almost for the place. When he'd looked at me, his hard expression had sent me scurrying to hide behind my mother's legs. We'd been sent to bed, but I'd known the exact moment he'd left. I hadn't been able to sleep that night, not for the sudden fear I felt at the sound of my parents arguing, my mother crying.

"*You* did it, old man. You brought this on yourself."

I guessed the unknown person was Raphael Amado.

Heavy footsteps echoed off the marble floors. I stood frozen at the bottom of the stairs. I couldn't make myself move, even though I knew I should. Holding tight to the banister, I don't think I breathed as the stranger came into view.

He didn't see me at first, he was so deep in thought. His face, tight and hard, betrayed his feelings, but he looked different than I'd guessed he would.

"Amado!" my grandfather roared.

Raphael Amado halted.

I must have made a sound because he turned his head. When his eyes met mine, I gasped and clung to the banister. A cold chill iced my veins. He was younger than I expected. Much younger. And... beautiful. Never before this moment had I described a man as being beautiful. He was tall with dark hair and olive skin, with steely blue eyes that didn't seem to fit with his dark features. They pierced me through, spiking me where I stood, so that even if I wanted to, I couldn't have moved. I don't think I breathed for as long as he held my gaze. I could see the anger raging, burning behind the ice of those glacial eyes.

"Sofia." My grandfather stopped short when he saw me. He didn't say hello. He didn't smile.

The stranger's gaze slid over my uniform before returning momentarily to my face. Then he looked away, releasing me from my prison.

"Go to your room." Although Grandfather spoke to me, his eyes remained on the man.

I opened my mouth to speak, wanting to say something, anything, against the command more fitting for a five year old.

I saw one side of Raphael Amado's mouth curve upward as he watched me.

"Now!" Grandfather barked.

I turned and bounded up the stairs, forgetting the reason I'd come down in the first place. Everything seemed suddenly so inconsequential.

"Six months, old man. I'll be back then to take what's due me."

I heard Raphael Amado say that right before I reached my room. The front door opened and then slammed shut. I went to my window, saw Raphael climb into the backseat of the SUV, and watched as it disappeared toward the property gate.

An hour later, my grandfather sent for me, summoning me into his study, a place I'd only been invited into a handful of times. When I walked into that dark room, I found him sitting behind his large, antique desk, his face gray, his eyes like steel.

I'd imagined a different sort of reunion after four

months away at school. I hadn't even come home for the Thanksgiving holiday. Although life was never any different here, even during the holidays. At least I went away to school. Lina had to live here. I sometimes didn't understand why he wanted that, why he bothered with the private piano lessons for her. I never got the sense he wanted to encourage it or her —he'd never been that kind of man—but once he'd discovered her talent, he'd hired her the very best teachers. I didn't like leaving her behind. Didn't like the feeling of my little sister unprotected and alone here without me. Thank goodness for Marjorie.

"Close the door and sit down, Sofia."

A deep sense of foreboding settled like a cement brick in my belly as the door clicked closed behind me. I took the seat he pointed to. He'd barely looked at me when he'd said it, and when he spoke, it was more like a business transaction than a handing off of his granddaughter to a stranger. I learned who Raphael Amado was, at least what Grandfather was willing to tell me. I learned my fate. A future decided for me, the reasons for which I was not allowed to know. And as my heart grew heavier and my stomach felt like it would heave the lunch I'd eaten, I knew my life would change—had already been changed–irrevocably.

I didn't even hear him after a while. He spoke almost on autopilot, like the cold, heartless machine he was, and all I could imagine, all I could picture, was a deep, dark canyon and me standing on a cliff that crumbled beneath my feet, moments from falling into the chasm, my life forfeit.

Six months.

I had six months before he'd come to take me.

I was the thing Raphael Amado felt he was due.

I was what he meant.

He'd come on my eighteenth birthday. The same day as my graduation from St. Sebastian. What should be a day of celebration would become the day of my sacrifice. Because I no longer belonged to myself. My life had been traded, exchanged. And I belonged to him now.

My grandfather, a man who should protect me, would give me to a stranger.

With the meager details Grandfather allotted me, I wasn't sure whom to hate, whom to blame, whom to pity. All I knew was that in six months' time, I would be taken out of my home and forced to marry Raphael Amado, to become his property, the payment of a debt my grandfather owed.

The image of the two of them in the hallway came to mind. I'd never seen a man stand nose to nose with my grandfather. Raphael Amado hadn't cowered. The opposite. He'd stood in my grandfather's house as if it was his. As if he had every right to it. And he'd told my grandfather what he would do, leaving no room for discussion, no doubt as to what would happen.

Any man who could cause my grandfather to yield was formidable.

I knew Raphael Amado was a man to be reckoned with.

And in six months' time, I'd be his.

2

SOFIA

June twenty-third. Just one week to graduation.

"That's all, ladies and gentlemen. Well done. We'll run through it again tomorrow."

Sister Lorelai excused us, and ninety kids, this year's graduating class, broke out into chatter, our shoes loud on the wooden platform erected in the east garden of the property.

"There's a party at the pool later," Cathy whispered to our group of five. "Invitees are handpicked. We're all on the guest list, of course." She winked, locking arms with Mary.

"Swimsuit optional?" Mary asked.

"Absolutely!" Cathy said, leaning her head in close.

They broke out in giggles. I didn't feel much like laughing myself.

"Sofia, come on. You've missed the last three parties! You can't not go tonight," Cathy said. "Exams are over, you have no excuse."

I smiled at her, my mind elsewhere. "Sorry, tonight?"

She raised her eyebrows. "Party? Boys?"

"Um..."

"I just got a new bikini in the mail yesterday!" Mary said. "I'll show you."

"I'm going to run to my room first," I said, breaking away from the group when we reached the mansion where we were housed.

Mary muttered something, but I didn't care. They had no idea what would happen to me in a week's time. And attending a party was the last thing on my mind.

It was a little after seven in the evening. Dinner wouldn't be served for another half hour, but I wasn't feeling very hungry. I climbed the stairs to the second floor where Cathy and I shared a room, grateful I'd be alone.

One week before my eighteenth birthday.

How would he do it? Would I get to go home first? Would he just show up to take me? Send someone for me?

I shuddered, the memory of his cold blue eyes still fresh in my mind.

I'd dreamed of those eyes often in the last six months and every night in the last two weeks. Those rage-filled, arctic eyes. He was my enemy, although I didn't know why. No, that wasn't true. I did know why. Because my last name was Guardia. All it took was my name for him to hate me because I shared it with my grandfather.

I'd always wondered why Lina and I had my mother's last name and not our father's. I understood now. It was required for the inheritance. The inheritors of the Guardia fortune had to carry the last name.

In the study that day six months ago, I'd learned my mother had run away from home to marry my father. And I knew I was right. That our grandfather had felt little emotion toward us apart from ownership of us. Taking us in was not a kindness. It was his victory over my dead mother. Over her sin of falling in love with a man he'd not approved of.

I'd learned that he'd had business with Raphael's father that left Lina and I exposed, vulnerable. That was all he'd said. He'd told me Raphael was in a position of demanding something *"quite dear"*—as if he'd ever held me dear—and that if I wanted what was best for my sister, I'd better comply. It was the only way to save Lina, he'd said.

That's all he'd needed to say.

After that one time, we hadn't discussed it again. I hadn't told Lina about it for a long time, and when I finally did, I only told her what I needed to and had kept my reason for agreeing a secret. That

Christmas had been as bad as the one when we'd lost our parents because now, I would be losing not only my sister but myself as well.

Since my grandfather couldn't afford to pay Raphael the money he owed, Raphael would take me instead. He would marry me for my inheritance —fifty percent of the winery would belong to me on my twenty-first birthday.

This...transaction, it wasn't about me. It was between Raphael Amado and my grandfather. I was collateral damage.

I knew my grandfather wasn't telling me the whole story. There had been too much anger, too much rage in Raphael's eyes for this to only be about money. My grandfather had done something terrible to Raphael. I knew it. I just hoped Raphael wouldn't punish me for his sins.

After returning to school in January, I called nightly to talk to Lina and didn't even go home for winter break. Lina had been allowed to come to the school to spend it with me, for which I was grateful. That was when I'd told her about the agreement that would bind me to Raphael Amado.

I finally reached my room, and my woolgathering ended. I frowned. The door stood open a crack. That was odd. Cathy and I were both good about locking up behind us. The sisters had a strict policy on not tempting anyone to sin—in this case, that sin being stealing. Each of the doors had locks on them. I guessed in all the rush and excitement, Cathy had forgotten to lock the door behind her. Although it could just as easily have been me. I was so distracted these days.

I pushed the door open and gasped, my hand going up to cover my mouth.

He looked too big standing here, my room suddenly too small and emptied of oxygen.

Raphael Amado closed the book—my book— and set it down on the nightstand. He'd cut his hair since the last time I'd seen him but had what looked to be two days of growth across the hard line of his jaw. He wore dark jeans and a navy button-down shirt with the sleeves rolled up, looking more casual than he had the last time I'd seen him. Dark hair dusted powerful, tanned forearms. My gaze traveled upward, and I imagined the contour of his biceps, chest, and wide shoulders.

All the while, he studied me.

And I stood like a trembling mute before him.

"Sister Amelia let me in," he said, his tone relaxed, his body at ease. He cocked his head to the side, and a small smile played at the corners of his lips. "I hope you don't mind."

When he spoke, I forced my gaze to his face. His eyes looked just the same as they did in my night-mares, although they weren't as fierce as they had been that day at Grandfather's house. Not as angry.

A hardness still edged them, though, and my mind screamed its warning inside my head.

This man was dangerous. His soul was dark. And if I wasn't careful, he would drag me down into his hell.

"I do," I managed, my voice quaking. "I mind."

He didn't respond. Instead, he let his gaze circle the room, making me see it through his eyes.

He took a step and picked up a bra hanging half off a chair, then dropped it back down. "You're messy. Or is that your roommate?"

"I wasn't expecting an inspection."

"Not an inspection. Not of your room, at least."

"What are you doing here?"

"Curious, I guess."

"It's not time yet." It wasn't, I was sure. I had until graduation. And I wasn't eighteen yet. He couldn't take me until my eighteenth birthday. I had seven more days.

He stopped his perusal of the room and turned his gaze on me, slowly taking me in from head to toe. I swallowed, blinking fast, lowering my gaze momentarily when his found mine but forcing myself to look at him.

I couldn't cower, no matter what.

I wouldn't.

"I like the uniform."

"What do you want?"

"Come inside. Close the door."

I shook my head.

"I said come inside. Don't worry. You're still safe from me. I won't touch you."

Touch me? God. He would touch me soon enough.

I bit my lip, searching his face, imagining this man close, his face to mine, his hands on me. His mouth...

"Sofia."

His deep, low voice made a command out of my name. I stepped into the room and closed the door behind me, keeping my hands on the doorknob at my back.

He walked over to my desk and picked up the small snow globe. It was a Christmas motif. A family around a tree: mother, father and two little girls, all holding hands, forming a complete circle.

"Late in the year for this, isn't it?"

I went to him to take it from his hands. When my fingers brushed against his, a spark of electricity jolted through me. I gasped, for a moment frozen. Blinking a few times, I finally found my voice. "That's not yours." I took the globe and set it down.

He smiled, moving a little to the side, blocking me between himself and the desk. He stood too close, his body too big. He used up too much of the oxygen, so all I could do was suck in gulps of air.

"But *you* are."

His gaze searched my face, settled on my mouth.

"Mine, I mean."

My skin prickled, every nerve ending alive, my body at attention. "Why?" I asked, unable to look away from him. His eyes, they held so much that I wanted to know, in spite of the warnings going off in my brain.

"Restitution." His gaze remained steady, watching me process.

But he and my grandfather spoke in riddles, giving me bits and pieces of a puzzle I couldn't put together without more information.

He stood so close. I picked up the scent of after-shave, alluring and treacherous and very, very wrong. Like him.

He smiled with one side of his mouth, and I flinched when he raised a hand. But he gave me a small shake of his head before tucking the hair that had come loose of its clip behind my ear.

"Soft Sofia. Pretty Sofia."

He leaned in close, his chest touching mine, making me gasp. He inhaled deeply.

"Sweet, innocent Sofia."

I shuddered, my nipples tightening, brushing against his hard chest. He stepped back, his gaze falling to the dark peaks I know he saw pressing against my white uniform blouse. I blinked, looking anywhere but at him, feeling too hot, sweat gathering under my arms, beading across my forehead. He was the opposite, collected and relaxed and fully in control of himself, of his body, while mine betrayed me, feeling things I'd never felt with anyone before.

I knew he was twenty-four years old. He was experienced. He was also a criminal, like his father. But one so charming, he'd fooled Sister Amelia into letting him into my bedroom.

"Boys aren't allowed in this building," I said stupidly, forcing myself to look up at him.

At that, his smile widened, reaching his eyes, as if he were suddenly, terribly amused.

"I'm not a boy."

No. No, he was not.

He stepped back, but barely. "Do I make you nervous?"

"No," I answered too quickly.

He reached to either side of me and placed his hands over mine. I realized I was white-knuckling the edge of the desk.

"No. Not at all," he said.

I broke eye contact, and he took two steps away. When I looked up, he was reaching into his pocket to take out an envelope.

"I actually came to give you something."

"What?"

He held it out.

"I don't expect your grandfather to have been forthcoming, considering. Although you probably know that, given the fact he raised you."

"He didn't raise me." Marjorie had.

He gestured for me to take the envelope. I did.

"What is this?"

He studied me. "Truth."

A shudder ran through me. I glanced down at the envelope in my hand.

"He won't miss me, if that's what you think. You won't hurt him by taking me."

He studied me but didn't reply to my comment. Instead, he reached out and took my hand, startling me. His eyes held mine, that smile remaining on his face as he twisted my class ring off my finger.

I shook myself out of my stupor. "That's mine!"

He slipped it onto his pinky. It went about halfway down.

"I need it to be sure your wedding ring fits."

Wedding ring. We were going to be married. Me to him. Him to me.

Every hair on my body stood on end at the thought of what he'd expect from me.

"I'll be here to take you home with me after your graduation." Raphael turned and walked to the door. "Make sure you're ready."

"It's not home. Not for me."

"And your grandfather's house is?" he asked with barely a glance in my direction.

"Can't you forget what he owes you? What, you think I should repay?"

He turned to me.

"Forget the debt," I added in a near whisper.

His eyes darkened. "Sadly, forgiveness must precede forgetting, and unfortunately for you, neither is an option."

His gaze flitted over me once more.

"You should eat. You're too skinny." He disappeared out the door.

I dropped onto my bed, clutching the envelope he'd given me, my heart pounding. Footsteps and laughter broke into the quiet, and Cathy and Mary pushed the bedroom door open.

"No wonder you're not interested in the party!" Mary said.

They had no idea.

They think I'm the monster. The beast who would steal the innocent girl, when all along, they're the animals. He's the beast who would sell her to save his decrepit neck.

I gave Sister Amelia a wink as I left. Outside, I climbed onto my bike, glancing up as I started the engine. Two faces peered out of Sofia's window, but neither belonged to her. Shifting into gear, I sped off the grounds and toward the city, needing the long ride. The freedom of speed. The danger.

The last was one of the few things that cleared my head.

Sofia had lost weight since last I saw her. Her face looked thinner, her uniform looser. It was expected, though. I imagined she was more than a little anxious about her future.

At least I wasn't a liar, though. At least I was up

front about who I was. She wasn't going anywhere worse than her home. Maybe even a little better. With me, she'd always know the truth. Life with me would not be easy, but it would be honest.

Another week to wait. Then I would leave this place. Go home.

Home.

Fuck.

What was that even? Where was that? Could vengeance be home? Because that fit. That was about all that fit.

I'd spent the last six years of my life behind bars. I'd killed my father with my bare hands. Although the ruling was overturned and the act declared one of self-defense, I knew better. I'd killed the man who should have protected us, who should have laid down his life to protect my mother, my brothers. Me. I killed my own fucking father after he destroyed us, after he set to flames the only good in our lives.

Between mine and Sofia's upbringing, we had great fucking family values. Almost made me understand my brother, Damon's, choice of vocation. Almost.

But that was neither here nor there.

Sadly for Marcus Guardia, I didn't rot in jail. And now that my life was saved, I would destroy theirs.

See, there was one thing prison did to a man. It gave you time. And in that time, I figured out my priorities. The things that mattered. Used to be family for me. But that was ash now. Now, my priority was punishing those who had been the catalyst for what had happened. For what had led to the fire that destroyed anything worth living for.

But for all Marcus Guardia's pomp and circumstance, he was a weak man. A coward. He'd all but offered up his granddaughter. Maybe he never thought I'd go through with it. Or maybe he just didn't give a fuck about her. But he did give more than a fuck about the money. I'd be taking a hefty share of the precious Guardia fortune, and I'd determine what the hell happened to the winery.

My mind wandered back to Sofia. She was innocent. I knew that. And if I had any humanity left, I would have felt for her. For her predicament. All her life, that man had been using her, abusing the trust as her caregiver and legal guardian. Hers and her sister's. And she didn't have the first clue.

I knew he not only lived off the money that belonged to her and her sister—his allowance wouldn't afford him the kind of luxury he was accustomed to—but he was outright stealing from his grandchildren. What in hell he planned to do with that money, I had no idea. The man had to be close to seventy by now. He couldn't live long enough to spend it. Although snakes like him never seemed to die.

I knew Sofia was as much a victim as me, but she'd have to endure her future. Her fate was sealed the day mine was six years ago. And ultimately, I was the one who'd paid the heaviest price. Who'd lost so much. I was the one who'd had to live among violent, raging men who would rape you or kill you and eat their dinner off your broken body when they were done. Thank God, it had taken exactly one time, one incident, for them to learn not to fuck with me.

I accelerated and shook off my thoughts.

That was all in the past now. I never had to go back there again.

And if I didn't sleep, not even the nightmares could touch me.

I ARRIVED LATE to the graduation ceremony.

I could have waited for her to go home with her family. Given her a few precious hours with her sister. But I didn't want to.

Sofia's grandfather and sister sat in the second row behind the students. The sun beat down on me, the sky clear, the June heat stifling. I didn't mind the warm temperatures. It was the humidity I could do without.

Tuscany would be hot, too, but not humid, not like Philadelphia.

Sofia glanced back to wave to her sister, but her smile faltered upon seeing her grandfather. I wondered how much her sister knew. She knew we'd be married. But had Sofia confided the details of this unholy union?

Had Sofia read what I'd given her, or had she'd buried her head in the sand, unable or unwilling to face and understand the reasons for her fate?

The ceremony commenced, and the hum of conversation quieted, leaving me to observe. I didn't bother to take a seat, choosing to lean against a tree behind the last row of chairs instead. Speeches were made, people applauding at the appropriate time. All very dull, quite frankly. Sofia shifted in her seat, uncomfortable, or more likely, nervous. The students stood one row at a time as names were called.

Sofia's turn approached, and I straightened once she stood and glanced back. This time, her gaze met mine. Even from this distance, I saw the strange, pale caramel-colored eyes widen, the delicate skin around them puffy and pink. She'd been crying.

She stumbled when the girl behind her moved faster than she did, but righted herself, looking straight ahead as she made her way to the platform. At the stairs, she stole one more glance. When they called her name, she slowly made her way across the stage, her legs seeming heavy as she took those last steps in freedom to shake the principal's hand and take her diploma. The families clapped and cheered, and Sofia held her head high, refusing to meet anyone's gaze, unable or unwilling to smile as she, instead of resuming her seat, walked toward me.

This was a surprise. I expected a meek, spineless, submissive girl.

I cocked my head to the side.

When she reached me, she took off her cap.

"Congratulations?" I said with a smile.

"Fuck you."

My smile widened. Not meek at all. I should have seen the fire burning in those usually soft amber eyes.

"Is that what you walked over here to tell me? If it's because you think I forgot your birthday—"

"You think what you gave me changes anything?"

I shrugged a shoulder "Not for me," I said more casually than she probably liked.

"You think it makes any difference at all?"

"I don't care, honestly. Like I said when I gave it to you, it's truth." I don't think she heard me at all.

"Do you think I even believe your lies?"

"Again, I don't much care."

"Know that I will fight you every step of the way."

"I hope so."

"Sofia?"

Her sister approached us. Marcus Guardia stood in the distance, conversing with one of the nuns but watching us. His face revealed nothing, the smile false. He was, after all, an upstanding citizen. A philanthropist who gave generously to St. Sebastian and many other institutions.

If only they fucking knew.

My hands fisted at my sides. I wanted to kill the motherfucker.

"I will never make this easy for you."

Sofia drew my attention back to her.

"I hope you won't."

Lina's cautious gaze fell on me. Even if this was the first time I'd seen them together, I would have known them to be sisters. Apart from eye color— Lina's were a mossy green—and Lina's dark hair, the similarity of their features was striking.

"Sofia."

This time, Lina physically turned her sister toward her. Sofia dragged her angry gaze from mine and wiped the backs of her hands across her eyes.

Good. At least she knew what to expect. Today's tears would be the first of many. I had years of hate to work through, and she'd be my whipping girl. Literally, if she wasn't careful.

"Hey." Lina took her sister's face in her hands and held her forehead against Sofia's.

I watched them, curious. My brothers and I weren't close. Damon being my twin, we had a special bond, even now, even through all the hatred and anger, but we weren't like them.

I snorted, shaking my head.

"Okay?" Lina asked.

Sofia nodded. "I have to go."

"I know." Lina released her and stepped back, reaching around her own neck to unclasp the necklace she wore.

Sofia shook her head. "Mama gave that to you."

"Shh."

I noticed they each had tears glistening in their eyes. She wrapped the necklace around Sofia's throat and clasped it. Sofia touched the pendant.

"I changed the picture," Lina said quietly.

"Christ, you act like you'll never see each other again," I said.

Both sisters turned to me.

I raised up both hands, palms up in mock apology.

"I don't want you here," Sofia said to me.

"That's too bad."

She fisted her hands and narrowed her eyes, and I knew it took all she had to say what she said next.

"Let me say good-bye to my sister." She gritted her teeth. "Please."

My eyebrows rose. "Wow. A please."

She pursed her lips. "Just go to the car and give me one fucking minute."

"Do the nuns allow that sort of language?" I taunted.

"Sofia."

Her sister tried to draw her away, but Sofia held her ground.

"I hate you."

"You don't even know me."

"I know enough."

I shrugged a shoulder.

"Go," she ordered, pointing to the car.

I laughed at first, but my face hardened in the next instant, and I stepped close enough that she drew back. "Speak to me like that again, and you'll be sorry," I hissed.

"I'm already sorry," she said, her voice trembling.

Lina caught her hands, forcing Sofia to look at her. I leaned away.

"Sofia?" Lina's eyes misted.

Sofia shook her head and tried for a smile. "I'll be fine. It's okay."

"Call me every day, okay?"

I could see the effort it took for Sofia to hold back her tears.

"We have a flight to catch," I said, checking my watch.

They hugged each other tight, and it was Sofia who broke away, sniffling.

"Do you want to tell your grandfather good-bye?" I asked, although I pretty much knew the answer.

"No," Sofia said. "I'm ready."

"I hope for your sake, you are."

Inside the envelope Raphael had given me were three sheets of paper, pieces taken from a larger document. When I'd asked him what it was, he'd said one word—truth. But it couldn't be that. There was no way. Grandfather wasn't that hateful. No matter what, we were his family, his only remaining family.

The night I'd first met my grandfather as a child had also been the night we'd celebrated my mother's twenty-first birthday. The timing of his visit made perfect sense, now that I knew the details of my own inheritance. For as all-powerful as I'd always believed my grandfather to be, this one thing he could not control. At least not wholly. Because on my mother's twenty-first birthday, she received majority control of Guardia Winery. My grandfather was merely given an allowance that she dictated.

One thing I hadn't known was that my grandfather had taken my grandmother's last name. She was Sofia Guardia, my namesake. He had never been head of the family. Not really. Even if he made it seem like he was. I guessed when my grandmother had died before I'd even been born, he'd continued to receive his allowance and lived in the family home, but only because of my mother. She was the heiress. He had nothing without her.

And now that she was gone, he had nothing without Lina and me.

That's what Raphael had given me. History. History and proof of my grandfather's dishonesty. He was stealing from us. He'd stolen from my mother, and now was stealing from Lina and me. He even had an offshore account into which he'd transferred sums of money too small to be noticed yet large enough to sustain a lavish lifestyle. Why did he need it, though? He already had everything he wanted, didn't he?

My mother running away meant my grandfather had lost control, at least for a little while. It was natural he would be our guardian once our parents died. And with us, Grandfather had taken back the control he'd lost.

As we settled into our first-class seats, I glanced at the man sitting beside me. This stranger I would be married to. A man I would have to live with. I didn't know what was expected of me. The marriage had to be in name alone. I represented half of the Guardia fortune for him. On my twenty-first birthday, I would inherit. And he would steal that inheritance, just like my grandfather had been doing all my life.

What would happen to me after the three years?

For the past six months, I'd spent all my free time learning as much as I could about Raphael Amado and the Amado family. I knew his age, twenty-four, and that he had two brothers, one a twin. His family had two homes, one in the states, and a second in Italy, where they spent most of their childhood. His mother was Italian, his father American, and Raphael and his brothers had been born in America. I knew that six years ago, he'd lost his mother in a fire intentionally set by his father at the house in Tuscany. And I knew that a few months after that fire, Raphael had been charged with the murder of his father. He'd spent six years in an Italian prison for it, and only eight months ago had the ruling been overturned and Raphael's name cleared.

He'd wasted no time in coming for me, had he?

But what did my grandfather owe him? That, I did not know.

I learned his father had been a criminal with ties to some bad people. I knew he'd been accused of arson, but he'd died before he could be tried. Raphael's mother had been killed in that fire, and I knew in my heart that her death, and perhaps the way she'd died, had been the thing that had brought about Raphael's rage. It had been what had caused the violence that precipitated his father's death.

But looking at him now, I didn't see violence.

I had to be careful, though. I couldn't romanticize this thug. Couldn't allow myself to be fooled by his appearance.

"Are you going to stare at me the entire flight?" he asked without looking up.

I blinked, realizing I'd been doing just that and it had not gone unnoticed.

"What does my grandfather owe you?"

He folded his paper and turned to me. "He didn't mention anything?"

He acted so casual, but I knew he was not. "You know he didn't."

"Did you understand what was in the envelope?"

"I'm not stupid, Raphael. I understand what you want me to believe."

"That your grandfather is a thief?"

I shook my head, not quite sure yet. Still processing. "The newspapers said you killed your father."

He remained so still, it was as though he were carved from stone. It took him a full minute before he cleared his throat and spoke, and I knew there was more here than what I'd read online.

"Did they?"

I searched his eyes, like deep and stormy seas.

Tumultuous waters that could pound me against jagged cliffs and decimate me.

"You told me you were giving me truth the other night. I'm asking for it now." I paused. "You owe me the full story—"

"I owe you nothing," he said calmly.

"Did your father set the fire? Was it proven?"

"The media loves to hype this shit up, don't they?"

He flipped the paper open again and turned away from me, effectively dismissing me.

"You blamed him for your mother's death," I said, although I wasn't sure. I'd only read newspaper articles and snippets of public record, most of which were missing.

"Does that absolve me, then? A life for a life?"

"I don't know that you're seeking absolution, Raphael."

He looked at me again and bowed his head. "Clever girl."

"The trial records have gone missing. I don't know anything more."

"Maybe that's for the best."

"You'd lost your mother a few months earlier. Your father was accused of the fire that nearly destroyed not only her home, but her entire legacy. Wiped out generations of history."

"Don't make a saint out of me. I'm not that."

"I know you're no saint. I just want to know what my grandfather has to do with this."

He folded the paper again and this time, set it in the seat pocket. "If you're so curious, then why didn't you ask him?"

Because I was afraid of his answer.

I dropped my gaze.

"Don't you have more relevant questions? Questions that pertain to you, your fate. My expectations of my wife?"

Wife.

I knew where he was going.

"Do I get a say in any of it?" I asked without thinking. "The contract," I clarified, looking at him. "The marriage." I faltered. "What will..." I cleared my throat. "Will it be in name only?" I forced the words.

His gaze swept over me, and a small smile lifted one corner of his mouth. "You surprise me. What exactly has your dirty little mind been conjuring up, Sofia?"

I gasped, drawing back.

He smiled fully. "Well, what? I'm definitely curious about this."

"No!"

As I felt the color drain from my face, the flight attendant came to take our drink orders.

"Champagne?" he asked.

"I'm eighteen," I reminded stupidly.

He smiled. "Vodka, then."

Was he joking? He turned to the server.

"Sparkling water for my fiancée and a whiskey neat for me, please."

Fiancée.

"Going to Italy to get married?"

Raphael smiled nodded.

"Oh, how romantic! Congratulations!"

She must have seen the look on my face because she quickly cleared her throat and was gone.

"I'm not a beast, Sofia," Raphael said, all playfulness gone from his features.

"But what you're going to do to me..."

"I spent the last six years of my life behind bars. Your grandfather's greed destroyed my family and almost destroyed me. Think about that instead of your petty little life for a change."

"I—" I what? What did I want to say? That my life wasn't petty? That I mattered? That I did think of other things and not only of myself?

"Ask me what it was like to be locked up for killing a murderer. Ask me what it was like to spend six years in prison only to have the verdict overturned."

"Raphael—"

"Ask me."

"I don't need to. I imagine it was terrible."

"Worse than you can imagine. Worse than I could have imagined."

I searched his eyes, which had lost all their cockiness, all their coldness. There was room for neither, not with the pain that filled them. It was that moment that shifted things for me. That made me see him as something else, something other than a beast.

"Don't make me pay for it. Please," I said, my voice as small as I felt.

He only watched me, and I could see the battle behind his eyes. This war of good and evil.

"Don't make a saint out of me. I'm not that."

I shook my head at the memory of his words. No. I couldn't do that. He'd warned me himself. I was an inexperienced girl. Raphael was a man. A man who'd killed. I was probably child's play to him. A bore. He would probably just fuck with me to pass the time.

"Why did you come to see me at the school? Why did you tell me about my grandfather stealing from us?"

"Because it was truth. That's one thing you'll get with me, Sofia. Truth. I won't lie to you."

"So what? I mean, it doesn't make it easier."

"This isn't about being easy. There is no easy."

"Do you hate me that much?"

"I don't hate *you*. I hate your name," he snapped.

His sudden anger startled me. The attendant returned with our drinks and dropped off a dinner menu. I took mine but didn't bother to look at it. I knew he didn't either, even though his attention seemed riveted on the thing.

"The last time we saw each other, you told me to forget what had happened. I told you it's not an option. That doesn't mean I don't want it to be," he said. "There are things I would give years of my life to forget, Sofia."

Those last words he spoke so quietly, they made me stop. Made me study him, his face, his eyes, which he kept on the menu rather than looking at me. Part of me understood. I understood why he felt he had to do this. It didn't make it right, not by a long shot. And I'd still be the one punished for sins I'd not committed. I'd be the one—

He cut off my thoughts when he turned to me suddenly.

"It doesn't have to be terrible for you. Three years, then you're free. A marriage in name only. I'll even make sure you're not out on the street afterward, if you're a good girl."

The blue of his eyes shone. So much emotion swirled like a deadly twister behind them.

"What if I say no?" I asked.

It took him a moment to answer, and he only did so after studying my face, my eyes.

"You already said yes."

"I can change my mind."

"This conversation is a waste of time. You won't change your mind, because if you do, I will destroy your family. Even if you don't care that your grandfather will rot in jail, you do care about your sister."

He said it with such spite, such hate, I physically felt nauseous at his words.

"You and Lina are very close."

It was such an abrupt change of subject, it surprised me. "I love her. I will do anything to protect her." I dropped my gaze to my lap.

"I know. That's what makes this so damn easy."

The flight attendant returned to take our dinner order, and the man I glimpsed, the one beneath the hate, vanished.

"I'm not hungry," I said, handing back the card.

"She'll have the steak. We both will."

"I said I'm not hungry."

"You need to eat."

"I'm fine.

"Steak," he repeated to the attendant.

"I don't eat red meat."

He looked at me like he didn't believe me but went along with it. "Make it the chicken for my fiancée, then. And another drink for me, please. I'm obviously going to need it."

She nodded and walked away.

"I'm not hungry. I won't eat it."

"You will. You've become too skinny."

"Anticipation of my future."

"Ouch."

"If it's true, what you said my grandfather is

doing—stealing from us—" To say it out loud made it real. "Can I protect Lina's inheritance?"

He shrugged a shoulder. "I can help you, or I can hurt you. Choose the battles you fight with me carefully."

What the hell did that mean?

"Tell me something." He leaned in close to whisper. "Pretty girl like you. You must have had boyfriends at that school?"

All seriousness had vanished. He was cocky, arrogant, asshole Raphael again. I glared at him then shifted my gaze out the window at the darkening sky. We'd be flying overnight.

"No boyfriends?"

"It's none of your business."

"Come on, it's a long flight. And it'll be a long three years."

"It wasn't allowed. Besides, the boys at school didn't interest me."

"I can see that. You seem older than your age. You need a man to manage you."

I faced him. "And you think you're that man?" I asked, cocking my head to the side.

"I do."

I licked my lips and sipped my drink. His gaze fell to my mouth, and the look in his eyes made my belly flutter, my face flush with heat.

"I've seen how your body reacts to me, Sofia," he said in a low, menacing whisper. "Did you know arousal even has a scent? Yours is lovely. Soft. Virginal, perhaps?" he asked, searching.

I didn't answer, but I probably didn't have to, not with how hot I suddenly felt.

Raphael's eyebrows rose, and he set his hand on my knee and slid it up along my inner thigh. I should have worn jeans. A big, baggy pair of mom jeans. Instead, I had on a cute summer dress.

I pushed his hand away. "Don't touch me. My body doesn't react in any way to you."

"I beg to differ." He tickled the back of my knee. "Even now, your pupils are dilating, your nipples are hard, you're licking your lips. And..."

He brought his mouth to my ear, then tilted his face to kiss the throbbing pulse at my neck, making my breath catch.

"Your heart is beating like crazy," he whispered.

I shuddered. His breath sent goose bumps down the back of my neck and heat between my legs.

I shoved him away as the attendant came to set our individual tables for dinner. He smiled at me, obviously enjoying my discomfort, and when the hostess left, he leaned in again.

"Have you ever had an orgasm, Sofia? Did you slide your fingers inside your panties and make yourself come while lying in your bed at night, pressing your face into the pillow to muffle your moans of pleasure?"

He licked his lips and picked up his glass, looking at me over the rim.

"Have you ever felt a man's touch?" He smiled. "The look on your face is telling me no. Don't tell me I'm right. That you're a vir—"

"Stop!" I cried out, trying to jump from my seat but caught halfway with the seat belt fastened across my lap.

"I don't think they want us to get up yet, honey."

Heads had turned to watch us, watch me. Embarrassed, I sat back down. "I hate you, Raphael Amado."

He rolled his eyes. "I don't care, Sofia Guardia. That's the beauty of this."

5

By the time we landed in Florence, we'd been traveling for over thirteen hours. The drive to the Amado property took another hour and fifteen minutes. Located outside of Florence near a town called San Gimignano, the house—or rather estate—came into view only a few minutes after we'd driven off the country road and through a large entrance, where tall iron gates stood open and stone walls separated the property from the road.

We sat in the back of a dark sedan with tinted windows. As the driver took us through, I looked back at the dragons on top of the two pillars. Each was posed differently, one perched on its haunches, the other ready to take flight with its wings wide. Both had eyes that seemed to follow me.

I shuddered and glanced at Raphael, who had a strange look on his face as he surveyed the land, the swelling hills, the green grass, the vast seeming acres of land.

"It's beautiful."

"Thank you." He smiled.

That was maybe the first authentic smile I'd seen from him.

"It's called Villa Bellini. It's been in the Bellini family—my mother's family—for centuries. It now belongs to me."

"Not your brothers too?"

He shook his head. "Always goes in whole to the firstborn."

"Wow. That's crazy. What about your brothers? And you're a twin, how does that work?"

"Damon is my twin, but he was born three minutes after me, which makes me firstborn."

"Tell me about them. Damon and Zachariah, right?"

"Damon lives nearby. You'll meet him soon. I'm sure he's dying to meet my future bride," he said sarcastically. "Zachariah joined the military when he turned eighteen. Can't blame him. I don't know where he is. Some mission somewhere, I suppose."

"You don't know? That doesn't worry you?" He didn't answer my question, seeming to drift into memory instead.

"We were born in Philadelphia—our parents wanted to be sure we had American citizenship—

but spent most of our time here. With the winery in full production, it was easier."

"Your English is fluent and you have no accent."

"We attended international schools."

"Ah. The name Amado is Portuguese?"

"My father is, or was, American-born of Portuguese descent."

"I looked it up. It means *one who loves God*," I said.

His face hardened and he turned to me, his voice tight when he spoke.

"I don't believe in God, Sofia. No God would allow what happened to my family to happen." He glanced out the window. "Which you'll see the irony in when you meet Damon."

"Raphael is the name of an archangel. That's an irony, isn't it, considering?"

"I guess your God is having a good laugh at my expense."

A few moments later, the house came into view. I didn't want to be affected, but before I could stop myself, I made a sound of utter awe.

"It needs repairs," Raphael said. "My brother had part of the house closed off. Money was...tight while I was in prison."

"We flew first class," I reminded. He went on, ignoring my comment.

"Seventeen bedrooms altogether, only six of which are useable at the moment, an interior courtyard, a large swimming pool, updated kitchen, etcetera."

"Etcetera? You take this for granted?"

He turned to me. "I take nothing for granted."

"The Guardia home here, from what I know because I've never been there, is more of a factory used for harvesting and production. This is beautiful. Elegant. Is that, or was it, the vineyard?" I asked as the car came to a stop outside a building that stood beside a vast field of what looked to be the charred remains of a vineyard.

"Yes." He looked straight at me. "The one my father burned down. To collect the insurance money. You wanted to know what your grandfather had to do with what happened to me. This is it. My father owed your grandfather money. He gave my father an ultimatum, life or death, and my father set the property on fire to repay him to save his worthless life. It killed my mother."

He spoke the words quickly, as if determined not to let them affect him.

"She wasn't supposed to be there," I said. I'd read that. That his mother had come home with a headache and had gone to lie down. His father hadn't known that.

"She was. That's all that matters. And if she wasn't, it would have killed her to know he destroyed her legacy. So one way or another, she was finished."

He took a breath and didn't look at me anymore.

"And the bastard couldn't even cover his tracks. Insurance didn't pay him a cent in the end, and he still died."

"Why did he owe Grandfather money? He runs the family business, why would he—"

"Truth, Sofia. Can you stand it?"

"Raphael—"

"Wondering why your grandfather agreed so easily to this? To handing you over to me?"

Could I take this truth?

"I have proof of his deal with my father, for one thing. He'd go to prison if it got into the wrong hands. He'd lose everything, and so would you."

God. This couldn't be true. My grandfather wasn't evil.

"I don't believe you."

"Facts are facts."

"Guardia Winery is a legitimate business. A successful one."

"Sure, he hides behind the *legitimate* business. Yes."

"Raphael..."

The car came to a stop. Raphael opened his door and got out. My brain whirled with Raphael's 'facts,' and it took me a minute to open mine. I climbed out and just stared at the grand estate, then took in the house, part of which was black from the fire.

It was a huge, two-story building, the stone and color of which fit perfectly into the Tuscan countryside. The front doors were recessed behind three arches, which were duplicated on the second floor. Large windows with intricate ironwork stood open on both floors, and I wondered if the house was air-conditioned.

Raphael went to greet the older woman who'd walked out of the house with a huge smile on her face, wiping her hands on her apron. I watched as they hugged, watched her rub his back then stand holding his hands and looking him over. She wiped her eyes and released him. When Raphael turned toward me, I didn't miss the look of tenderness on his face, even if it did disappear when he laid his eyes on me.

Then someone else walked out of the house. I did a double take and glanced at Raphael. I knew they were twins, but to see them in person, it was weird. Amazing, that nature could duplicate life so flawlessly. Damon stood as tall as Raphael, his hair just as dark, his build big and powerful. The only difference between them was in the eyes. Damon's seemed kinder.

He greeted his brother with a handshake, and I could see from the expressions on both their faces that their relationship was strained.

Damon looked at me and smiled. The brothers approached together. Watching them was almost surreal.

"You must be Sofia."

His voice was as deep as Raphael's but had a different tone altogether. I wondered if this was how Raphael would sound if he hadn't spent the last several years of his life behind bars. If circumstances had turned out differently for him.

"I'm Damon Amado, Raphael's brother. Welcome to Italy."

"Thank you. It's nice to meet you, Damon."

"Damon is the slightly nicer version of me."

Raphael came to stand beside me and wrapped a hand territorially around the back of my neck while he held his brother's gaze.

"Holier than thou and all that."

Damon didn't reply to his brother's jab but shifted his gaze to me.

"Raphael's been very secretive about you."

I knew from the look in his eyes, he knew this was no normal romance. Not a romance at all, actually.

"I'm looking forward to getting to know you," Damon added.

Raphael snorted. "Amazing how two people sharing a womb can be so different, isn't it?" he asked of no one in particular.

Damon continued, taking me from Raphael and leading me toward the house.

"You will always have a friend in me, Sofia," he said quietly.

I wasn't sure if I was the only one meant to hear it, but the way he said it, it made my eyes mist.

"What did I say? Holier than thou," Raphael grumbled, knocking Damon's shoulder with his as he passed.

"This is Maria, she's the cook and pretty much manages everything having to do with the house," Damon said, introducing me to the older woman. "She's been with our family for as long as I can remember."

That's why there was the obvious bond between her and Raphael.

She gave me a courteous smile and said something in Italian.

"Only speaks Italian, though."

Raphael took me from his brother. I felt like a yo-yo.

"I studied a little Italian." I said. Freeing myself from Raphael, I greeted the woman with my passable Italian, which I could see from the look on her face she appreciated.

"I'll take you inside. Maria made lunch, so you'll have to wait to get settled."

As we walked in, three men came around the corner. Raphael spoke to them in Italian and shook their hands, then turned to me to tell me their names, not quite introducing me, just telling me who they were. Cousins, apparently, who worked for him. Whom I gathered would be around a lot. I only remembered the first one's name: Eric.

The scent of food wafting from the kitchen made my stomach growl. Even though I was dead on my feet, I could eat whatever it was this woman was cooking.

"I can't stay. I'm expected at the seminary," Damon said. "I wanted to be here to meet you, though."

Seminary?

"I'll be back in a few days' time. If you need anything—"

Before I could answer, Raphael did.

"She won't," he said, cutting him off.

Damon took out a card and handed it to me anyway, as if Raphael hadn't spoken at all. I guessed not many people did that with Raphael.

"My cell phone number is on the back, and you can also always find me here."

I looked at the card. *St. Mark's Seminary* with a Florence address.

"You're a priest?" Was that the irony Raphael mentioned?

"Studying. Not yet ordained."

"Oh." I looked at him with fresh eyes.

Raphael pulled me close, and, as if he'd read my mind, said: "He's not all that good. Don't be fooled, Sofia. I can tell you right now to be wary of any Amado male."

Damon rolled his eyes at his brother. "Good-bye, Raphael. Believe it or not, it's good to have you back home," he said. "I think it'll be good for you to be here."

Raphael studied his brother, and for a moment, I thought he might say something remotely human, but he didn't. Instead, he broke his gaze and dismissed him.

"Good-bye, brother."

Damon left, and Raphael ushered me inside where the driver was already carrying our bags upstairs. I had a momentary panic, wondering what the sleeping arrangement would be. Our marriage would be on paper alone, but did that mean he wouldn't try to touch me? Would that mean he'd have other women?

I glanced in his direction, realizing he'd have no trouble finding as many as he wanted, married or not.

"Can I have a few minutes?" It came out stiffer than I intended.

Raphael turned to me.

"I'd like to splash water on my face and change out of these clothes before lunch," I added.

He nodded. "I'll take you to your room."

My room. Did that confirm we weren't sharing?

Raphael said something to Maria, who went into the kitchen, and he led me up the stairs to the second floor. I looked around as we went, taking in every detail.

"How old is the house?"

"Over three hundred years."

"The oldest building at St. Sebastian was seventy years old."

"I'll give you a tour later." On the second-floor landing, I saw how the arches that matched those at the front door let in the bright sunlight framed by the bluest sky.

"You must have amazing views on a clear night."

"We do."

Raphael looked nostalgic. Sad almost. At least for a millisecond.

"This way."

I followed him down the hall to the third door. He opened it, and I stepped inside. My suitcases were already arranged on luggage holders, which were the only modern things in the large room with its king-size bed, draped by curtains hanging from the ceiling with high, intricately carved wooden head and footboards. Blues were the theme here, and the curtains at the picturesque windows matched that of the headboard. The windows stood open, and I realized that for as warm as it was outside, the house itself felt reasonably cool, even if it had a slightly musty smell. Raphael seemed to notice it the same moment I did.

"The room hasn't been used in a while."

"It's beautiful." I turned in a circle, wondering how old the furnishings were.

"Bathroom is here."

I followed him to an adjoining room, not very large but big enough to house a bathtub separate of the shower. White marble veined with gold covered floor, ceiling, and walls, although the fixtures looked quite old. He turned the tap.

"Completely updated. You should be very comfortable."

"Once we're... Um... Never mind."

"What?"

I hesitated, cleared my throat, and asked the question. "Will I keep this room once we're married?"

"Does the idea of sharing my bed repel you?"

"I...you said..."

He chuckled. "Don't worry. I'm not used to having to force my women."

I guessed that meant a yes, I'd keep this room. But I also felt like a jerk.

"I didn't mean—"

"Don't take too long." He walked out of the bathroom. "We'll have lunch out back. Can you find your way?"

"I think I can manage one set of stairs and an exit."

"I guess that private-school education will be of some use after all."

And I was the one who felt like a jerk?

He left me alone, and I went to the window to watch Maria and two women setting up a large banquet that I swear would have fed a dozen but was set for only two. Raphael's dark head appeared, and I watched as the two girls helping Maria almost curtsied to him. He shook their hands, and their laughter resonated up to my room. For some reason, a feeling of something close to jealousy tightened my stomach.

He looked up a moment later, surprising me. I stepped away, embarrassed, shook my head, and opened one of my suitcases to get something to change into before heading down for lunch. I needed a shower and a nap, obviously. Exhaustion was making me think and feel things there was no way I should think or feel.

THE TRAVEL between time zones made sleep difficult, so when I woke at close to three a.m. the next morning, I wasn't surprised. After tossing and turning for half an hour, I gave up. I was wide-awake. Throwing the covers back, I got up and went to one of the windows, pushing the curtain away to look out at the rich, velvety midnight-blue sky dotted with sparkling stars. More than I saw at home, more than at school. It was a clear night, and I felt like I could see forever. The few clouds that floated past shone silver in the moonlight.

The gardens were quiet, and I saw once again the shadows of the ruined vineyard. It seemed impossible that Raphael's father would burn it down. And more impossible that he would do it to repay my grandfather for a debt.

I didn't know much about the process of growing grapes or making wine. It seemed strange now, considering that was where my family's money came from. I wondered if he could replant, revive the land. It seemed like a waste and a shame to leave it dead, like it was.

Although it fit, in a way. Part of Raphael was dead too.

I shuddered and dropped the curtain, hugging my arms to myself. I picked up a sweater I'd hung on the back of a chair, put it over my shoulders, and slipped into a pair of flip-flops. I'd go to the kitchen and make myself a cup of tea.

I glanced both right and left but the hallway was quiet. I wondered which room was Raphael's as I made my way down the stairs and around the living room to the kitchen, which had been expanded and, judging from the wall, looked to be about twice the size of the original. I pushed the door open and walked inside, switching on the light. It seemed almost eerie now with only me there, but I set that thought aside and found the kettle, filled it with water, and set it on one of the six burners. I then set about looking for mugs and tea bags. That was when an outer light came on, startling me. A motion detector? The door opened before my imagination could carry me off, and Raphael walked inside. He stopped short at the door, just as surprised to see me as I was to see him.

He looked different, his hair messy, his face relaxed, the usual cockiness gone. He wore jeans and a tight-fitting V-neck white T-shirt that hugged his shoulders and arms, giving me a glimpse of cut muscle beneath.

I swallowed.

He stomped dirt off his shoes and took them off, then stepped inside and closed the door.

The tea kettle whistled, but all I could do was stare at him. He raised his eyebrows, and when I didn't move, he came toward me, stepping a little too close, closer than he needed to. His chest touched mine, and I picked up the faint scent of sweat and grease before stepping backward as far as the counter allowed.

He grinned.

I knew he liked it, liked making me feel uncomfortable. He seemed to take some sick pleasure from it. It was probably more that he liked messing with me because I made it so damn easy.

He switched off the burner.

I cleared my throat, blinking away. "I couldn't sleep. I thought I'd make some tea."

He nodded and reached over my head, one corner of his mouth curling upward as I shrunk away. Being this close to him, it felt strange.

"Why do I make you so nervous, Sofia?" he asked, setting a mug on the counter.

I turned around and looked up and found an array of tea bags in the cupboard. "You don't," I said weakly, focusing on reading every box.

"I told you I don't expect to bed you. I thought that would ease your mind."

I concentrated on opening a tea bag.

"Unless you wanted me to, that is. I'm open to the idea, of course."

"You like messing with me," I said, watching the water as he filled my mug.

"I do. It's so easy."

He set the pot down and went over to the sink. On his way there, he glanced down at his shirt, which was smeared with dirt. He pulled it over his head and dropped it down a chute along one of the walls. A laundry chute. I had one in my room too. He stood with his back to me, scrubbing his hands and splashing water on his face. I wasn't sure if it was the marks I noticed first, thin silvery lines crisscrossing flesh, or his powerful back flexing with muscle at the movements.

When he turned to me, I swallowed, forcing my

mouth to close. I'd never seen a man that looked like him in person before. He was perfect, his face, his body—perfect apart from those countless scars.

"Can you toss me the towel?"

"What?"

"The towel. Behind you."

I turned. "Oh." I felt stupid, flustered. Like an inexperienced fool. I threw the towel, and he caught it. All I could do while he dried himself was watch him, focusing on his hands.

His hands.

Big and calloused and...

I shook my head to clear my thoughts. How could I be attracted to this man? "I'll go upstairs."

"No."

He walked to another cupboard and found a glass and a bottle of what I guessed to be whiskey.

"Sit."

He took a seat at the table, then, when I still hadn't moved, he pushed a chair out with his bare foot.

"Sit, Sofia. I don't bite."

With heavy legs, I joined him at the table. He watched me while he uncorked the bottle and poured about two fingers worth into his glass. He then tilted the bottle and poured some into my tea.

"What are you doing?"

"It'll help you sleep." He leaned back in his chair and drank.

"I don't drink."

"Maybe you should start. Lighten up a little."

"Lighten up? You...you kidnapped me!"

"Don't be dramatic. I don't remember knocking you out and dragging you away. Besides, this isn't exactly a dungeon I've brought you to."

"You know what I mean."

"Give it a rest, Sofia. The whiskey will help you sleep. That's all." He seemed suddenly tired.

"It's just," I started, picked up the mug, and sniffed it, feeling a little embarrassed. "I just have never really drunk very much."

His eyebrows went up. "Are we adding drinking to the list of things you haven't done?"

I gave him a glare, then dropped his gaze. I knew exactly what he was referring to. Determined not to give him one more thing to tease me about, I took the smallest sip. My lips burned.

"Define much. You had to have parties at that school of yours even if your stuffy old grandfather locked away the liquor."

"Of course we had parties." I just didn't attend them most of the time. I'd never been much for them, preferring to spend time reading or studying. "I've had some beer and wine."

"Have you tasted any of your family's wines?"

I smiled. "Lina and I snuck a little at Christmas."

"Bad girls," he said, his expression again mocking.

"Don't make fun of me."

"You like to follow the rules?"

"You like to break them?"

"It's a lot more fun than always doing what you're told."

Why did I care what he thought of me? If he found me ridiculously boring? Why did I care? "I just never gave not following them much thought." And why in hell was I defending myself?

"That so?"

"I'm sure I'm very dull, considering your colorful history." His face hardened, and I wished I hadn't said that. What happened with his father, it wasn't his fault. I knew that. "I'm sorry. I didn't mean to…"

"It's fine." He finished his glass and poured another.

"Where were you?" I asked, painfully aware of his naked beauty just across the table, trying hard not to stare.

"Maria told me they've been having some trouble with the work truck. I wanted to have a look."

"Work truck?"

"There are fields on the other side of the property. We sell hay to local farmers. I'll show you around later."

"Does that money sustain the house?"

He chuckled. "Not even close. When my mother passed away, she left my brothers and me a sizeable inheritance. Most of it has gone to repairing the house. Not much left over for maintenance after the fire. Luckily, I have other sources of income."

"Other sources like arrangements like mine?"

"Well, I don't have other brides in the closet, but yes, I suppose."

"Did you get it fixed?"

He looked confused.

"The truck, I mean?"

"You really want to know about the truck? You have no other questions, nothing else you'd rather talk about?"

I had about a million. I just had to muster up the courage to ask them. "I lied earlier. You do make me nervous, Raphael." I didn't know why I said it, I just knew I had to.

His expression changed. He hadn't expected that. "What do you think is going to happen to you? What do you think I'll do?"

"Anything you want."

He sat forward, resting one elbow on the table, his chin in his hand. His eyes, the blue so bright, studied me closely, making me wonder if they could penetrate through me, pick my thoughts right out of my mind before I'd even had a chance to process them.

"I'm not going to hurt you, Sofia."

"Why did you have to take me, then?"

He leaned back in his seat. "That again."

"Sorry to bore you, but this is my life we're talking about."

"I did you a favor. I opened your eyes."

"By telling me my grandfather is a thief. That he's been stealing from my sister and me."

"Do you prefer to bury your head in the sand? It doesn't change things. Grow the fuck up." He drained his whiskey.

I pushed the chair back. "Screw you, Raphael. You try putting yourself in my shoes for a split second, then tell me to grow the fuck up," I said, standing.

"Sit," he growled.

"No."

"Just fucking sit. Ask me a question. A different one."

"Are you going to stop being a jerk?"

He gave me a lopsided smile. "I'll try, but no promises. It's my nature."

I hesitated.

"Sit down and talk to me," he said finally.

I wasn't sure if it was his tone or his words that made me do it, that made me sit back down and meet his eyes and feel at least a little closer to equal footing for the first time with this man.

He nodded in acknowledgment.

"Is this home for you?" I asked.

He inhaled deeply. He took his time to answer,

and I thought about what he'd told me earlier, what he'd promised. Truth.

"Yeah, I guess it is."

"Why?"

"Because it's where things were good. It's where I remember my mother. Where I remember my brothers and me as kids." He paused. "I remember being happy mostly."

Hearing him say that last part, it was strange. In a way, it almost hurt me to hear it. I felt the loneliness coming off him, and I realized it was always there, every time I was with him. No matter what, no matter the insane reasons I sat in this beautiful house in Tuscany across from this beautiful beast in the middle of the night, that was what I always felt from him. Loneliness. Maybe that was why I had questions to ask. Maybe that was why I wanted to know him. It was naive, I knew it, and that little voice inside my head sounded its warning again, but I felt his pain lying just beneath that cool, detached surface.

Raphael suffered. He suffered greatly.

"It's normal to miss your mom," I said. "And your brothers and the past."

He looked confused for a moment, and all I could do was think of how much what I'd just said applied to me.

We sat quietly, and I finished my tea. Raphael tilted my mug to glance inside it, and before I could stop him, he'd poured more whiskey into it. Not much, maybe half what he had. He handed it back, and I picked it up. Sipping it straight was harder than when it was mixed with the tea, but I did it, liking the warmth, the tingling feeling in my spine, relaxing a little even.

It was me who finally broke the long silence with a confession of my own.

"When my mom was seventeen, she eloped with my dad. She ran away from Grandfather to do it because she was pregnant with me." I felt him watching me, and I wondered why I told him that. Although, he probably already knew the story. In fact, it seemed like he knew more about me than I did. "Do you ever think about your father? About why he did it? Even though he had no intention to harm your mother physically, didn't he know how much it would hurt her, even considering his circumstances?"

The temperature in the room seemed to drop by about a thousand degrees, and I regretted asking the question the moment the words were out.

"My father was a bastard, a coward, a cheat, and ultimately, a murderer. But he was also desperate."

Silence hung heavy in the air between us until, finally, I found my voice. "I'm sorry."

He raised his eyebrows and tipped his glass toward me before drinking it down.

"Do you only want me for the money? Is that

why you took me, because my grandfather couldn't pay?" I had grown a little bolder after swallowing the last of the whiskey. "I mean, you have to wait until I'm twenty-one to get it. What if I don't sign over the shares?"

"Do you want me to want you for more?" he asked.

I raised my gaze to his, surprised by his question.

"Truth, Sofia."

My face heated both from the question and the intensity of his gaze on me. I couldn't answer him; I didn't know myself what I wanted.

"I never thought I'd be married…like this. That's all." I reached for the bottle and tilted it to pour in a little more.

"Too much truth?" he asked, studying me. Seeing right through me.

I swirled the whiskey in my glass then drained it and poured myself a little more.

"You probably shouldn't drink so fast," he said.

"You said I should ask you my real questions. I'm asking. Now you have to answer."

He smiled. "I asked if you had things you'd like to talk about. I didn't say I'd talk about them."

He took the bottle and corked it.

"That's not really fair," I said.

"Life isn't fair."

His eyes told me how deeply he knew that truth.

"Will you hurt me if I refuse to sign?" I asked,

forcing down more whiskey, unsure why or where that particular question came from.

He studied me, then shook his head with a snort. "That's enough," he said, standing. "Up to bed."

"I'm not done." I reached out for the bottle, but he gripped my wrist.

"I said it's enough."

I looked at his huge hand wrapped around my tiny wrist. He could snap it in a second. It probably wouldn't even cost him that much effort or energy.

"Come on."

He walked around the table to my side. Could he see what I was thinking? Perhaps, because he released my wrist and slipped his hand down to take mine instead.

"I'll take you up to bed."

He pulled me to my feet.

"I mean, you're going to hurt me anyway, aren't you?" I tugged myself free and sat back down. Well, more like fell into my chair, my legs too wobbly to hold me up.

He watched me with a deep exhale.

"What about our wedding night?" It came out a whisper. "This isn't how it's supposed to go."

"Remind me to never give you whiskey again."

I wiped my eyes clean. Would he answer?

"Did my grandfather think you'd bed me?"

"Come on, get up."

"I mean, you can make me do whatever you

want. You're bigger than me. Stronger than me." My eyes wandered over the now blurry expanse of his chest. "Maybe you even like that kind of thing."

"I'm not used to forcing women, Sofia, and I have no intention of making you do anything you don't want to do." He paused. "I told you already, I'm not going to hurt you."

"Maybe you like having power over me. Making me submit."

"You're not making any sense."

"Will you? Is that what you want? To make me?"

He chuckled. With one hand on the edge of the table, he leaned over me, his eyes seeming to forever study me.

"I think you're curious, sweetheart, more curious than you like."

Had he just called me *sweetheart*? My head felt heavy.

"But tonight is not the night for this discussion, although I'd love to have it with you. Come on. Get up."

"I'm not tired." Why did my words sound slurred?

His smile spread across his face, and he winked as he reached down for me. "Hell, maybe I should give you whiskey more often, not less." And he pulled me to my feet.

Sofia looked so completely confused sitting there, it was charming. Almost endearing, even.

"Up. I'm taking you to bed." I hauled her to her feet. It was the first time I'd really held her, and she felt smaller, lighter than I expected. More fragile.

"That's what you'd like, isn't it?"

She tried to stand on her own and stumbled, her little hand shooting out to grab hold of me to steady herself. The moment we made contact, we both stopped. I looked down at her hand, pale and delicate against my chest. I'd been working outside since late spring, so my skin had been tanned a rich golden brown, making her soft white a beautiful contrast.

I thought she'd pull away, and maybe if she

hadn't drunk that whiskey, she would have. Hell, she'd be smart to. I'd been messing with her up until now, but something about her innocent, maybe naive directness, intrigued me. And when she let her hand move over my chest, softly feeling the touch of my skin, sliding it over to my shoulder, then bicep, then up toward my face, to the stubble at my jaw, I knew what I'd said was more right than she probably liked to admit. She was curious.

"You feel nice." She swayed on her feet. "Softer than I thought."

I smiled and wrapped an arm around her waist. "You feel nice too, but you are so going to regret telling me that in the morning," I said, lifting her up in my arms. Her eyes fluttered closed, then opened again a moment later as I carried her out of the kitchen and to the stairs.

"I'm not sleeping with you," she said, slurring her words, her eyes closing again.

I chuckled. "Don't worry. I don't like my women dead to the world."

We were halfway up the stairs when she put her hand flat on my chest again and lifted her head. "A lot of women?" she asked.

"You're drunk, Sofia." We reached her door, and I pushed it open. She turned her face into my chest.

Her expression turned worried. "I'm a virgin," she said, shaking her head. "Stupid, huh?"

"Not stupid. And for your information, I figured that out already."

"It's stupid." She smiled. "You smell good, all worky and like a man."

I chuckled. "I really, really hope you remember this tomorrow morning." I pulled the covers of her bed back and sat her down, slipped her flip-flops off her feet and took her sweater off. I couldn't keep my gaze from roaming over the little tank top and shorts she wore and all that skin they left exposed. I lay her down and drew the blanket up to her chin. I looked down at her, already asleep, snoring quietly. It made me smile and for some reason, I leaned down to kiss her forehead. She didn't stir. I shook my head and walked out the door, closing it behind me, then headed to my bedroom, where I took a cold shower before climbing into bed.

She was sweet and innocent and scared.

And I would still tear her world down brick by brick.

She didn't realize what I would do to her family's business. She thought I'd take her inheritance and run. She thought she was saving her sister by sacrificing herself. Well, if she didn't hate me by the time the inheritance came due, she would once she understood what I would do. It would be too late by then, though.

Not that it mattered. She was right when she said

I wasn't seeking absolution. I had no interest in forgiveness. Hate and betrayal had burned any goodness, any honor, right out of me.

And I couldn't care less if she hated me.

IT WAS after ten in the morning when Sofia came downstairs. Maria and her staff were already busy baking, and I had just come inside to get a second cup of coffee. She'd wound her wet hair up into a messy bun and wore a pale pink sundress and looked more than a little uncomfortable walking into the kitchen.

"Good morning," I said.

She flushed, then cleared her throat. "Good morning."

"Coffee or tea?"

"Um, coffee, please."

"Fresh baked bread for breakfast?" I asked.

She glanced at the counter where Maria had set a basket of breads and small cakes. "It smells wonderful." She looked at Maria and repeated the same in Italian. It was heavily accented, and the sentence was out of order, but it worked. Maria nodded her thanks.

"Headache?" I asked, making sure she knew I remembered the night before.

"I'm fine."

Liar. "Well, if you happen to get one later, there's aspirin in that cabinet. Come on, we'll eat outside."

I carried our coffee cups, and she followed me out. I watched her take in the surroundings, the beautiful rise and fall of the hills, the vast green fields. The dead vineyard. We sat down at the table, and she took a piece of bread and buttered it.

"Your brother said he was going to the seminary?"

"Yes. He wants to become a priest."

"He's only twenty-four. I guess I've only ever known priests to be old men."

"Our mother was a devout Catholic. She must have passed some of that to him."

"And you don't even believe in God."

I shrugged my shoulder.

"You're not close with either of your brothers. Really? Not even with Damon being a twin."

I shook my head.

"I guess I can't imagine that. I don't know what I'd do without Lina."

An awkward silence stretched out between us.

"I have some business at the neighboring farm, so I'll be gone most of the day.

"Can I come with you? I don't want to sit here alone all day."

"The seamstress will come in the afternoon to fit the wedding dress."

"A wedding dress? I assumed it would be a civil ceremony."

"In front of God and man."

She didn't pursue that conversation. "You said you'd give me a tour."

"Later." I checked my watch.

"I'm finished now. I won't make you late."

She swallowed her coffee and left the bread. She really did need to eat. "Finish your breakfast. I can wait a few minutes."

After she ate, I led the way to the large garage. It was built in the same style of the house and had enough space for three cars, but two of those were loaded with old equipment for the vineyard we no longer used. In the third stood the truck I'd been working on, a 1970s Chevy.

"That's very old. Does it still run?" she asked when we neared.

"I hope so. I spent last night and two hours this morning working on the thing." I'd been up since half past five.

"You didn't get much sleep."

I shrugged a shoulder.

She touched the rust and peeled off a layer of old paint, then opened the door and climbed in as I settled behind the driver's seat.

"Is it safe?"

"I wouldn't drive you around in it if it wasn't."

She stole a glance when I said it, then fastened

her seat belt. The engine hiccupped then roared to life, and we drove off.

"I hope you don't mind the wind." I had both windows rolled all the way down. "Couldn't quite get the AC working."

"No. I like it. How big is the property?"

"About two-hundred acres. A hundred of that is vineyard."

"That is no longer in use. What a waste."

"It is a waste."

"Maybe you could start again, replant...rebuild your mother's memory."

My throat felt tight, and it was hard to swallow. "These fields here are rented by neighbors," I said, ignoring what she'd just said.

"Are those cows?"

"Yes. Half a dozen or so. They don't have the space, and we do, so it's an easy trade."

"And it's nice to see the animals. Any horses?"

"Do you ride?"

She shook her head. "Just a handful of lessons, but I like it."

I nodded.

"What's that?" She pointed in the distance to a stone building.

"Chapel. It's been there as long as the house." We pulled up to the building, which was missing part of its roof. I shut off the engine, and we climbed out.

"This is amazing."

Sofia stepped up the two stairs and pushed the heavy wooden door open. I remained at the back, watching her take in every detail, touch every surface as she made her way toward the altar. There were only six pews, three on each side. It was very small. The roof had caved in at one corner, but the altar and most of the building was still protected against rain or snow. An overgrowth of green crept along the outside and some of the inside walls.

"The altar is intact."

She bowed her head and made the sign of the cross, then climbed the three stairs to touch the stubs of candles and wax stuck to the stone altar, the crucifix that still hung there.

"This place has an energy to it," she said more quietly, not quite looking at me. "Do you know when it was last used?"

"When my mother was alive."

"Oh."

She walked around to where a confessional stood, the wood rotting.

"It's almost as though incense clings to the space like it was burned yesterday."

She peeled what was left of the old, dusty curtain back to look into the confessional, then turned to me.

"Do you feel it, that energy?"

I had my hands in my pockets and shook my

head. There was a time I had. But that was past. "Not anymore." She looked at me like she felt sorry for me. "We should go."

"If you let the past go, maybe it will let you go."

Her words startled me, momentarily rendering me mute. Her gaze held me, and for an instant, I felt envious of the hope that flashed inside those innocent eyes.

But then reality reminded me why she was here. "Who says I want to let it go?"

Sofia looked physically deflated. I gestured to the door. "Let's go."

"Will you repair it? The chapel?"

"No."

"Can I ask you a question?"

"Are you asking my permission now?"

She shrugged a shoulder. "I guess I am."

"I can't promise I'll answer, but you're free to ask."

"What kind of things do you think my grandfather is involved in? On the plane, you said 'for one thing.' That means there's more."

"Does that mean you believe me?"

"You have to understand how hard it is to grasp. He took Lina and me in, he paid—"

"He's living off your inheritances. *You're* paying for it all."

She bowed her head, shaking it once. I dropped

it. It would take her time to accept this. I could give her that. Hell, time was all we had.

"Don't ask questions you don't really want to know the answers to. Believe it or not, it's not you I want to hurt."

"I'm collateral damage. I know."

"Let's go."

This time, she came without resistance. We drove in silence until I pulled through the gates of a neighboring farm. "Come on" I said, switching off the engine and watching about six children huddled in old man Lambertini's shed. His dog had recently had pups.

"Where are we?"

"This is the Lambertini farm. They're the ones who rent the land for their cows. I have some business with Lambertini. You'll have to wait for me."

Lambertini stood, wiping his hands on a towel, his pipe hanging from his mouth, the smile wide on his weather-worn skin as he came toward us and held out his hand to shake mine.

"Raphael."

He pulled me to him, hugging me with a pat on the back.

"Good to see you home," he said in Italian.

"It's good to be home, Mr. Lambertini."

He turned to Sofia and held out his hand.

"This is Sofia, my fiancée."

Sofia smiled and said hello when he took both of her hands in one of his.

"Are those puppies?" she asked.

"Why don't you go see them while I have my meeting," I told her.

She nodded and went. I followed Lambertini inside, where we discussed the business of the farms before his face grew serious. He told me there had been men there a few weeks back. I guessed it was Moriarty's men, looking for me now that I was back. He didn't know who they were, but from the look on his face, they weren't overly friendly, which only confirmed my suspicion.

"I'll take care of it," was all I said. My father had enemies, which meant I had enemies. If he owed money, and I was pretty sure he did, they'd come after me to pay his debts.

We walked back outside, and I found Sofia trying her Italian with the kids, one of the pups in her lap.

"Take it," the old man said, gesturing, smiling.

She glanced at me.

"He's telling you you can have one."

"What?"

She looked from him to the pup to me. She didn't want to ask permission from me. I could see the pride in her eyes.

"I had a puppy once," she said instead, petting the little thing.

I didn't say anything. She turned her big caramel eyes to mine.

"Can I?" She bit her lip.

I nodded. I could do this one thing for her. Hell, it wasn't much.

"Really?"

Her eyes sparkled, and she gave me the biggest smile I'd seen yet.

"Are you sure?" she asked Lambertini.

He nodded.

"Thank you so much. Thank you!"

"We have to go," I said, heading to the truck.

She stopped me, coming right up to me. "Thank you."

Flustered, I looked at her for a minute, then nodded, feeling uncomfortable. Awkward, even. It was just a dog. No big deal.

"Just keep the thing under control," I said, stepping around her to open the passenger door.

"I will."

She climbed in, her attention fully on the puppy. She waved good-bye as we drove out.

"Lina and I had a brand-new puppy when our parents died. They'd just given him to us three weeks before they'd left. Grandfather wouldn't let us bring him with us to the new house. It broke Lina's heart to say good-bye. Mine too."

I kept my eyes on the road. We all had fucking sob stories.

"Yeah, well, what can I say? Your grandfather's a jerk."

She reached out to touch my shoulder, startling me. I looked at her.

"Thank you, really."

"Don't be so grateful yet. Nothing comes for nothing. I'll think of some way for you to repay me later."

When I'd woken up this morning with a headache and bad memories of what I may have said last night, I hadn't expected to be smiling from ear-to-ear later that same day. But here I was, carrying my brand-new puppy into the house. I decided to name him Charlie.

Raphael surprised me. Even if he did end on that cryptic *"I'll think of some way for you to repay me later."* The memory of it made me shiver.

Last night, the whiskey had hit me hard. For one thing, I was an inexperienced drinker, to say the least, and for another, I was jet lagged and exhausted. I remembered almost everything but hoped I'd dreamed parts of it, especially the last part when I'd told him he smelled good, and worky —what kind of word was *worky*—oh, and like a man. God. How embarrassing. And if that wasn't enough, I also clearly remembered telling him I was a virgin.

Raphael had said he had work to do and left me at the house to wait for the seamstress.

Maria gave Charlie a little pat on the head, but from the way she jumped when his wet nose touched her hand, I knew she wasn't used to animals. She gave me a bowl for water, and I set it in the corner for Charlie to drink. The two women who worked for her, Tessa and Nicola, couldn't get enough of him.

I looked at them while Maria pointed them to some food to give him. They were pretty. Probably around my age, maybe a year or two older. These were the same women who'd tripped over themselves for my soon-to-be husband. I didn't want to like them, but I had to admit, they were nice to me and fell instantly in love with Charlie, like I had. They were nicer than Maria was, at least. The older woman seemed to stand back and watch. I knew her bond with Raphael was probably like that of a mother. Did she see me as a threat? Did she know anything about our situation?

When the doorbell rang right at noon, I asked if Charlie could stay in the kitchen while I had my fitting, which Maria allowed. I opened the door, and an older woman with white hair stood just outside.

"Hello."

The seamstress introduced herself in broken English and came inside.

"I'm not sure where the dress is—"

"I was told it would be in your room."

"Oh." She knew more than I did. "I guess we should head up. Would you like something to drink?"

"No, thank you."

"Okay. This way, then." She followed me up the stairs, and I admit, my curiosity grew. When we got to my room, I saw the long white garment bag hanging from the closet door. "I haven't seen it," I said while she set her things down.

"It's beautiful," she said, moving confidently toward the bag and unzipping it. "Raphael's mother, Renata, wore it."

His mother had worn the wedding dress he wanted me to wear?

"Terrible how she died," she continued.

I only nodded and watched her lift the long lace gown out of the bag. She looked it over and smiled approvingly.

"Perfect condition. It was in Renata's family. Worn by at least four women."

I touched the delicate, intricate lace, wondering at its age. Wondering why in hell he'd want me to wear this.

"It's beautiful." The dress had long sleeves and a deep V-neck with a fitted waist that dropped straight to the floor with a slight train at the back. It looked to be close to my size.

The seamstress looked me over. "It should fit you. Come."

I undressed, and she helped me step into the gown, then buttoned what seemed to be an endless number of pearl buttons that went from my low back up to my shoulders. Only then did she permit me to look at myself in the mirror.

I had no words. I never would have thought I'd wear a lace gown. Not that I'd given my wedding much thought while at school. Some girls did, but that wasn't me.

It had to be taken in just a little, but not much. I smiled when I reached up to push the hair back from my face and noticed the sleeves widened at the wrists, making it look more medieval. The length would be perfect with the high-heeled shoes Raphael had also arranged for me to wear.

I stood still while the seamstress worked, wondering where exactly we'd be married. He'd said in front of God and man. Did he mean we'd be married in a church? And why did he want me wearing this? Wouldn't he be better off to save it for when he really got married? After me, after the three years had passed and he had no use for me and could find his true happily-ever-after?

The thought made me nauseous, actually.

The seamstress didn't stick me once with the

hundred or so pins I swear she used before finally, she was satisfied. She then opened another bag I hadn't seen. It was behind the one the dress had come in. This one contained a simple white veil edged with lace of the same pattern. She took the clip from my hair and laid it over my head. I noticed then how the veil was yellowing along the edges, but the result was no less stunning.

The door opened at that moment. There was no knock first. We both turned to find Raphael standing there. His mouth fell open, and he didn't speak for a long time. Finally, I moved, sliding the veil from my head, and facing him.

"It's bad luck for the groom to see his bride before the wedding," the seamstress said with a wink.

Was she oblivious to the tension between us?

"This is no ordinary wedding," I muttered.

Raphael cleared his throat and dragged his gaze from me. "Do you need anything?" he asked the seamstress.

"No, I should be fine. I'll have it back within a few days. Not too much to do."

"Good." He looked me over again, his expression strange, tight. He then nodded, walked back out, and closed the door. The seamstress helped me undress and carefully placed the gown back in its bag. After gathering her things, she said good-bye and left.

Feeling the weight of jet lag, I lay down to close

my eyes for a few minutes, but those few minutes turned into two nightmarish hours.

I dreamed of Lina and Grandfather back home, but Grandfather had a set of horns growing out of his head in my dream. That and yellowed, decaying teeth. Lina was smaller, younger. More vulnerable. And even though I was there, it seemed as though I wasn't. I was able to watch, but I couldn't reach out and touch her, and she couldn't hear me when I spoke, when I told her to run because Grandfather was stalking her through the house.

It was when I caught a glimpse of myself in a mirror that I finally woke, and when I did, I was sweating and the sheets had knotted around my body.

I was wearing that wedding dress in my dream, but it didn't look the same. It was bloodied and blackened by fire and death, and there was a stench so strong that I swear I could still smell it now as if it clung to my nostrils.

After unraveling myself from the sheets, I picked up my cell phone and called Lina. She answered on the second ring, whispering.

"I'm so glad I caught you," I said.

"Me, too. I've been waiting for you to call. I didn't want to call you, figuring you'd be messed up with the time difference."

"Don't worry about that, just call me whenever."

"You too."

"Why are you whispering?"

"I'm hiding in the bathroom. Piano lesson."

"Oh." Her schedule was grueling, and the only thing that gave me comfort was knowing she actually enjoyed the work, or at least the end result.

"How are you? How is it there?"

"Okay," I said. It's a really nice property, actually. His family has an estate here, or I guess it's his now."

"Did you meet his brothers?"

"Just the one. Damon. He wants to become a priest!"

"A priest?"

"I know, I was shocked too. I mean, this is the Amado family. The only legitimate thing about them was the winery that's been destroyed. It's no secret who their father was, what he did."

"Don't judge them all by their father's actions."

She was more right than she knew, considering Grandfather's actions. "You're much nicer than me, Lina."

"How is he? Raphael, I mean?"

I shrugged a shoulder. Honestly, I couldn't figure him out. What did I tell her? "I don't know yet, I guess. He gave me a puppy."

"He did? Wow! That's nice."

"It was one kind act. He's not a nice man, Lina. We can't ever forget that."

"Maybe he's trying?"

"I don't want to be naive." But I did want to believe it. It would make things bearable.

"Give him a chance."

"How can I do that when I know the reason for this is my inheritance? He'll marry me for it, keep me prisoner, and then what? What will happen after three years?"

"Three years, then you're free. A marriage in name only. I'll even make sure you're not out on the street afterward, if you're a good girl."

"No one knows what will happen in the future. You're the one who always told me that when I was down."

"He wants me to wear his mother's wedding dress."

"What?"

"I don't get it, Lina. I think he likes messing with me, but that's just weird. Why would he want that?"

"Sofia, I don't like him for taking you away. I don't like what he's doing to you, to us. But he could be really awful to you. He could lock you up and throw away the key. It's not like Grandfather could stop him if he wanted to—"

"I know he can't."

"My point is, give it a chance. You don't know him. He's been through hell and back. Maybe he's searching for something too. Maybe he's trying to find his peace."

"Or get his revenge."

"You have to give it a chance to figure it out. Figure *him* out."

"Whose side are you on?"

"Yours. Always yours. But for the next three years, you're stuck. I don't want it to be hell for you."

"I wish you were here."

"Grandfather will never agree to that. You know that."

"I know."

I heard her teacher's voice calling for her. "Just a minute," she called out. "I have to go," she said to me. "I'll call you back after the lesson, okay?"

"Okay."

"Hey, don't be sad."

I nodded, but tears filled my eyes.

"Send me photos of the puppy. What did you name him?"

"Charlie."

"Like our Charlie."

"You remember him?"

"I remember losing him," she said.

"I'm sorry."

"It wasn't your fault. You were five."

"I know."

"I have to go, Sofia. I love you."

"I love you."

We hung up, and I climbed out of bed. It was close to five in the afternoon, and the heat was oppressive today. I dug through my suitcases, found my bikini, and slipped it on. I'd check on Charlie and go for a swim. A little exercise would clear my head. Then I'd focus on getting Lina photos of everything.

She was right. I didn't know him. I only knew he'd been through hell. I just didn't want him to put me through it now. But for the next three years, I was bound to him.

I grabbed a towel from my bathroom and stepped out into the hallway. At least he wouldn't expect me to share his bed. That should have been a comfort, a relief, but for some reason, it only made me feel a little...less. Like I wasn't good enough.

After checking on Charlie, who lay sleeping on the cool tile floor in the kitchen, I went out to the swimming pool. I didn't see Raphael until it was too late. Until he'd seen me, and I couldn't sneak away.

He leaned against the edge of the pool at the far end. I guessed he'd been swimming laps, because he looked to be breathing hard. The muscles of his arms and back flexed as he pulled his body out of the water and climbed out. He wore tight swim trunks, and sun glistened on his wet skin. I quickly looked away, forcing my legs to move as he picked up his towel to dry off while watching me.

I sat down on the chair farthest from his on the opposite side of the rectangular pool. The water sparkled in the sun. I longed to submerge myself but felt self-conscious as he approached, stopping just in front of my chair. Water dripped from his wet hair onto me. I hadn't worn anything but my bikini and had wrapped the towel around myself on my way out here, so now I perched on the edge of the lounge chair, holding the towel tight to me.

Raphael sat with an exhale, then stretched out on the seat.

"If you clutch that towel any tighter, you might pop a knuckle."

I softened my hold on the towel and turned to him.

"Where's your puppy?" he asked.

"Sleeping in the kitchen. It's probably too hot for him out here."

"Too hot for anyone. Get in the pool and cool off."

"I'm fine."

"So you just came out here to sit and *watch* the pool?"

I shrugged a shoulder.

He chuckled and lay back, closed his eyes, and turned his face up to the sun. "Suit yourself."

I turned my attention back to the water and, after a few minutes of silence from him, I undid the towel from around myself, checked that his eyes were still closed, and quickly walked to the edge of the pool. Testing the water with my toe, I stepped in, descending the five stairs before floating out, ducking my head under and swimming to the far end before coming up. I glanced at Raphael, who now sat watching me. I went under again and swam, coming up for air only to find he'd joined me in the water.

My heart beat hard as he swam out to me, his dark head parting the water like a shark as, with two powerful strokes, he was at my side, then had me cornered, his arms trapping me at the edge of the pool.

"One thing I learned early in life is never let your enemies see your fear." He moved in closer, his wet face inches from mine. "Never let them smell it on you because it's like a fucking drug." He inhaled deeply. "You can get high from it, Sofia."

"Are you my enemy?" I asked, focusing on that one word. Unable to think about the rest. Knowing it was true.

"I'm not your friend, am I?"

"No."

"Your eyes betray your desire, Sofia. Your hunger."

"You don't see very clearly, Raphael."

"I see very clearly. And I read you like a fucking book."

I looked away, very aware of his body so close to mine, very aware of how my lips parted and my tongue darted out to lick them. And how he watched that little involuntary movement so knowingly.

"You're curious, Sofia. At least admit it to yourself. Or are you a coward?"

"I'm not a coward. And you're wrong."

"Am I?"

"Let me go."

"I'm not touching you."

His gaze roamed over my face, then dropped to my lips.

I dove down and slipped under his arm, swimming to the shallower edge of the pool. But before I could climb out, he was behind me, and this time, he was touching me. His body pressed against me, his chest to my back, trapping me.

"You want me to touch you," he whispered in my ear. "Don't you?"

When his lips closed around my earlobe, I sucked in a breath. It was like the sensation shot right through me. Shot down to my core, awakening something else. Something he seemed to do just by being around me.

One of his hands slid down to close over my waist, and he turned me so I faced him.

"What are you doing?" I asked, breathless, trapped.

"I told you I'd find a way for you to repay me."

"What?" I panicked, looking to either side of him for an escape but knowing I'd go nowhere if he didn't allow me to. Physically, I was no match.

"Shh. Just be quiet."

Water dripped into my eyes, and I blinked. In that moment, his mouth closed over mine, wet and cool, the taste of chlorine clinging to his lips.

I made a sound and pushed against his chest. It's what I should do. I should resist. But he didn't budge and he didn't release me, not with his body, not with his mouth. Instead, his lips teased mine open, the stubble on his jaw sharp against my cheek as he slid his tongue inside my mouth. Against my conscious will, I opened. He eased his tongue deeper, and I did something so against what my brain told me to do, which was to resist. Instead, I tasted him. I tasted his tongue, his lips, his breath, and for one brief moment, I kissed him back.

That was when Raphael broke the kiss.

I opened my eyes to find him watching me, his eyes darker, the victory inside them a mockery, shaming me.

"You want it, Sofia. You want it so fucking bad, I can smell it on you."

"Get off me," Sofia shoved at me, but I wasn't ready to let her go just yet.

"Make me."

She tried again. "I mean it."

"Or what? What will you do if I don't let you go?"

Frustration lined her forehead. It took her a full minute to answer my question with her own.

"What *can* I do?"

She searched my face as if truly seeking an answer from me.

From *me*.

"Nothing. That's the point," I said.

"I'm a game to you."

"No, not a game."

"Then what? I don't understand what you want with me. You tell me this marriage will be in name alone. You tell me you hate me, yet—"

"I told you I hate your name. There's a difference between hating your name and hating you."

"Does it matter?"

I could see her confusion and frustration visibly mounting as she frantically searched around her.

"I'm cold."

She gasped when I wrapped my hands around her tiny waist and instantly tried to push them off. When I lifted her out of the pool and set her on the edge, she exhaled, her face flushing red, probably embarrassed at her panic.

I climbed out and got her towel, wrapping it over her shoulders as I sat beside her.

"Thanks."

I nodded.

"I don't understand what you want," she said.

I looked at her sitting there, hugging the towel to herself, shivering in the heat. Her wet hair clung to her skin, and she refused to look at me for a long time.

What did I want? What did I want with her? This was a business transaction, ultimately. Money owed. She was here to pay off a debt.

But did I want to take it out of her skin?

What did that make me if I did? This wasn't how I thought it would go, but having her here, having her close, warm and soft and so fucking innocent... I could have her, that was the point. I didn't even have to make her. She wanted me, and I was using her desire against her. Taunting her with it.

"Look at me, Sofia."

She did, and her pale eyes searched mine. Inside them I saw humiliation. I saw sadness. Uncertainty. I saw vulnerability, and I saw a loneliness, a longing, a hope, that I recognized. One I couldn't ignore. One that threatened to resurrect a part of me I'd buried long ago.

One I intended on keeping buried.

I knew only one way to shut it down, and I needed to shut it the fuck down. Now.

Anger boiled inside me. Rage at my own weakness. My weakness around her.

"I own you," I said, gripping her jaw harder than I needed to and bringing her face to me.

"Stop!"

"When I want to fucking kiss you, I'll fucking kiss you." To prove my point, I mashed my lips over hers. This time, they didn't open. They didn't yield like they had just a few moments ago.

Good. That was good. That was the point.

I released her, and she tried to scramble away, scraping her thigh on the edge of the pool as she tried to slip out of my grasp but ending up on her back instead, with me on top of her.

"Stop it."

She struggled beneath me, but the sick thing

was, it only excited me. Her fight turned me on, and I knew the instant that fact registered for her.

"You don't fucking want me to stop." I kissed her again, this time slipping one hand between her legs and gripping her sex.

She gasped, and I tightened my hold on her pussy.

"You. Don't. Fucking. Want. Me. To. Stop, Sofia."

The next kiss was rough, my teeth cutting into her soft lip, the metallic taste of blood, of her blood, making me groan.

"Admit it," I demanded.

"I don't want it!" she cried out, frantic now beneath me, her little fists pounding my shoulders, her hands curling into my hair, pulling hard.

"More," I said, kissing her again, squeezing her cunt. "It only makes my cock harder."

"This isn't you. I know it. I know it."

"You know nothing. I could make you."

"You won't! You said it."

"I could. And you'd be wet for me."

"No."

"What if I slip my hand into your suit, Sofia?"

She shook her head frantically but only managed to spread her legs wider in her effort to free herself from me.

"Would it make you feel better if you pretended I made you do it?"

"Please," she begged.

"Please? Is that a yes?"

"No. Raphael, let me go. This isn't you."

I shot up, straddling her, released her pussy, and wrapped my hand around her throat. "This is exactly me!" I roared, years of anger vocalizing now. How in hell did she think she knew me when I didn't know myself?

I squeezed, and she gripped my forearm, trying to pull me off. Her face reddened, her eyes wide as saucers, and the sick thing was, the fear in them only set ablaze a thing already burning like a fucking brand inside me.

"I killed my father with my bare hands, Sofia. You think I *won't* hurt you?"

"Self-defense isn't the same as murder," she managed, tears streaming out of the corners of her eyes.

"Your fear makes me hard," I whispered close to her face. "That should scare the fucking shit out of you." I squeezed once more, then let go of her throat and straightened to loom over her. She brought her hands to her throat and turned her head, coughing. I watched until finally, she shifted her gaze back to me.

"It does," she muttered. "You do. You scare the shit out of me."

Her eyes trapped me, the tables turning, even in the sound of defeat in her voice.

"You win, Raphael. Don't you think I know that? That you've already won?"

I sat up straighter, my weight on my thighs, so I no longer crushed her.

"You told me you wouldn't be a beast to me, but look at you," she said. "You can make me do whatever you want. We both know that. You can take whatever you want, you can take every single thing away from me. You can force me—"

Her voice broke, and she never finished that part.

"You can lock me away, and there wouldn't be a thing I could do about it. But you know what's even more fucked-up than you getting off on my fear?"

Her voice cracked, tears pooled in her eyes.

"The fact that I know, that I believe with all my heart, it's not what you want. It's not who you are."

I blinked several times and ran a hand through my hair.

She shifted beneath me, slid her legs out from underneath mine, and stumbled to stand. She grabbed her towel and held it to her chest, another barrier between me and her as I knelt at her feet. Unable to move. Unable even to look at her.

Beneath her.

She kept a wide berth as she staggered backward and away, toward the house. I turned to watch her go, watch her run, water dripping from her as she disappeared inside.

And all I could do was sit there. All I could do was nothing.

I was a monster. I knew it. I had known it for a long time.

Take care when fighting the monsters you don't become one.

My mom used to tell me that. Her favorite fucking quote from Nietzsche.

I fought for her too. I fought him. I always lost. I always knew I'd lose, but I did it anyway, and I took the penalties, endured the consequences.

I guess I didn't realize when the transformation had happened. When the monster had beaten me. Had taken me over and made me like him. Like my father.

I staggered to my feet like a drunken man and went into the house, up to my room, unable to even look at her closed door. I didn't bother to shower. I just pulled on a pair of jeans and a T-shirt, got into my car, and drove, not sure where I was even going until I pulled up to the seminary gates. I'd never been here before. It was while I was in prison that Damon had told me his plans. We hadn't really talked much before that. Damon and I, we were as opposite as could be. I guess, though, in a way, we were both surviving.

My father was a two-bit criminal. Never organized enough or smart enough to be on top of his game. Always in debt. A thug for hire. But charming.

Always charming. The man could talk, and he put on airs. Made people believe anything he wanted. That's how my mother had fallen in love with him, I was sure. That or the fact that love truly is fucking blind.

The physical abuse didn't start until I was twelve. I'd always been a big kid, so I guess he'd felt like I was a match. Like he could beat the living shit out of me because I'd fucking take it and survive. I wondered how long he'd been beating mom before I really saw the evidence of it. She'd shielded us from that side of him as long as she could.

Seeing Sofia's face, her fear, her courage through it—because she was courageous, she wasn't the coward I accused her of being—it reminded me of her. Of my mom.

And the reflection of myself in her eyes scared the ever-living shit out of me because what I saw there, it wasn't me. It was him.

I looked at my watch. It was almost eight o'clock. Way past visiting hours, but I didn't care.

When I found the doors locked, I scrolled through my cell phone to find Damon's number and dialed it. It rang four times then went to voice mail. I walked around the property, trying all the doors when finally, a few minutes later, my phone rang. It was Damon.

"Raphael?"

He sounded surprised. "Yeah. It's me."

"Are you all right?"

"I'm outside."

"Outside?"

"Outside the seminary. Doors are fucking locked."

"Wait there. I'll be right down."

We hung up, and I went back to the front door, which opened a few minutes later. Damon stood on the other side wearing his cassock. I had to look twice. It was so strange, seeing my twin brother dressed like this.

"Are you fucking sure you want to do this?" I asked. "Throw your fucking life away."

"Lower your voice and watch your language in here."

He let me in and locked the door. I followed him to a private room. He offered me a seat, but I paced instead. "You have something to drink?"

He nodded and took out a bottle of whiskey from a cabinet. He poured us each one. I drained my glass in one go. Although he raised his eyebrows, he re-poured for me and sat back down. I remained standing.

"What's going on?"

"I'm like him, aren't I?" I asked, not sure what I was doing here. Feeling weak for having come.

He studied me. "Like our father?"

I nodded once.

"Tell me in what way you're like him. Give me one fucking thing."

I smirked. "Are you allowed to say that? Won't your God strike you down or some shit?"

He gave me a stern look. "One thing."

I shook my head and swallowed more of my drink. "I scare the shit out of her."

The look on his face changed, but he didn't quite smile. "Well, stop."

"It's not that easy."

"It's exactly that easy. What did you do?"

Fuck. "Nothing," I mumbled without quite meeting his eyes.

He raised his eyebrows. "Is she hurt? Physically?"

"No."

"Again, how are you like our father?"

Damon knew about the abuse. He'd seen me take it. He'd been made to watch. Our father was a wicked, manipulative, evil man.

I stopped pacing. "I'm not sorry he's dead," I said finally. "I only wish I'd done it sooner. Before mom—"

"That's not your fault. None of it is your fault. When are you going to get that through your thick head?"

"I knew what he was doing to her."

"You found out too late. We all did."

"I should have known earlier. I should have known when he stopped with me." My father only picked on those he could overpower. He never took a chance he might lose. And when I got bigger than him, he left me alone.

"Stop blaming yourself. She didn't blame you."

"I went to the Lambertini farm. He said some men were out there. Men who'd had business with our father. I'm guessing Moriarty."

"Call the police. Let them deal with it, Raphael."

"I'm going to make an example."

"Like you are with Sofia? Fuck with Raphael Amado and pay? Is that the message you want to send?"

"I don't have a choice."

"Yes, you do. You can choose to leave the past in the past. Let the police handle this."

"I'm a murderer."

"Self-defense. Our father would have killed you. That was obvious to everyone, including the judge."

"Still, I spent six years—"

"And the ruling was overturned." Damon emptied his glass. "I guess you have to figure out what you want, Raphael. Figure out who you are. Whether you want to continue the life our father led or bury it. Do good instead. You have the land. You can replant, make an honest living."

I snorted at the mention of honest.

"It would make mom proud," he added. "And it would be the ultimate revenge. Take back what our father stole."

"Death is final, brother."

"You think I don't know that?"

I drained my glass and studied him. I guess I never thought of my brother mourning, but he was. We all were, Zachariah too. Still. Six fucking years later. "I have one question for you." He waited for me to ask it. "Why aren't you telling me to let Sofia go?"

He studied me back, his eyes narrowing a little, and for the first time in a long time, I glimpsed the Amado blood running in his veins.

"Because as wrong as it is what you're doing, I think she's good for you."

I laughed outright at that. "What the hell does that make you, brother, if not an accomplice?"

He stood and came to me, smiling. "I'm your brother first," he said. "I want you to be happy. Finally."

9

SOFIA

It wasn't hard to avoid Raphael after the incident at the pool. He seemed to be avoiding me too. He seemed to have always eaten before I did, and I kept to my room when I didn't have to go downstairs to take care of Charlie. I didn't know where Raphael was most of the time, and I didn't want to care. But I did.

He had two sides to him, and he flipped with deadly precision on a dime. His demons were so dark and so deep that when they reared their heads, when they overtook him, he was the scariest beast of all. A man filled with hate and vengeance. But wasn't it those very things that had broken him?

But that fissure, it only made him more dangerous because that hurt, it could swallow me up too. It could destroy me like it was him.

I could still feel him on my lips, his mouth on

mine, his tongue inside my own when I'd opened to him. Like some fool, I'd yielded and so fucking easily. He hadn't even had to make me. If he made me, it would be easier. If he made me, I could hate him. I wouldn't have to hate myself then because he was right. I did want him.

Two days after my first appointment, the seamstress returned for another fitting, and soon my dress was ready. I let it hang in my bedroom hidden inside the garment bag. I didn't want to think about it.

On the third night, once again, I took my dinner with Charlie in the kitchen. I was half afraid of Raphael walking in at any minute, dreading it, but also fed up with being on my own, ready to face him. Ready to get this over with.

But the house was still quiet apart from the light rain tapping against the windows. It felt strange to be alone in such a huge, old place. Charlie devoured his food and curled up at my feet to sleep again. I kind of envied his life.

I dumped more than half my plate in the trash can and rinsed my dish, then left Charlie to sleep while I went to look around the house, taking care to leave the kitchen door propped open for him.

The living and dining rooms had been freshly dusted and vacuumed. I bypassed them, knowing Raphael's study was at the end of the hall. I wasn't sure what I'd do, not really. Not until I stood directly outside his door. Guilt made me glance over my shoulder before I reached for the doorknob and turned it. I don't know if I felt relieved or disappointed to find it locked.

I walked back toward the kitchen. Maybe it was a good thing I couldn't get into the study. I noticed a light from beneath a closed door I hadn't yet opened. Knocking once, I waited, but when no one answered, I opened it. It creaked, and my heart raced, unsure what I'd find, equal parts nervous to run into Raphael as I was to run into a ghost.

But neither greeted me. Instead, I stood looking down a stone staircase, the scent and chill telling me this was the cellar.

"Hello? Is anyone down there?"

No answer. I took two steps down, then another two until I could peek into the cool, dank space. It was large and well lit, with stone walls that looked like they were older than the house itself.

My ballet slippers made no sound. I counted as I descended fourteen stairs total. I looked around, wrapping my arms around myself at the sudden chill. Along the walls stood covered pieces of what I assumed was old furniture or equipment. Some of the covers had been pulled back recently. I could tell from the dust someone had been here not too long ago. At the center of the room stood a pillar. Drawn to it, I crossed the floor. It was old, like everything else here, the wood intricately carved, even if it was decaying a little. It was sturdy and probably beautiful once. It had been dug deep into the ground, and when I looked up, I knew exactly what it was used for. The chill I'd felt earlier now trailed an icy finger up along my spine and settled at the back of my neck.

Iron chains hung from above. Bracelets with locks stood open.

The image of Raphael's back flashed before my eyes. I shook my head.

No. Not what you think. Not possible.

The sound of footsteps startled me, and I jumped, noticing for the first time an almost cave-like opening in the far wall, realizing that was where the scent of damp earth came from. Panicked, I wanted to run, every horror movie I'd ever watched playing before my eyes. But terror paralyzed my legs, and I stood glued to the spot, watching, my hands at my throat, my mouth open, holding my breath.

Would I scream? Would any sound come at all if I tried? Or would fear render me mute?

The sound came closer, and a moment later, Raphael appeared at the mouth of the tunnel. I cried out, and he stopped short, his wet shirt and hair clinging to him.

"Sofia?"

I covered my face, only then realizing how tense I'd been, how afraid. It made me laugh a strange, almost manic sound. "I thought..." I drew in a shaky breath and wiped my eyes. Why was I crying? Why now?

"You look like you've seen a ghost," he said.

"I thought you were one."

He stepped into the light. His cheeks and the tip of his nose were red from cold, the scent of the tunnel clinging to him.

"No ghost."

His gaze fell to the pillar, and when he moved deeper into the room, I had the feeling he took care to leave a wide berth between it and himself.

"What are you doing here?"

I shook my head. "I was just looking around the house and saw the light on."

"You shouldn't be down here."

He stepped closer. I smelled alcohol on his breath.

"Where did you come from?"

He pointed behind him. "The tunnel leads to the chapel."

"You went to the chapel? Now? It's nighttime, and it's raining."

He walked to a table, his back to me when he replied.

"I haven't seen my mother's grave in six years."

"Oh, God." I went to him, raising my hand to his shoulder but stopping short of touching him. "I'm sorry." I noticed the flask he'd tucked into his back jeans pocket.

Raphael pulled back one of the sheets but drew it closed again. When he turned to me, I saw how his eyes had darkened, how intensely his gaze bounced from corner to corner, landing inevitably back on that pillar.

"You don't belong down here, Sofia."

His voice dark and low, he took a step toward me. I took one back. His wet, cold hand wrapped around my arm and stopped my progress. He stalked closer, his damp body almost touching mine. He searched my face, my mouth, my neck, the swell of my breasts as I drew heavy, shuddering breaths. His gaze returned to mine, and we stayed like that, eyes locked, for an eternity. His shirt wet my dress. The hand that held my arm lowered to my wrist, and his other one wrapped around behind me to my waist, then higher, between my shoulder blades, icy on the back of my neck, cradling my head. Without a word, he leaned down and cool, wet lips covered mine.

I gasped, but he swallowed the sound, his hand at the back of my skull holding me in place as his lips moved over mine, slow and soft, tasting me. When his tongue probed, I opened, and he slid inside. I tilted my head, and he pressed against me. When he did, I felt him, his hardness, at my belly.

I would have stopped the kiss.

I did.

But he held me and reclaimed my mouth, and this time, urgency replaced the gentler exploration of moments ago. His kiss was hungry, ravenous almost, and his desire only seemed to wake the same inside me. I raised my hand and laid it against his arm, liking the feel of hard muscle there. Feeling somehow safe for it. My body eased, relaxing into him, and my eyelids fluttered closed.

But then he broke the kiss and leaned his forehead against mine.

His breath came heavy. His hands moved to my hips, holding me.

"I'm fucked up right now," he said. "You need to go upstairs."

I raised my head to look at his face, into his eyes. They told so much he didn't say, and it felt strange that I'd only known this man for days. I should hate him. Fear him. And I did fear him, but there was something else, a pull too powerful to ignore.

As dominant as he could be, as much as he commanded me, Raphael's vulnerability seemed to touch the edges of his hardness, to soften it, even if he tried to hide it, to bury it, and all I could think was that he was lost.

With trembling fingers, I touched his face.

One of his hands moved lower, then rose upward, sliding over my stomach, his skin burning through the thin cotton of the dress as he caressed belly then breast, and when his knuckle brushed against my hardened nipple, I felt it at my core, as if he touched me between my legs.

"I want you, Sofia. But I'm drunk, and I need you to go upstairs to your room and lock your door, understand?" His warm whiskey breath tickled my face.

"You won't hurt me." Was I so sure?

"I will. You don't know me."

"You keep telling me that."

"Maybe you should start believing it."

He cupped my breast over my dress, and I gasped, watching his hand move, fingers playing with my nipple, neither the dress nor the bra offering protection.

"You could have hurt me the other day, but you didn't," I said.

Eyes locked on mine, he tweaked my nipple, as if to prove his point. When I made a sound, he released it and stepped back to pull his T-shirt off with one hand.

"Touch me."

I looked at him, swallowing, something inside my belly fluttering. We both watched as my hands shook, as my fingertips touched his skin damp with rain. I caressed him lightly, softly. I wondered if he'd laugh at me, at my inexperience, but he didn't. He stood letting me touch him, letting me feel his heart beat beneath his skin. But when my exploration emboldened and my fingers trailed downward over ripped muscle to the trail of dark hair that disappeared inside his jeans, he grabbed my wrist roughly.

I gasped, my head snapping up.

"I told you to go upstairs to your room and lock your door. I'm drunk. I'll hurt you."

"You also told me to touch you."

He squeezed my wrist.

"You were right the other day. I want it. I want you." I swallowed, not sure what the hell I was doing, where this was going. "Kiss me again, Raphael."

A fire burned behind his eyes. My lips parted, and I licked them. Raphael pushed me against the wall, his mouth crushing mine in a kiss so intense, so full of everything, it hurt, it seared. It was as if he were leaving his mark. Claiming me. He pressed the flat of one hand against my belly, the back of my head against the cold, painful jagged stone.

"If you weren't a virgin, I'd fuck you here and now, against the wall."

The words came out in a ragged, hoarse voice. He didn't give me a chance to answer. To tell him to do it. Because some part of me, it liked this side of him. This damaged, dark, broken soul. It longed to touch him. To touch that fractured part of him. The one that left him open and lost and dangerous.

Instead, he smashed his mouth over mine again. I made a sound, not a protest, but also not a yielding. I knew he was drunk. I could taste it on his tongue. I liked it, I wanted it. I wanted him. But not like this. Not the first time.

Raphael drew back, his breathing hard. He gave me one hard glare then stepped away, turning his back to me. Even from behind him, I knew his gaze locked on that pillar.

"Your back, Raphael," I said, stepping closer, touching the bumpy, uneven skin. Scar tissue.

He whirled around and grabbed my wrist so hard I stumbled.

"Don't. Touch. Me." He squeezed. "Not my back."

"You're hurting me now," I squeaked after a moment.

It was as if it took him time to process my words, because it took him time to release me and step away. He dropped his gaze and ran a hand through his hair.

"I told you I would," he mumbled, then straightened and pulled the flask out of his back pocket. "Whiskey?"

He wasn't really offering it, but I shook my head anyway. He swallowed a large gulp. Hardness was slowly returning, laying concrete over broken ground. I watched it happening before my eyes.

"You shouldn't be down here, Sofia. This place," he looked around, shaking his head. "It's haunted."

"Haunted?" I wanted him back, the man I'd just seen, the one I'd glimpsed for mere moments. He wasn't making sense, and he wouldn't look at me.

Something told me I needed to get him upstairs. Get him out this cellar.

"Too much pain and suffering and hate." He spat the last word.

"Come upstairs with me, Raphael."

He shook his head. The light glistened against his too bright eyes. "Go."

"Not without you."

"I belong here."

He drank.

I went to him again, tentative this time as I raised my hand to touch his arm, the back of his hand. He watched it, watched the progress of my touch.

"You don't belong down here. No one does," I said.

He only looked at me.

"Come upstairs with me. Please."

"You don't know me. You don't know anything about me. You don't have the first fucking clue of what I'm capable of."

"I think I may know you better than you think. And you're right. There's too much hurt here. You need to come upstairs with me."

"Why? Why do you care? I mean, look what I'm doing to you."

I didn't answer that. I couldn't when I didn't know the answer myself. All I knew was that I couldn't leave him down there alone. Not now. Not ever.

"It's cold." I took his hand and dragged him, or tried to, toward the stairs, but it was like trying to move that pillar. "I'm cold. Take me upstairs."

He didn't answer, just watched me. I wasn't sure how much of the whiskey he'd already had. He didn't seem drunk, but he wasn't himself.

"Come on, I'm cold."

Just then, Charlie's yappy bark came from the top of the stairs. I looked up at him. He stood at the edge of the stairs still too small and maybe too frightened to take that first leap down. When I turned back to Raphael, I found him watching me with the strangest look in his eyes. I couldn't name it. Couldn't put my finger on what it was.

"Come with me, Raphael." This time, he let me lead him up. "Charlie will get hurt if he tries to come down." Slowly we went up, and Charlie circled our ankles when we got to the top. I turned out the light and closed the door behind us. He let me lead him through the house and up to the second floor. "You're freezing," I said when we got to my bedroom.

He just stood watching me.

I opened the door and pulled him in with me, not sure it was the best idea, not with that strange look in his eye. From the bathroom, I grabbed a towel and dried his hair, shoulders, and chest and set the towel on the bed. Unsure what I was doing, uncertain I should do it at all, I began to undo his jeans, first the button, then the zipper. He stood still, and I knelt to take off his shoes and socks so he stood barefoot, bare-chested, his jeans open, the dark gray of his briefs visible.

I pushed the jeans down off his hips, the wet denim sticking to his thighs. Swallowing, I bent again, and he stepped out of them.

"Sofia," he said once I straightened.

"Shh." I pulled the covers back. "We're just going to sleep." I meant it. Nothing would happen. Not yet.

His forehead had furrowed, and his eyes had lost some of their strange brightness. He nodded, and when I pushed on his chest, he got into bed. I drew the covers over him, watching how the thick muscle of his arms and shoulders bunched when he turned to his side.

Charlie tried three times to jump on the bed. I picked him up and lay him at Raphael's feet before grabbing my tank top and shorts and changing in the bathroom. Raphael lay watching me when I returned. I drew the covers back and climbed into bed, turning my back to him, taking care not to touch him. But then his heavy arm draped over my waist and pulled me to him. My heart raced and my breath hitched as he tucked himself around me, his big body wrapping around mine, his arm settling, his hand splayed open at my belly, holding me tight to him.

Neither of us spoke, but I knew he didn't sleep for a long time.

Eventually, his breath evened out, and I closed my eyes, my body too tired to fight the fatigue any longer, his body too warm for me to not curl into, to soften against.

"I haven't slept holding a woman like this. Ever."

I blinked my eyes open but didn't speak.

"I never wanted them to stay," he finished. He pulled me in tighter.

"Raphael—"

"Sleep, Sofia. Nothing's going to happen."

I reached my hand down and touched the back of his and closed my eyes and slept, and when I woke in the morning to sunlight coming through the curtains, he was gone, his side of the bed cold.

I sat in my study with the door locked, reading for the hundredth time the amendment to the contract that her grandfather had made. As much as I hated him for it, part of me wanted it, rejoiced in it.

That was the sick part. The part I tried to warn her about. The part she felt sure didn't exist.

I shook my head, my thoughts wandering again to last night. I should put a lock on that cellar door. I couldn't have her go down there again. I couldn't have her see what lay beneath those sheets. Hell, I should seal that door. Maybe then I could forget the things that had happened in that room.

Last night was the first time I'd been there in more than six years. It was raining, and I had needed to go to the chapel. To the cemetery behind it. I hadn't shown Sofia that part when I'd shown her the small church. It seemed too personal, too private. My excuse to use the tunnel had been the rain, although it was flimsy. I didn't care about getting wet, and if I did, I could have driven.

I wanted to see if that room still held power over me. If the horrors of it still haunted me. I thought I was stronger. That time would have toughened my skin. That six years in fucking prison would have squashed those memories, but they hadn't. Nothing ever could. Whenever I went down those stairs, I would become that little boy again, that scared little boy pissing his fucking pants.

I gritted my teeth.

It could be worse. I could be like him instead. Like my father. Hell, I wasn't sure I wasn't. Wasn't it better to be the victim?

No. Fuck, no. It was never better to be the victim. I needed to remember that, and maybe what I needed were more fucking visits to that hell, not less. Maybe what I needed was to have someone take the whip to me again. To teach me. To harden me.

Sofia's warm body pressing against mine all night, the sound of her quiet breathing, the feel of her softness as she finally relaxed in my arms, had finally let me exhale.

In my arms.

Fuck.

She'd surprised me when I'd returned to the cellar. That was the last place I ever expected to

find her. I ever wanted to see her. She didn't belong
in that world. I meant what I said, the past
haunted that cellar, and that past was full of
horrors. She did not belong there, and I'd be
damned if I'd let it touch her. Dirty her. Take her
innocence.

But wasn't I doing the same? Stealing that from
her? I didn't need the past to dirty her. I would do a
fine job myself. I wanted her. And the way I wanted
her was different than what I expected, what I had
planned. She was supposed to be afraid of me. That
was the plan. But holding her last night, holding her
in my arms, her taking care of me...taking care of
me? Why had she done that? I didn't understand. It
made no sense.

I stood and walked to the window. In the
distance, far enough from the women to not be
intrusive but close enough to do his job, stood Eric.
After my talk with Lambertini, I'd thought about
hiring a few more men.

From behind the curtain, I watched Sofia. She
wore a short turquoise sundress, her long hair in a
clip wet from a shower. I'd have to talk to her about
her wardrobe. The thought of anyone else looking at
what was mine bothered me.

She'd just walked outside. Charlie, whom I'd let
out at five this morning while she'd slept, ran to her,
and she grabbed him in her arms. A smile lit up her
face, but I saw how she looked around, and when

Nicola went outside and Sofia spoke with her, I knew she was asking about me.

I'd told Maria I wasn't to be disturbed. I told her to say I was gone.

I was truly fucked up. An asshole, really. Last night, she'd seen me. Really seen me. And she hadn't run. Not even when I'd let the darkness own me, just for a little while. The opposite, in fact. She'd stayed with me and refused to leave me behind in that place. She'd told me I didn't belong there. That no one did.

She doesn't know you.

She sat down at the outside patio table and sipped her coffee. When she glanced toward the study, I ducked behind the curtains.

I wanted her. I wanted more than just to fuck her. I wanted to have all of her.

Maybe it was prison. Maybe it was being locked up like some animal.

I'd told Sofia this would be a marriage on paper, but then I'd started fantasizing about her. About our wedding night. About prying her legs apart, making her mine. But I didn't want that. If she said no, I would stop. I wouldn't hurt her, not like that. But it made me fucking hard to think about it, and that was the part that scared me the most. I couldn't let it take hold of me, no matter what.

Maybe it wasn't prison after all that did it to me. Maybe it was her innocence. Her purity. Maybe it was some feeble attempt on my part to cleanse myself. Hell, maybe I sought absolution all along and didn't even fucking know it.

All I did know was that this wasn't how this was supposed to go.

But why couldn't it? Why couldn't I have her ? She belonged to me already. Why couldn't I have all of her?

I shook my head and returned to my desk. I picked up my pen and signed the amendment, then lifted the phone off its cradle to call my attorney. I needed to get things in order. Prepare. I needed to force myself to focus on that, not on the things Sofia had said, not on the look in her caramel eyes, not on the softness of her touch, the smoothness of her skin.

Not on the thought of how much she would hate me when she learned what I had just agreed to.

11

SOFIA

I didn't see Raphael for three days after what happened in the cellar. Maria just said he'd gone out on business. I don't know how I'd missed him leaving the bed that morning. I wondered what time he had left. I hadn't even felt him move when he'd climbed out of bed. All I knew was I'd slept like a rock in the warmth and safety of his arms. This man who would steal me away—he was the one who made me feel safer than I'd felt in years. Ever since my parents had died.

I'd been so young, but with Lina being younger, I'd become her protector, in a way. It wasn't even a conscious thing. It felt good to finally let go. So good, it made me realize how I'd been holding on for so long.

But what about Lina now? What would happen to her, now that I was gone? Who would protect her?

This idiocy about feeling safe in Raphael's arms, what was that? Shouldn't I feel the most afraid there?

But the image of him that night in the cellar, of his eyes, I couldn't get it out of my head.

Raphael Amado was broken. I wondered how long ago he'd been broken. Who'd done the breaking. The marks on his back told a horrifying story. How old had he been when it had happened? Judging from the scar tissue, it wasn't a one-time thing. Not even close.

It was late afternoon on the third day and the shadows had begun to grow long. When Eric went inside to eat dinner, I snuck away, tired of constantly being watched. I needed fresh air and exercise to clear my head, and quite frankly, I hoped I'd run into him. I wanted to see Raphael, to face this—whatever this was.

I didn't realize I was heading to the chapel until I got there. I wondered about the tunnel that led from the house here but shuddered at the thought of being underground for that amount of distance. I'd never been claustrophobic, but that scared me.

Instead of walking to the front door of the church, I headed around back. It felt a little wrong to do so, to come here without Raphael knowing, but I wanted to see his mother's grave. See where he'd been that night.

The overgrown path didn't help my progress, but

I pushed open the creaky little gate around the side of the church. I wondered how I'd missed the grave-yard the first day we'd come here, when he'd shown me the chapel, but with the thigh-deep grass, the grave markers were well hidden. Pushing weeds aside, I counted over a dozen grave markers, most of them flat stones in the ground, some taller. Finding his mother's wasn't hard. It was the only one with the weeds and overgrown grass cleared—literally pulled apart—and a single wilted dandelion lay before it.

He'd left a dandelion. He'd probably plucked it from the ground beside the grave. I felt sad to look at it, to think of him here, realizing he'd come empty-handed to visit his mother after all this time. I thought of him alone. Sitting in the spot where I stood now. And all I felt was lonely. It was almost too much.

The sound of a branch breaking startled me, making me spin around, my hand to my heart.

"I didn't mean to startle you."

For the briefest of moments, I thought it was Raphael. But then Damon smiled, and I hoped he didn't see my disappointment.

I forced a smile. "No, you didn't. I'm just jumpy." Embarrassed, I gestured around me. "Dusk in a cemetery. Probably not my smartest move."

Damon walked toward me. "I got here early. I like to come to the chapel when I'm here." He looked at the grave. "He won't let anyone maintain it."

I followed his gaze to the dandelion.

"Why not?"

Damon shook his head and looked at me, and the similarity in their features struck me.

"If I know my brother, he feels guilty over her death. He's like that. As hard as he is on the outside, he takes it all on on the inside. Always did."

A sudden gust of wind made me shiver.

Damon took off the sweater he was wearing and draped it over my shoulders. The gesture was kind, and maybe it was the fact that he was almost a priest that I didn't take it any way other than that. I noticed that he wore a black T-shirt beneath it, noticed he was built like his brother, and I quickly blinked away.

"Come on, let's go inside. It won't be much warmer, but you'll be out of the wind."

I climbed the stairs with Damon behind me. He pushed the door open, and I entered.

"How did you manage to get here on your own, anyway?"

"You mean Eric?"

He nodded.

"He was having dinner."

"Raphael won't like that."

"Too bad. I don't see why he needs to have me watched anyway."

"It's for your protection. And Maria's and the staff. Our father had enemies."

"I know. It's still odd." We sat down in a pew. "Can I ask you something?"

"Sure."

"I know it sounds strange, but the priest thing…" I shook my head. "I'm sorry, it's none of my business really, but I just want to understand."

"It's fine. I think it's a normal question to have, but I don't really have an answer. Not one that makes sense. It's just…a feeling."

I nodded, although I wasn't sure I understood what he meant.

He continued. "I like it here. It always soothes me somehow. Even though I live in a seminary and attend mass daily, this little chapel makes me feel something different."

"It's a special place."

"Maybe I like the ceremony of the Catholic church. The discipline. It too soothes me, I suppose. But maybe I'm just trying to escape the past. Who I am. The blood in my veins." We both looked at the altar as he spoke.

"You hold onto guilt too."

"No, it's different."

"Have you ever been in love?" I asked before I could stop myself.

He smiled at me and shrugged a shoulder. "I

went through a period of falling in love nightly with a different woman on each night."

I felt myself blush.

"How is my brother treating you?" he asked.

"He's...different than I thought he would be."

"He's not a monster, Sofia. When I met you, I thought you might be able to help him see that. But you have to see it first."

"I do. That's the thing. I just don't understand him, I guess. I expected him to be cruel. Or crueler. It would make more sense if he was." We sat quietly for a minute, our eyes on the altar. When a small mouse scurried over the top of it, I startled.

"I think he lives here," Damon said with a smile. "He seems to be here every time I am."

"I guess it's good the chapel is used by some... thing, even if it's just a mouse." I turned to him. "Damon, I'm sure this is very personal but... I don't know how to ask it actually."

"Just ask it."

He was so frank and so easy to talk to. "Raphael has marks on his back."

Damon's face darkened, and he shifted his gaze away from mine.

"And I was in the cellar the other night. I found him there. He said he'd been to your mother's grave, and I know he was drinking, and he—he wasn't himself." I hesitated, but decided to tell him what I thought. "I saw the pillar."

He nodded and returned his attention to the altar. "Our father was not a gentle man, Sofia," he said gravely before looking at me again. "And Raphael was a good brother. A protective brother to me and Zachariah."

"What—"

"The rest is for him to tell."

The door slamming against the wall startled us both. I jumped, gasping, and we both turned to look behind us. Raphael stood at the entrance of the chapel, one hand flat against the door he'd just smashed into the wall, the other fisted at his side, his face hard.

Damon stood. "Brother."

"Cozy in here," Raphael said, his gaze shifting from his brother to me, the accusation in his eyes chilling. "I was looking for you."

"You weren't home," I said, feeling guilty but not sure why.

"You shouldn't come out here on your own. It'll be dark soon."

"You just disappear and expect me to sit around and wait for you?"

Raphael ignored my comment but didn't deny it. He turned his attention to Damon and cocked his head to the side. "What were you telling her?"

"He wasn't telling me anything," I folded my arms across my chest. "You disappeared," I repeated.

Again, he didn't look at me. This was between the brothers.

"I always come to the chapel, you know that. I just happened to run into Sofia this time," Damon said.

"What do you expect me to do alone here day after day?" I asked. "When you're just gone without a word?" I felt annoyed at being ignored, irritated with myself at the emotion, the hurt, in my voice. But hadn't he felt something the other night? When he'd held me like he had, hadn't it meant anything?

Raphael and Damon glared at each other.

"Raphael, don't be stupid," Damon said as if they were somehow communicating without words.

"I'm being stupid when I can't find *my* fiancée anywhere, and when I do finally locate her, she's sitting cozy with my brother's sweater wrapped around her shoulders, the two of you whispering?"

"What the hell are you suggesting?" Damon asked, stepping into the aisle toward Raphael.

Raphael dragged his gaze to me. "You don't belong here, Sofia."

I let out a short exhale and stepped out of the pew too. "That's two places I don't belong. I don't even know why you want me here."

"I'll take you back to the house," he said, his tone level, empty of emotion.

I walked toward the door, then realized I had Damon's sweater on and tugged it off to hand back to him. "I can find my own way." But he stood in the doorway and didn't budge.

"No, you can't." He took my arm.

"Let me go."

"Raphael," Damon started, stepping toward us.

"You stay out of this. She belongs to me."

"I'm a human being! I don't *belong* to anyone!"

"Wrong."

With a quick, cold smile, Raphael marched me out of the church and down the steps. Night was falling fast, and I had to admit, he was probably right that I couldn't find my own way back.

"Why are you doing this?" I asked when he wouldn't release me but kept walking at a pace too fast for me to keep up without stumbling. "Let me go. I'm not a child. Or a prisoner for that matter. What's wrong with you?"

He stopped.

I tripped behind him.

Once he righted me, he opened the passenger side door of the truck, but I dug my heels into the ground.

"Get in."

"No. Not until you tell me why you're being so weird."

"I was looking for you," he finally said, his eyes hooded, any emotion shielded.

"You're the one who left in the middle of the night. Left and never came back."

"It was morning. That dog of yours was yapping. Get in the truck. Maria's waiting with dinner. Eric shouldn't have let you slip away."

"I don't like being followed and watched all the time."

"It's for your protection."

I didn't want to talk about Eric. "I don't understand you, Raphael. I thought after that night…"

"After that night?"

The way he asked it, so casually, like it had been nothing. Like nothing had happened. It made me feel so fucking stupid, I faltered.

"I don't want you hanging around with my brother," he said.

"We weren't hanging around. I just wanted to see—"

"My mother's grave? You wanted to see why I'm so fucked up?"

He grabbed me by both arms, his grip too tight.

"You're hurting me."

"Get in the damn truck."

"Why are you so angry?"

"Goddamn it, get in."

He lifted me up, put me in the truck, and closed the door before I could protest. He walked around to the other side and climbed in. I saw Damon watching us from the chapel door.

"What about your brother?"

Raphael reached over to strap me in, then turned the truck around and drove off too fast.

"He's a big boy. He can find his own way back."

"Why are you so angry?"

"I told you the other night, Sofia. I'm fucked up. That's all. Whatever you imagine happened between us, forget it."

"What I imagined?" I asked, feeling angry myself now.

He gave me a sideways glance.

"Slow down."

"You want to know about my back? About the scars?"

He didn't slow down, his hands fists on the steering wheel as we drove by the house and toward the gate leading off the property.

"Is that what you were asking Damon?"

"Where are we going? Slow down."

"My father whipped me. It was his special punishment just for me. I'm sure my brother told you all about it."

I watched his face, feeling truly afraid now as we bumped onto the road, wheels spinning, kicking up dirt.

"Dozens of times. Down there in that cellar. And that's not the worst of it."

"Raphael—" I reached over to touch him but drew my hand back.

"I needed to see it again. That's all that night was. I was drunk."

"Please slow down. You're scaring me." Just then we hit a pothole. I let out a small scream, my seat belt tightening as I shot my hands out to the dashboard.

He laughed, but the sound was strange, not a laugh at all, but he slowed the truck down.

"Are you scared of me or my driving?" he asked.

"Both," I answered honestly. "He didn't tell me anything about your scars. He told me you were a good brother. A protective one. That was all."

He looked at me, studying my eyes in the dim light of the dash.

"I asked him, and he said it was your story to tell. That's all, Raphael."

That seemed to calm him a little, and we drove in silence for ten minutes before he took a turn off to a winding road leading up toward what looked to be an abandoned, crumbling village.

"And it wasn't nothing," I said, collecting my courage. I studied his profile. "What happened the other night, you weren't just drunk. It was something."

He didn't reply. We both sat silent as we drove. He finally parked the car along the outer walls of the village. He switched off the engine and sat looking at it. I kept my eyes on him.

"What did Damon mean when he said you were

a protective brother?" I had to ask it. But I knew the answer, didn't I? I could guess.

Raphael turned to me, the pain in his eyes the same pain I'd seen the night before. He didn't answer my question. Instead, he climbed out of the truck. I undid my seat belt and followed.

"This is Civitella in Val di Chiana."

"It looks abandoned." It was so dark.

"It's not. Not completely. There are a few festivals during the summer, then again in September at the harvest, but apart from that, it's quiet."

I followed him up through the crumbling stone gate, looking around, reading the signs of the shops —a baker, a butcher, several little cafés. When I stumbled, he caught me and held my hand the rest of the way until we were at the top of the village in an open area, which must have once been part of the house that now lay in ruins. Grass had long covered the ground, and at the very center of the now small field, he stopped and looked up. I followed his gaze and stared in awe at the black sky dotted with diamond stars.

"No light pollution," he said and sat down.

I sat beside him.

"It's amazing."

"My mom used to bring me out here." He lay back. "On the bad nights."

I followed, and we both watched the sky.

"Take care when fighting monsters you don't become one," he said.

I turned my head, but he wasn't watching me.

"Nietzsche," he added.

"You're not a monster."

"You don't know me."

"You keep telling me that." He turned on his side to face me.

"You know what I want to do right now, Sofia?"

His gaze slid down to my mouth, then back to my eyes, and his hand came to my belly. Watching me, he slowly began to bunch up my dress, the fine cotton tickling my thighs as it rose higher and higher.

I put my hand over his. "Stop."

"Why?"

He took both my wrists and dragged them over my head before rolling on top of me.

I held my breath, gasping when I realized what I felt pressing at my stomach.

Raphael's mouth came to mine in a brief but lustful kiss.

"I want to make it hurt, Sofia."

His voice was so quiet, and desire burned in his eyes as he brought his mouth back to mine, his lips not soft, but not quite hard. He transferred both of my wrists into his one hand, and his other one slid to my thigh as he opened my legs with his knees, watching my face as he did so, watching my eyes with a darkness that both terrified me and made me want.

"Stop," I tried again, sounding unconvincing to my own ears.

"Maybe it's because of how I grew up."

His grip on my wrists tightened when I began to struggle as the fingers of his other hand roamed my inner thigh, rising higher, just brushing against the edge of my panties.

"Raphael—"

"There's been a change."

"What change?"

He shook his head, as if setting that thought aside. "It won't make a difference if I take you tonight or tomorrow night or the next night. You're mine. That's all that matters."

He swallowed hard and licked his lips, and I could hardly breathe for the look in his now dark eyes.

"Does it scare you that I want it to hurt you? That I want you to feel me take you. Feel me tear you."

I bit my lip.

"That I want to hear you cry out."

I gasped when his fingers slid into my panties, tickling the hair there.

"You don't know how hard I get when I think about your tight little pussy squeezing my cock. Imagining how warm your virgin blood will feel. What I want to know is—"

He kissed my mouth again as he lifted his hips a little, and his fingers closed over my sex.

"If you're wet for me."

He grinned, and I squeezed my eyes shut and turned my head to the side.

"Mmm."

He breathed against my ear as his fingers began to stroke me, making me suck in short, quick breaths as he tickled my clit.

"Please."

"Please, what?"

He slid a finger into my opening, and I stiffened. He rolled his weight off me but kept my wrists pinned over my head. We both looked down at how my dress lay wrinkled on my belly, my thighs parted, his fingers working inside my panties.

I should tell him to stop. But I couldn't do it. I couldn't tell him to stop. Because I wanted him. I wanted him as much as he wanted me, and I didn't care about the rest of it.

"Look at me," he commanded with a whisper.

I did.

He slowly drew his hand out of my panties and began to drag them down.

"Tell me to stop."

Down, down, down, off my thighs and past my knees and over my ankles.

"Tell me to stop, and I'll stop. I'll stop right now."

He released my wrists. I didn't move as he sat up,

and his gaze slid to my sex. He brushed his fingers through the dark curls then looked back at me.

"Tell me, Sofia. Tell me you don't want this. Tell me you don't want me."

I couldn't. God, I couldn't.

He smiled as if he already knew it. "You can't."

I didn't move, and he grinned.

"Open your legs."

I shook my head a little. That was all the resistance I could muster. He smiled and then, without breaking eye contact, he pushed one leg to open me up and returned his gaze to my sex. I lay there unable to move or speak as his fingers trailed through my hair again before he lowered his dark head to kiss me there.

My gasp was a muttering of his name. He then licked me, a quick flick of his tongue, then a slow circling around my clit. When he sealed his lips around it, I moaned, and my hands moved to his head, pulling at his hair as he knelt between my spread legs and looked up at me.

"I smell you," he said

Then, with his fingers on either side of the lips, he pulled me open.

"Your pretty little pussy is dripping for me."

He closed his mouth over my clit again and began to suck and lick. I gripped his hair and pulled and pushed—off and on and wanting him, wanting his mouth, wanting the feel of him on me, sucking me, his tongue so soft, the stubble at his jaw so rough. It took me only moments to come, the sound I made foreign to me as I squeezed my eyes shut. He sucked hard, making me gush, draining me of everything, swallowing up my pleasure, my denial, my want, all of me, until finally, my arms fell to my sides, and I exhaled loudly, the sound more a deep sigh as Raphael straightened, wiping the back of his hand across his wet lips, smiling down at me, victorious.

"I like the way you taste," he said, drawing my dress further up to reveal my bra. He pushed the cups down beneath my breasts and studied me, reaching for the zipper of his jeans as he did.

The sound of it suddenly animated me.

"Wait!"

He shook his head and planted one firm hand on my belly.

"Stay." He knelt. "Don't you fantasize about what it will feel like?" he asked, pushing his jeans and briefs down.

I looked at it, at his cock against his tight belly, thick and long, the tip wet. He gripped it and began to slowly pump, and when I met his gaze, he was watching me.

"Don't you wonder how it will feel to have my thick cock stretch your tight little cunt?"

I swallowed. I did. Every night. Every single night as I slid my fingers between my legs, I imagined just that. And the look on his face told me he knew it.

"You're mine, Sofia."

He pumped harder as he said it, and with his other hand, he reached to tweak one nipple, hurting me, making me cry out. It only seemed to excite him more, though, as he squeezed tighter and pumped faster. I bit my lip watching him, imagining the taste of his glistening cock, my gaze moving from his dark, shining eyes to his hand moving so fast, so hard, making me want. I leaned up on my elbows, and Raphael knelt over me. A sound came from deep inside his chest, and he came, ropes of cum splattering across my belly, my pussy, my chest, and neck, warm against my nipples as he emptied on me, before falling back onto the grass, spent, drained, like me.

I moved to cover myself, but he gripped my hand and shook his head and watched the sky.

"There's been a change to the contract," he said without looking at me.

The breeze felt suddenly cold against my skin, and I shuddered. "What change?"

Raphael squeezed my wrist and turned to me. "We'll be married in two days."

"Two days?" Why did I panic at the thought? I knew it was coming.

He nodded. "Don't look at me like that. At least you get to see your sister."

"Raphael—" I began to rise, but he stopped me. He sat up, took off his T-shirt, and began to wipe me clean. He didn't speak as he did, and once he was finished, he pulled the dress down to cover me.

"The change, Sofia," he said. "It's not the date. It's something else."

I sat up, the look in his eyes a warning.

"It's an amendment to the contract."

"What amendment?" I asked, knowing what he'd tell me, what he'd agreed to, it would be a betrayal of me.

"The marriage will be consummated."

Confused, I waited.

"Your grandfather requested the change."

"I don't understand."

"He wants your blood on my sheets."

The detachment in his tone left me cold.

I shook my head, pulling away from him. I would consummate the marriage. I wanted it. He had to know that. But didn't *he* want it? Was tonight...would he make love to me—no, he wouldn't make love. He would fuck me. I should never make that mistake, not with him. He would fuck me to fuck my grandfather. That's all this was about, and I'd been a fool to think otherwise even for a second.

He stood. "Let's go. I'm hungry."

I could only stare up at him, not believing what I was hearing.

"One night, Sofia. You'll survive it. Don't look at me like that. Don't pretend you don't want it."

He reached down to grab hold of me.

"Get away from me," I said, scrambling backward.

"Christ."

I stood, backing away. "Why didn't you just tell me? Why humiliate me like this?" I looked at my panties discarded on the grass, and that shame I felt made my skin burn.

"Don't be dramatic. Let's go."

"You're going to take something that could be beautiful and make it ugly. You have no right." I tried to process, to understand how this could be happening. "Do I repulse you?" I finally asked.

"What?" he asked.

I snorted, shaking my head. "You're going to fuck me so you have bloodied sheets to prove the marriage is binding? To ensure my grandfather doesn't contest your supposed rights to my inheritance?"

He inhaled deeply and watched me, as if confused himself.

"You don't repel me. Far from it," he said.

"I can't believe you. God, I am such a fool, aren't I?"

"Calm down, Sofia. Let's go home."

"I already told you, this isn't my home. It will never be my home. You've just made sure of that."

"All right, that's enough."

He grabbed hold of my arms.

"I hate you," I said, tears blurring my vision. "I hate that you're going to do this to me."

"It's not like you don't want it."

"I'm not talking about the fucking, you prick!"

Without answering me, he turned, keeping hold of one of my arms and walking us back to the truck.

"Let me go. Get off me."

"And what, leave you here? Call for my brother to come get you? You'd like that, wouldn't you? You two sure got close fast, Sofia."

I fought him the whole way back to the truck, even though it was futile.

"Well, news flash. He's going to be a fucking priest. He's celibate. Or should be."

What the hell did that mean? "I don't want your brother. It's not like that."

"No?" He opened the driver's side door and lifted me up, then pushed me across the bench to the passenger side. "What's it like, then?"

"I keep thinking you're one way, but you're not," I said as he started the engine and put the car in gear.

"Put on your seat belt."

"I keep thinking you're just lost and hurt and—"

"Well, maybe you should stop thinking that. Maybe you should just accept the fact that I am a fucking monster. That I will fuck you, so I can show your sick grandfather the bloodied sheets he wants to see."

"You're both sick." I covered my face with my hands.

"Well, look on the bright side. One night with me and it's done. You don't ever have to touch me again."

"You're right," I said, not even caring he was driving too fast. "You were right all along. I shouldn't have ever thought anything else. You are a monster. Just like your father."

After the evening in Civitella in Val di Chiana, I doubted Sofia would appreciate that we'd be married in the Basilica of Santa Croce in Florence, alongside the resting places of Michelangelo, Galileo and Machiavelli, before the eyes of God and a handful of witnesses and fucking throngs of tourists. Tourists were unavoidable this time of year. I could almost tolerate them.

It had taken an exorbitant contribution to book the basilica, but it only concretized my thinking. Money was what everything came down to and that included the church. But I had to admit, this was a magnificent display of devotion and art, even if it was wasted.

I stood at the altar, waiting for my bride. The rope did little to keep curious visitors at bay. Beside me stood Eric as witness and another man arranged by my attorney. I didn't know who he was. In the front pew sat Sofia's grandfather, the great Marcus Guardia, his expression unreadable. At his side sat Lina. Smaller than Sofia but not by much. As pretty as her. The old man had kept his end of the bargain after I'd signed the amended contract. Across the aisle sat Maria. I hadn't invited anyone else to the wedding.

About two dozen strangers, worshippers who most likely were not expecting a wedding, dotted the other pews, giving the appearance of being guests. The priest cleared his throat and made a show of checking his watch.

It took another five minutes before the doors were opened, and someone stepped in to signal the music. The organist began to play the wedding march, and I took a moment to straighten my tie. I'd worn black on black. It was fitting.

Two men secured the large doors of the worshippers' entrance. From the waning sunlight outside, I could make out the two forms, the white of the dress casting a sort of halo around Sofia. Beside her stood my brother. My fucking brother. Tall and proud in his suit, Sofia's arm tucked into his. I could almost see him patting it, telling her it would be all right. Reassuring her when he had no business to.

I didn't know when she'd asked him to walk her

down the aisle. I understood she didn't want her grandfather. That made perfect sense. But this? It pissed me off, actually.

The organist started the march again, and they took their first steps. Once they stepped fully into the church, I could make out their faces. My brother, for all his support of a few nights ago, now condemned me with his gaze. I wondered how much he knew. How much she'd told him.

Sofia gazed at the floor. Her veil shielded her from me until she was about a third of the way down the aisle. That was when she hesitated. Damon paused too, then whispered something to her. She seemed to take a full minute to compose herself, and before my very eyes, she straightened, standing taller, her spine straighter. She looked directly at me.

I met her gaze, felt the unnatural chill inside her eyes, accepted the accusations she threw like grenades. But she had never looked more beautiful to me than in that moment.

The dress fit as if it were made for her, hugging her delicate curves, the antique veil with yellowing edges not quite concealing her but adding an almost ethereal air to her, to her beauty. Her hair had been intricately braided, only a few soft strands falling around her face, over her shoulder, and her golden eyes shone as if covered over by a layer of ice crystals.

She never shifted her gaze. Never faltered again

as Damon walked her toward me. As he faced her, the look they exchanged made me fist my hands at my sides. It wasn't attraction or affection, not more than that of friendship, but it seemed as though a bond had been formed between them, and I knew in the way he looked at me, the way he looked at her, that he knew what had happened between us. What would happen still.

I hated him for it in that moment. I hated him for having something of her that I did not. That I never would.

My brother lifted her veil and gave her a gentle smile, a kiss on the cheek. A whispered word. I'd fucking kill him for it.

He then turned her to me.

Tears didn't shine in her eyes. Her lip didn't tremble. When she looked up at me, all I saw was hate. A hate that came from betrayal. From a budding trust destroyed.

And in spite of it, or perhaps because of it, she took my breath away.

I turned her toward the altar and stood quietly by her side, listening to her breathe, listening to the priest but not hearing his words. Hearing her quiet "I do." Speaking my own. Catching the slight tremble of her hand as she handed her bouquet of blackest lilies—appropriate if not dramatic—to my brother, who remained by her side. She then faced me again, and I took her hand. From my pocket I retrieved her wedding band. A ring of thorns made of iron, black and rounded to slide onto her finger, jagged to remind her of her place.

She looked down at it once it was fully seated on her delicate finger, and I wondered what thoughts circled her mind.

The priest cleared his throat, and I wanted to slap him. To tell him to give her time. To let us be.

Sofia met my gaze. I handed her my ring. She took it, and I held out my left hand. As she slid the serrated ring onto my finger, she gasped, hesitating at the sudden sight of blood, faltering.

Her mouth fell open, her eyes wide when she met mine.

"Do it," I said.

She shifted her gaze back to my hand and dragged the spiked band upward, her eyes now fixated on the lines of red that appeared along my finger. The first dark droplet fell, soiling the snow-white of her dress, and when she pulled her stained fingers away, she looked up at me again, the ice in her eyes different, less cold. Confused now. Lost.

Lost again.

I gripped the back of her neck and forced her attention back to the priest who had gone a little pale at the blood.

"Finish it," I spat.

He met my gaze, swallowed, fumbled with his

Bible—fucking idiot—and then pronounced us husband and wife.

I kissed my bride with a hunger that would devour her. A warning to her. A promise of what would come.

"What did you do with the ring?" I asked when we got into the car. "Your finger—"

"It'll heal."

"Why did you do that? Why would you?"

"I thought it would be a constant reminder of you," he said with a smile not meant to be one at all.

"I don't understand you."

"What do you have with my brother?"

"Nothing. Are you jealous?"

"Not jealous. Remember, truth. I want truth, always."

"Well, he's not crazy. That's one thing we have, I guess."

"He's a different kind of crazy. I'm warning you now to be careful with him. You don't know my brother."

"And I already like him better than you."

"Isn't that a shame for you, then."

Silence.

I pulled the pins holding the veil on my head off and folded it on my lap. I glanced out the tinted windows, watching as Lina and my grandfather got into another sedan. Lina looked over at our car and waved. I waved back, watching as we drove away that they followed.

Lina had called me in a panic just days ago. She'd told me Grandfather wouldn't bring her to the wedding. Something had changed his mind. I wondered what.

Dinner would be catered at the house tonight, and I understood that the party at the reception would be larger than those gathered at the church. But I was surprised to find over a dozen cars parked at the house upon our arrival.

"Who are all these people?"

"Cousins. Business associates. Local people from the farms nearby. People I need to see, now that I'm back."

"Oh." I looked into the brightly lit house, saw people moving inside. The pool area and back veranda were lit by candles and lanterns. As Raphael helped me climb out of the car, I could see tables set for dinner with pretty white tablecloths and ornate centerpieces. Black lilies. Like my bouquet. That was the only piece I'd had a say in, and I was determined

to make my mark. Let him know how I saw this
unholy union.

"I arranged for your sister to stay with us for a
few days," Raphael said out of the blue.

"What?"

"Your sister. I know you want to spend time with
her."

"But my grandfather—"

"Your grandfather is welcome to leave whenever
the hell he wants. She's staying. I arranged it," he
said, cutting me off. "I told you I wouldn't be a beast
to you."

"Why?"

"Why won't I be a beast?"

"Why would you do that for me?"

"Just say thank you," he said as we rounded the
corner. All heads turned to us.

"Thank you."

I didn't have a chance to say more because we
were swept up by the crowd, too many people I
didn't know coming to us, congratulating us in Italian, kissing my cheek, handing us envelopes I hadn't
expected. As if this were a real wedding.

Raphael smiled beside me, talking to people,
hugging some, shaking hands with others. He
seemed relaxed, more relaxed than I'd ever seen
him. And he never took his hand from my back,
keeping me close to him, introducing me to too
many people, none of whom I'd remember.

My sister and grandfather had arrived. Damon stood with Lina. Grandfather hovered behind her like a dark shadow. I shuddered at the image but was distracted when I was handed a champagne glass and someone made a toast.

I looked at Raphael, who seemed to watch me through it all, as if one eye were constantly on me.

"Drink," he said.

I did.

An extravagant dinner followed, only breaking up when coffee was served. Raphael and I greeted more guests who had come after the dinner. An SUV with tinted windows, including the windshield, driving onto the property caught my eye. Raphael stiffened beside me. When three men in suits descended, I turned to ask him who they were.

"Go inside with your sister," he said, barely looking at me. Dismissing me even.

"Raphael—"

"Go."

He nodded to Eric, giving him an order in Italian. Eric glanced at me with a tight smile.

"Take your sister and go inside, Sofia. I have to take care of some business."

I didn't even have time to ask a question before he walked away to greet the men. I went to my sister, feeling my grandfather's eyes on me but unable to look at him.

"Lina," I said, drawing her away and into the

house. "Raphael arranged for you to stay here for a few days."

"I know. Grandfather told me he agreed. Said it was your wedding gift."

"I'm so glad."

"Me too. You look really beautiful by the way. You make a really good-looking couple."

"Don't say that."

"You'll make beautiful babies too."

"It will never come to that, I swear," I said and led her to the living room, where she immediately went to the piano.

"You never know," she taunted, letting her fingers run over a few keys.

"Oh, I know."

She turned to me and looked me over from head to toe.

"Really, you're so beautiful right now."

"Thanks."

"He can't take his eyes off you either," she said, nodding behind me.

I turned to see Raphael's dark gaze on me even as he headed toward his study. The men who'd approached as he'd sent me away followed him, and I didn't miss the way they scrutinized me and knew Raphael didn't either.

It was another half hour before Raphael's door opened again. Lina sat playing the piano with a group collected around her to listen. I watched the men leave, their faces tight. Raphael followed close behind, and I didn't miss how he held his hands fisted at his sides. I watched them walk out the front door, noticed the quiet murmur of whispers and sideway glances and wondered who they were. I would have asked Damon, but Raphael came to me then, taking me by the arm and giving me an elaborate smile and bow that called the attention of every man and woman in the place.

"Time for me to take my bride to bed," he said to the delight of all present. All but me. When he met my gaze, though, I saw the shadow in his eyes. This casual attitude, it was a front. Something had happened with those men.

I let him lead me toward the stairs. I glanced back and saw Lina and Damon watching, concern in her eyes, a warning in his, a warning to his brother. One I knew Raphael would not heed.

Up we went, Raphael and I. Up past my bedroom, disappearing down the hall to the last room, the one with large double doors which he opened then stood back and gestured for me to enter.

Our gazes locked, and although I knew I had no choice, that neither of us did, I knew stepping into his bedroom would change everything for us. I didn't even know what I wanted anymore. What I didn't want. It was too much to make sense of. Too much to take in.

And so when he called my name, drawing me back to the present, I took that step, and he followed. The door closed behind us, and the lock clicked, slipping into place, and I turned to him to begin our dance.

W as it possible to hear a heart beating?

Sofia's pounded at a frantic pace. She stood just inside my bedroom. Her gaze slid from mine, and I watched her take it in, seeing it anew from her eyes. It was the biggest bedroom of those not damaged by fire. The one I'd grown up in was all but destroyed. The furnishings here were few and brand-new: dark carpet, dark curtains to match, a king-size bed against the far wall, and a table holding a lamp on the side I slept, a chair and table in one corner on which I tossed my jacket. That was all.

She turned her gaze back to mine.

I loosened the tie at my neck and pulled it over my head, hanging it over the back of the chair, then undid the cuffs of my sleeves one by one. I set them on the table before rolling each sleeve up. All the while, Sofia and I watched each other.

"Who were those men?" she asked.

Her question took me back. I turned away from her and took the lid off the bottle of whiskey on the small table, pouring us each a tumbler. She only hesitated for an instant before taking the glass I offered her.

"Business associates of my father's."

"Not friends or family?"

"No."

"Why were they here, then?"

"Did they upset you?"

"No. Just...I didn't like how they looked at me. And they felt... I don't know. They weren't invited guests, were they?"

"No." No sense in lying.

She took it in.

"You're safe, Sofia."

"Am I?"

I didn't reply but touched my glass to hers and drank. She did the same. Once our glasses were empty, I took hers and set them both down. "Get undressed."

"Oh, that's right. Down to business."

I smiled and wrapped an arm around her waist to pull her to me. "I'll make it good for you."

Her hands pressed against my chest. "Do you

have any idea how humiliating this is for me? To know my grandfather—"

"Forget the old man. Forget everything. You want this. And so do I."

My hands worked the topmost buttons of the back of her dress. She drew back. "Stop."

"Don't make me take it from you, Sofia."

"Would you?"

"I don't want to."

"That's not what I asked."

"I'll make you come. I promise."

"You think this is about an orgasm?"

"If only it were that easy," I said, releasing her, stepping away to run a hand through my hair, thinking. Thinking. I faced her. "This thing, Sofia...this amendment...Your grandfather is testing my weakness. He's testing to see if *you* have become my weakness."

"What do you mean?"

"He used Lina. He said he wouldn't allow her to be here with you to see what *I'd* do. See if I'd give in to this demand, or tell him to go fuck himself. If I told him to fuck himself, then he'd know I didn't give a shit about you."

She bowed her head, her hand coming to her throat. "I need to sit down for a minute."

She perched on the edge of the bed, not moving for a long time, probably trying to make sense of what I'd just told her. She began to undo the pins holding her hair together and set them on the night-stand. I counted twenty-seven by the time she was done and her hair fell in waves over her shoulders.

"Why didn't you tell me that the other night?" she asked.

"Because I was pissed I'd been played. I was pissed at finding you and my brother—"

"That was nothing like what you thought."

"I know. I know now."

"Is there more?"

Now wasn't the time for the "more." "Forget him. He's not why we're here, understand? Not anymore."

She didn't reply but watched me thoughtfully.

"Come here, Sofia."

She rose to her feet and crossed the room.

"Turn around."

She did, obedient. She knew this had to happen as much as I did. I didn't want to take it from her. I didn't want her to make me take it.

I stepped to her, and she kept her back to me. Touching her as lightly as I could, I lifted the mass of hair over her shoulder. She still trembled, though, at that lightest brush of skin on skin. I looked at her neck, delicate and so fucking fragile. It made me realize how vulnerable she was. How easily she could be hurt.

My mind traveled to the men who'd come, the ones she'd asked about. Moriarty and his goons. I hadn't missed the way he'd looked at her. In marrying her, she could become my vulnerability. Or my strength, depending. If she were viewed as a debt owed to me, it would show my ruthlessness. If she were viewed as someone I felt for, a woman I possibly cared about, then she was a weakness.

Was this to be my next war?

I would not be weak.

I could not.

Not if I wanted to survive. Not if I wanted us both to survive.

My eyes were drawn to the exposed skin at her back, each vertebra making up her spine, the perfect skin stretched over bone and muscle. She gasped, stiffening when I moved to undo the pearl buttons one by one, enjoying the painstaking process, wanting to make this moment last. Once I had unbuttoned down to the middle of her back, she moved her hands to keep the dress to her chest. I pulled it apart a little and looked at her, swallowing when, as if of their own accord, my hands reached to touch trembling flesh, tracing the lines of her shoulders, shoulder blades, spine.

She turned her head so she could see me from the corner of her eye. Even in profile, with her upturned nose, high cheekbones, and full lips, she was perfection.

"Wisdom," I said absently, slowly unbuttoning the rest of the buttons, lower and lower until I could see the top of her lace panties.

"What?" she asked, her voice a whisper.

"Your name. Sofia. It means *wisdom*."

We locked gazes, and I pushed the dress off her shoulders. She hesitated but dropped her arms and let it slide to the floor, let it pool around her ankles. She wore no bra and now stood with her hands covering her breasts. My gaze slid down her back to her lace-clad ass. My cock twitched, but it wasn't just a fuck I wanted. It was so much more. A claiming. A taking. An owning. But even that wasn't enough, not if it was only her body.

I wanted more.

I wanted everything.

"You are so beautiful," I said, tracing the curve of her spine, liking how her body reacted, how she tightened, aware of my every fleeting touch. I leaned my head closer and kissed her shoulder, at the soft bend at her neck. She made a sound, and I turned her around and took her face in my hands.

"Sofia. Innocent and wise and so fucking beautiful." I kissed her mouth, wanting to taste her, taste her sweetness before the fire, before the intensity, before the pure need would overtake me. I kissed her softly. She opened, and I slipped one hand to the base of her skull, cradling her head. Her hands rose to my chest. I took one wrist and dragged it down my cock. When she gasped and tried to pull away, I tightened my hold on it and broke our kiss so I could watch her face.

She opened her mouth as if to speak, but nothing came.

"I want you so fucking badly, you have no idea."

"Raphael—" She tried again to pull away. "Not this way. Not because of some contract."

"Fuck the contract. I don't care about the contract. It doesn't make any difference. I want to make you mine, Sofia. That's all. Mine."

She moaned as I took her face in both hands and kissed her again, then pulled back but held her close.

"Take off my shirt."

Cautious, unsure, her curious eyes met mine then blinked and shifted to the buttons on the shirt. She gave me a slight nod, and her fingers trembled when they touched the first button, undoing it, fumbling as they slid to the next, her touch making my cock harder.

I wanted to have a bath to calm her, but I wasn't sure how long I'd last with her this close. The thought alone of her naked, sitting in the bath cradled between my legs, was difficult enough.

She moved slowly, the trembling of her fingers making the task harder, but soon, she was pulling the shirt out of my pants and, once all the buttons were undone, she pushed it apart, her eyes following her hands as she stroked my chest and pushed the shirt off my shoulders. She looked up at me, her hands curled over my biceps.

Her smile vanished when I faced her again and this time, grabbed hold of either side of her waist and dragged her backward toward the bed. When the backs of her knees hit the mattress, she sat. I spread her legs and knelt between them, my gaze moving from her face, over the small mounds of her breasts, down to the lace panties, the hair, and the slit of her pussy visible through it. With one hand, I dragged the crotch of her panties aside, exposing her pussy to me. She gasped, but I took hold of one leg and drew her forward so she sat on the very edge of the bed.

I brought my mouth to her clit and licked, then sucked. Sofia's legs spread a little wider, then closed around either side of my head. "You want it as much as I do. Forget about everything. Nothing matters but this."

I pushed them wide again and pulled away, sliding her panties off and discarding them, so she sat naked. I then stood and while she watched, stripped off the rest of my clothes.

"You're going to come with my cock inside you tonight, sweetheart."

Sweetheart. I liked it. It fit her.

Pushing her backward, I climbed between her legs and kissed her mouth again, liking the feel of her against me, her nakedness pressing against my own. My cock ached to be inside her, but I held back, wanting to taste every inch of her first, her lips, her cheek, the pulse pounding at her neck, her collarbone, the space between her breasts, her taut nipples, the flat of her belly, the hair at her pussy, her thighs.

Sofia was panting by the time I drew up on my knees and pushed her legs apart, taking one and bending it up beside her, exposing her wholly to me.

"I want to fuck you hard, Sofia."

She shrank away a little, fear and desire warring in her eyes.

Watching that, watching her face, I brought my cock to her wet entrance and pressed the head into her.

Her hands came to my chest, but she didn't push. I did, though, stretching her slowly, inch by inch, watching her eyes as I did, holding on as her tight pussy squeezed my cock until I hit her barrier.

"Raphael," she started, panic edging her voice.

"Sofia," I groaned, wanting so badly to thrust, knowing how it would hurt her if I did.

I drew back, letting go of her leg, setting her thighs on top of mine so I could still see her face.

"Eyes open. On me," I said.

She shook her head, but her nails dug into my shoulders as she braced herself. I pumped in and out slowly, not yet breaking her barrier, sliding two fingers over her clit and rubbing.

"Open your eyes," I reminded when she bit her lip and closed them. "Look at me."

At the next thrust, I pushed deep, feeling the resistance, feeling it give, hearing her little cry as warmth engulfed my cock. I closed my eyes for a moment, that feeling of owning her so complete yet so fleeting, I wanted to hold on to it. When I opened them, I found her watching me. I began to work her clit again, turning pain to pleasure as I thrust deeper, harder, drawing all the way out then in again, watching her face. I lay my weight on top of her and closed my mouth over hers.

"Fuck, Sofia." I grunted as she closed her eyes and made a sound, the same one she'd made the night under the stars. Her cunt squeezed around my cock, and I watched her face, saw it tighten, then soften, her eyes slowly blinking open, her fingernails breaking my skin.

Seeing her come pushed me over the edge, and with one final thrust, I stilled inside her. I watched her watch me as I emptied, blood and cum from her and me mixing, smearing together, taking everything from me until finally, I collapsed on top of her, holding her, my cock sliding out of her, soiling the perfectly smooth skin of her thigh and reddening my sheets.

I WOKE at my usual time, three o'clock in the morning, and lay listening to Sofia sleep, her naked body pressed against mine. I opened my hand wide on her belly, holding as much of her as I could.

Last night had been good. Better than I expected. The physical attraction between us was mutual, but there was more than that. I wanted to hold on to it, to that thing, whatever it was. I knew it was important.

And impermanent.

Because I couldn't have that, and the reason I'd done this in the first place. It was one or the other.

The old man's test only strengthened my resolve.

I couldn't forget why I was doing this. Why she was here.

I wouldn't.

Rolling over onto my back, I stared up at the sliver of moonlight that slipped between the split in the curtains and streaked the ceiling. Sofia made a sound, and for a moment I thought I'd woken her, but then she curled up against me, the top of her head burrowing into me, her body hugging into itself, little fists and knees close. Unmoving, I watched her until she stilled and then wrapped my arm around her again, holding her to me. I wondered if she would consciously do this, nuzzle against me, if she were awake.

Thing was, I thought she might.

Maybe that's what made this so hard.

Marcus Guardia had used Sofia's love for Lina to test *me*. To test *my* weakness. He'd probably been planning it all along. The bastard had read me like a fucking book, and I'd fallen right into his trap.

If for a single moment I thought he might feel some modicum of emotion for his granddaughter, the ease with which he'd sacrificed her body obliterated that notion. We were all pawns in his twisted game.

But I'd turned it around. Managed to use it to my advantage with Sofia.

I guess I too was a master manipulator.

Telling her about consummating the way I had had been cruel. But giving her the gift of her sister at the wedding, it had turned her back around. Probably confused the fuck out of her, but hell, this whole thing confused the fuck out of me.

Sick fucking bastard, her grandfather. I wondered if he thought I wouldn't go through with it if she refused. Maybe that was his reason for asking it. Maybe he thought she'd cry rape. Put me in fucking prison again. Or maybe he truly just didn't give a shit about her.

Last night happening the way it had, though, it changed everything. She'd given herself to me. I hadn't had to look in the mirror this morning to find a monster more terrible than Marcus Guardia staring back.

But there was more. More that didn't concern Sofia, not yet anyway. I'd hold on to it, use it when I needed to.

Marcus Guardia wanted five percent back. Lina could come and spend a few days with her sister if I agreed to forfeit five percent, receiving only forty-five percent of shares, not fifty. This way, he ensured they kept control of Guardia Winery.

He wasn't a fool. He suspected I'd drive the company into the ground as soon as I could, as soon as I had the ability to. And I still would. I'd just do it differently than I imagined. He'd still pay. Hell, this way, he'd lose it all, not just half.

And I'd lose Sofia once it all came to pass.

But there was more to consider than Marcus Guardia. My meeting with Moriarty hadn't gone well. I hadn't realized how deep in debt my father had been. And Moriarty wasn't about to forgive that debt just because my father was dead. He still had every intention of collecting.

I couldn't give him what he wanted, though, because what he wanted was my mother's legacy. This house. The land. All of it. He'd even pay me for it, at least the portion my father didn't owe him.

Moriarty was a business developer. Well, that was the legitimate front. He had a way of getting what he wanted and didn't have any problem using whatever means he needed to. When Damon had told me to call the police and let them handle it, he didn't realize Moriarty had the police on his payroll. I'd have to deal with him, and I couldn't have Sofia be a part of that.

I felt like two boulders pushed at me from either side, squeezing the life out of me. All while I held Sofia, trying to keep her from getting crushed.

I got up out of bed.

Sofia stirred but settled quickly. I covered her with the blanket and slipped on a pair of jeans, then, from my closet, I retrieved the soiled sheet Maria had folded and placed there on my instruction while I'd washed Sofia. I took it downstairs, into the living room. There, I lit a fire in the fireplace and watched it take, watched the kindling burn, watched it set the wood aflame. I studied that fire for a long while. I don't even think I consciously decided. I set the sheet in the flames, destroying it, watching it burn, all evidence of our wedding night turning to ash.

In a way, it was symbolic because inside, I too was ash.

15

The next morning when I woke, Raphael was gone. I wondered if he slept, how many hours he slept. Last night, after making love to me—and he had made love to me—he'd washed me so tenderly, so carefully, it surprised me. Although maybe it shouldn't have. Maybe duality was the norm with him. Maybe knowing he had a capacity to be tender would make a difference, would make tolerating him when he was terrible bearable. Because I also knew he would be terrible.

Or maybe that knowledge would only make those moments that much harder.

After the night in Civitella in Val di Chiana, I didn't know how I'd be able to go through with the wedding. The wedding night. But then he'd told me why. My grandfather had used Lina like a pawn.

He'd seen a window, my weakness, and had used it against Raphael.

I needed to talk to my grandfather. I needed to confront him and hear from him his side of the story, about the stealing, about his agreement with Raphael. But I wasn't fool enough to think he'd tell me the truth. At least not all of it. But there were two sides to every story, and he had raised me. The man had given us shelter, if not love, for thirteen years. He'd given us the best that money could buy. He couldn't hate us.

He sold you out.

Literally.

Yes, he had. But if I were honest with myself, the way he felt about me wasn't the same as what he felt for Lina. Maybe it was because she was younger. Maybe it was her nature, that she forced some affection, even if it was the slightest bit of it from him?

Lina aside, though, I couldn't forget or deny that he had gone against me. And if what Raphael said was true, that he was stealing from me, from Lina— he had to be stopped.

But he was still my grandfather.

I rubbed my neck, trying to soothe the headache that was forming.

Another thing had been niggling in the back of my mind for a few days. Ever since the flight to Italy. I was eighteen now. I was married. Together with Raphael, I was capable of supporting my sister.

Could I request and be granted guardianship of her? Could I bring Lina here to live with us? If my grandfather didn't allow it, which I felt would be his response, would I fight him in court? Could I? How public would I be willing to go—if what Raphael said was true? How much would it hurt Lina? Her relationship with him was different. They lived in the same house. I'd been gone for four years.

But there was another question too. Would Raphael allow it?

He'd given me the gift of time with her. He knew how much she meant to me. But to bring her here to live with us?

Would Lina even want to? She'd have to leave everything behind. How would she feel about leaving our grandfather alone? And could I cast doubt on her faith in Grandfather, when I wasn't sure myself what was true?

It was a lot to think about. I climbed out of bed, then remembered that when Raphael had been bathing me, someone had come into the bedroom to change the sheets. My face heated at the thought of it, of someone—Maria, I would guess—knowing. Is that where he was now? Showing them to my grandfather?

I shook my head, forcing that thought away. I wouldn't think of it. I couldn't. It was too terrible. And as much as I didn't want to, I knew I had to talk to my grandfather this week before he returned home.

I picked up my cell phone and found his number, but I put it away again. I wouldn't call or make an appointment. I would show up at his hotel. Surprise him. Maybe catch him off guard.

Besides, I had more important things to do today.

Realizing I had no clothes in Raphael's room— the person who'd changed the sheets had even taken the wedding dress—I opened the door to his walk-in closet. I switched on the light and deeply inhaled, the scent of him strong here. I wasn't sure what I expected to find, but it wasn't much. A few suits were hung neatly, all dark, some pairs of jeans were folded and stacked, and T-shirts. A mountain of them. All were either black or white.

I chuckled. Ironic. Black and white. Good and evil. He was both.

Turning, I found a discarded black T-shirt on top of the laundry basket. Glancing around to be sure I was alone, I picked it up, brought it to my face, and inhaled. Without overthinking it, I pulled the shirt over my head. It fell to midthigh, which would do. I left his bedroom and tiptoed down the hall to mine, aware of the ache between my legs, of how he'd taken me, how he'd been almost gentle. At first.

I still wondered if I had said no, would he have forced me?

Once in my room, I quickly got changed into a pair of shorts and a tank top, brushed my teeth and washed my face, pulled my hair into a ponytail, and headed to Lina's bedroom. She was already in the hallway when I stepped out of my bedroom, dressed and carrying Charlie, cooing to him as he nuzzled against her, his little tail wagging.

"I love him so much," she said when she saw me.

"Me too. He's wonderful."

She looked at my face and smiled.

"You look good." She winked.

"Shut up," I said, taking her by the arm and leading her to the stairs. "I'm starving. You?"

"Yes."

"How did you sleep?"

"Great. I didn't sleep on the flight, and I was dead on my feet."

"Did you talk to Grandfather today?" I asked.

"Not yet. I told him last night that I'd call him today for lunch. It would be good for you too. You can't avoid him forever. Maybe give him a chance to explain."

I linked my arm through hers, and we walked down the stairs and into the kitchen. "I know I have to see him. It'll help to have you there."

"Then it's decided," Lina said.

Nicola handed me a note as soon as I walked into the kitchen.

"For you."

"Thanks," I looked at the folded sheet of paper, confused, then opened it.

Sofia,

I hope you slept well. I had business early, and I won't be back until late. Eric has been instructed to take you and your sister wherever you want to go.

Be in my bed tonight.

Raphael

I quickly folded the note and stuffed it into my pocket, trying not to think about the words. *"Be in my bed tonight."*

I decided I'd be irritated about Eric instead. I could drive a car. But he didn't want Eric there as a driver. He wanted security. I thought back to the night before, to those men who'd come late, the ones he'd met with in his study. I shivered at the memory of how the one had looked at me.

"What is it?" Lina asked.

"Nothing. Just that we have a driver," I said with resigned smile.

Lina studied me for a minute. She knew I was hiding something but thankfully, she didn't comment.

"You're not going to wear those sandals, are you?" I said, looking at her feet. "It's a lot of walking." She had on a pair of beautiful, brand-new sandals with a two-inch heel. I'd slipped on a pair of well-worn Toms.

"They're cute. I have to break them in somewhere."

"Siena's probably not the place to break them in."

"Beauty doesn't come free," she said, shrugging a shoulder.

"Nerd."

She stuck her tongue out at me.

After breakfast, we left Charlie behind. Eric drove us to Siena, where my grandfather was staying. Lina had arranged for us to meet him at his hotel for lunch, which gave us a few hours to shop and sightsee. It felt great to be with her again. Alone in a beautiful place, I could almost forget the reasons we were here.

My grandfather was staying in the nicest hotel in the ancient city. As we walked toward his table at the back of the restaurant, I couldn't help wondering if Lina's or my inheritance was paying for it. I watched him as we approached, sitting behind the elegantly laid table with its white cloth, a smile on his face, his white hair perfectly styled, his suit impeccable as he rose to greet us.

"Lina and Sofia," he said, smiling, holding out his hands to us.

Lina smiled back and took it. "Hi, Granddad." She kissed his cheek, and his smile widened.

I felt that usual pang of envy at her relationship with him. I didn't want to feel it, but I did. Even if he'd never be like other grandparents, his affection for Lina was obvious, as obvious as the fact that he'd never felt quite the same way about me.

"Exactly your mother's eyes. It's remarkable," he said once they'd broken away.

Although we looked very much alike, Lina had inherited mom's eye color as well as her olive skin and darker hair, whereas I had my father's coloring and eyes. I wondered if that's what it was. If that was why he loved me a little less.

"Sofia," he hesitated. "You look well."

I couldn't answer, my thoughts too confused with all I'd learned. With all he had to answer.

"Sit down, ladies."

He raised a hand to call the waitress. We ordered drinks, water for Lina and me, and a glass of white wine for my grandfather, then sat studying our menus in silence for longer than was comfortable. While I hid behind the menu, I thought about how I'd do this, how I'd ask him my question, how to do it without screaming. My heart pounded, and I was sweating. And I hated myself for it.

Remarkably, we ate lunch without a mention of Raphael, of what had happened to lead us here. Lina did most of the talking, obviously nervous to leave even one awkward moment. Even though she didn't know all the details, she knew the agreement of my marriage had been made between Grandfather and Raphael.

At the end of the hour, she stood to go to the ladies' room.

"Should we go together?" she asked.

It would have been easier to say yes. To bury my head in the sand. But I couldn't do that. "No, go ahead."

Lina smiled and squeezed my shoulder. No matter what, she didn't like conflict. Maybe she thought he and I would make up in these next few minutes.

I watched him as he watched her go. He then turned to me.

"How are you, Sofia?" he asked.

"Well, considering."

"I want you to know that I acknowledge I chose poorly."

He surprised me.

"I should have found another way."

"Wow. You *chose poorly*." I shook my head. "Yes, you should have found another way."

"I'm trying to fix this."

"Fix it how? Isn't it too late for that?"

He didn't answer. "I'm extending my trip, so you can spend time with your sister."

"How generous of you." I couldn't say that I knew why. Like a fool, I felt too ashamed.

"Sofia—"

"Is what he said true? Are you stealing from us?"

There was a flash of something close to annoyance in his eyes, but he masked it quickly.

"Stealing from you?"

"And Lina."

"You know the money is in your names, always will be. I married into the family. You two were born into it."

"Are you stealing from us, then? Just tell me the truth."

"I'm using funds required to bring you up the way you should be brought up," he answered sharply.

"And you? You're not setting any aside for yourself?"

"Don't be ungrateful, Sofia. It's not becoming."

"Becoming?" I shook my head.

He picked up his glass of wine and took a sip. He'd hardly touched it throughout our lunch.

"Why do you hate me, Grandfather? What did I ever do to you?"

He shook his head. "I don't hate you, Sofia."

"You don't love me either. Not like Lina."

"Your jealousy is unfounded."

"Is it because I'm the reason mom ran away to marry dad?" I blurted out. It was a question I'd had for a long time, one I never had the courage to ask. I'd done the math after finding letters from my mom to my grandmother. She and dad weren't married when she got pregnant.

My grandfather's face hardened. He tilted his head to the side. "I'm trying to amend my actions, Sofia. Trying to fix what I've done. Believe it or not, I don't want to lose my granddaughter the way I lost my daughter."

I faltered, not sure what I'd expected. It certainly wasn't that.

"Are you looking for forgiveness, then? Do you expect mine?" I asked, this whole thing ridiculous.

He smiled and shook his head. I heard Lina's sandals clicking on the marble floor.

"Don't you think I know I don't deserve that?" he asked. A moment later, he pasted a smile on his face, hiding any emotion he felt, and stood to help Lina into her seat.

We left twenty minutes later. I hadn't spoken more than a few words once Lina had returned to the table, my mind too full with what grandfather had said. He'd seemed remorseful, which was strange for him. All this time, did he regret what had happened with my mother? Did he regret losing her because he couldn't accept her choice of husband?

It was two hours later when we were on our way out of town that Lina realized she didn't have her cell phone.

"I wonder if I left it in the ladies' room at the hotel when I washed my hands."

"We can go back. It's just a few blocks that way."

"My feet are killing me in these sandals," she said.

I took her arm, and we turned toward the hotel. "Next time, wear smart shoes. Not pretty ones."

"Yeah, yeah."

We walked into the lobby of the hotel, and Lina went to check the bathroom. She emerged with a smile on her face a minute later.

"Got it."

"You're lucky. Let's go." Grandfather had said he had meetings the rest of the day, so I didn't expect to see him and was grateful I didn't. But then, just on our way out of the hotel, I heard his voice. We both did and stopped. He was speaking with someone, and the other man laughed. Something told me to hide. I dragged Lina into an alcove and signaled for her to be quiet. From our hiding place, we watched my grandfather and the strange man who'd come to the wedding the night before walk into the lobby. They both looked serious and not quite friendly, but when the man held out his hand and my grandfather shook it, I felt a chill run down my spine.

"We have to go," I said once the men had gone.

"What is it? Who was that? He was at the house last night too."

I shook my head, confused myself, questioning my loyalties. My grandfather had just shaken hands with my husband's enemy.

By the time I got home, it was well past midnight. I went directly to my room, not sure if she'd have done as she'd been told or not, but there she was, asleep in my bed. She was still dressed and on top of the sheets. Her arm hung over the side, and a book lay facedown on the floor.

She must have been waiting up for me. Or trying to.

I watched her for a few minutes. She wore white shorts and a yellow tank top, and long wisps of chestnut hair had fallen all over her back and arm. Her legs had tanned a little, and looking at her bare feet turned in a little at the toes, it made her look like a child. Like she needed protection.

And she did.

More than she knew.

I touched her face. She made a sound and

turned away, still asleep. I picked up her book. *When Nietsche Wept.* I raised my eyebrows.

"Interesting choice."

After setting her bookmark in the page that was open, I placed it on the nightstand, then sat on the bed and pushed the hair off her face to look at her.

She wore no makeup and slept so soundly. I couldn't remember ever sleeping like that. Nightmares had ruled my childhood and carried well into my adulthood. Always evolving while at the same time, always staying the same. I was envious of Sofia. I didn't begrudge her. I was simply envious of her.

She rolled over onto her back at that moment, her arms falling open on either side of her. She wore no bra, and her tank top stretched across her chest, emphasizing the small, round mounds, the dark nipples. Her short shorts showed off her nicely toned legs. I sat on the bed beside her and, feeling a little like a creep, I undid her shorts. When she didn't stir, I dragged them down off her legs. She wore pale pink lace panties. My cock was hard at the sight of it, at the little triangle of dark hair just beneath the lace.

Clearing my throat, I adjusted my cock and stood.

"Sofia," I said softly.

Nothing.

"Sofia."

Again, no response. The girl could sleep.

Lifting her to sit up, I pulled her tank top over her head. At that, she stirred, blinking several times, giving me a half smile, then closing her eyes again. I smiled back, stupidly, knowing she couldn't see me. She was asleep.

I drew the sheets back and lay her down and slid her panties off as well, liking her naked in my bed. Liking looking at her. A moment later, I forced myself to cover her again, then went into the bathroom to shower and climbed into bed beside her.

"I'm in your bed," she muttered, rolling toward me and throwing her arm over me. "Like you said."

"I see that."

But she was out again. I wrapped an arm around her, holding her close to me. Did I feel guilt over what I would do to her, to her sister? I would destroy Guardia Winery to punish her grandfather. I knew it meant I would destroy her in the process. I had no doubt my promise not to leave her on the street didn't absolve me.

How ironic, how parallel our lives seemed. How strangely the same. Our paths didn't merely cross. They moved along exactly the same path. What her grandfather had precipitated, the loss that had killed my mother, I would repeat it. I would repeat history knowingly. I would set fire to the Guardia lands. Obliterate the vineyard and the Guardia name.

I fell asleep to these thoughts running through my mind, and the nightmare I'd had a thousand times before was different this time. I knew it by the way it began, knew it as I choked on the smoke, trying in vain to reach her, knowing I'd be too late.

I was always too late.

This time, the house was different.

This time, there were no sirens, only the sound of fire and destruction in an already destroyed house. This time, when I reached the bedroom and pounded on the door and heard her inside, I knew it was too late, knew what I heard was her dying.

And this time, when I broke the door down, it wasn't my mother's charred body I found. It wasn't hers at all.

I shot up in bed, breathing hard, sweat covering me. My eyelids flew open, banishing sleep, leaving only the carcass of this version of the nightmare that had been repeating for six years. I looked over at Sofia beside me, who somehow still slept.

Would she be the Sleeping Beauty who would turn to ash this time?

Would it be me to strike that match and set the fire?

Who else but me who would destroy her?

I told her I wouldn't be a beast to her, but wasn't that my intention all along? Wasn't her destruction central to this plot of vengeance? Wasn't it in motion now, fully in play, after that change her grandfather had made to the contract?

I was a monster. I knew that. But to destroy her?

Her?

While my mind warred, she lay sleeping, oblivious and unconscious beside me. She held such a strange power over me.

Why couldn't I hate her? I was supposed to fucking hate her.

I got out of bed, angry and irritated and frustrated as fuck, and went downstairs, through the kitchen, taking old faithful—my favorite bottle of whiskey—with me. I didn't bother with a glass. Didn't need one. I knew where I was going. To that hated place.

Still no fucking lock on the door. I couldn't do it. Couldn't chance not being able to get in there.

I opened the cellar door, the smell already taking me back years and years.

Was this a twisted sanctuary of sorts? A tangled, dark thing, one I couldn't escape, one I dreaded that drew me back time and time again?

I drank gulps of whiskey as I made my way down the stairs. No lights tonight. I didn't need them. I knew every inch of the place, and the two small windows at the top of the one wall let in enough moonlight. It fucking highlighted the whipping post, as if it were a spotlight shining on the thing.

I drew back the cover of the first table, letting it fall to the ground. A spider crawled away, its long legs delicate on the worn leather. Whips lay all coiled as if waiting for their turn. They wouldn't get it, though. Never again. Not on my back.

For a long time, I stood looking at them. I knew the feel of each one and flinched at the remembered pain.

The whippings only took place at night. Always after I'd gone to bed. Maybe I was still conditioned to wake up at the same time as those nights. I think he liked it. Liked knowing I slept with dread, never sure if I'd be shaken awake and dragged to this place to be punished for sins I didn't even know. I don't even think it mattered to him whether or not I'd done anything. Whether or not any of us had.

I drank again, swallowing half the bottle this time. My throat burned, but I didn't care. I needed it. I needed that burn as I reached out and touched the long fine leather of one of the whips, the one he'd used the most. Without thinking, I wrapped my hand around the braided handle. It was worn, the sweat from his exertion a part of the thing now. Lubricating it. Keeping it supple even years later.

When I drew my arm back, I watched, transfixed, as leather slowly uncurled like a snake. I snapped my arm back, cracking it on the floor, flinching with the sound, a thing I could never forget. Memory made my back tense in its attempt to protect itself.

I drank more of the whiskey. Then, keeping the bottle at my side, I turned my attention to the whipping post. It, too, was worn in places. The carvings were softened where flesh had hugged it time and time again. I drew my arm back and struck it, heard the sound of leather wrapping around wood, remembered how the tail would circle back as if each stroke would count for two.

As if the leather itself were greedy. Ruthless.

But what did it feel like for him? To stand here behind me, or behind her, hearing our cries, seeing our pain, watching blood slide down our backs. What did he feel to stand here and hold all that power? To be master of our pain? What?

"Raphael."

Her voice broke the silence of the room. Disrupted the chaos of my mind.

I knew she'd come.

"I want to know," I said, looking at the worn wood, as if she'd heard my thoughts, and I was just continuing the conversation. "I want to know what it felt like for him."

When I did finally shift my gaze to her, I found her standing at the bottom of the stairs barefoot, my T-shirt hanging to midthigh, her arms wrapped around herself. She watched me, her gaze veering to the post, the whip, to my white-knuckled fist around the handle.

"Are you drinking?" she asked.

I realized I still held the bottle in my other hand and brought it to my mouth, draining it, then sent it smashing against the far wall.

Sofia jumped.

I faced her, took a step toward her. Then another.

"Come here," I said.

"Put the whip down," she said.

"I like holding it. I like how it feels."

"No. You don't."

"I do. I really do."

"What happened tonight? Why are you down here? It's after one in the morning."

"Come here."

She eyed the whip and shook her head.

"Are you afraid of me?"

She studied me, her forehead furrowing a little. "No."

A lie.

"Then come to me."

It took her twice the steps it should have to cross the space between us.

"Did you undress me? I woke up naked."

I nodded and touched the curve of her waist, bunched up the T-shirt in my fist, and pulled her to me. "I like you naked." I snaked my fist around behind her, holding her to me, and leaned down to kiss her.

One of her hands wrapped around my shoulder, the other clutched the wrist that held the whip, keeping my arm at my side.

Her lips trembled a little, betraying her caution.

Drawing her closer, I pressed my face into her

hair, inhaling the scent of shampoo. I closed my eyes and breathed deep. "I want to feel it," I whispered against her ear. "It's sick, isn't it?"

The hand that had circled my shoulder now moved to my face. She looked at me with pity in her eyes.

I hated pity. I fucking hated it.

I wanted it gone.

And it was, in the next instant. I felt my face change, my eyes darken, and knew the moment she processed the change because fear replaced that pity.

To be pitiful was to be weak. I would not be weak. I'd decided that the night I'd killed him.

"Don't feel sorry for me, Sofia. I accept myself as I am."

"No, Raphael. This isn't how you are. It's not what you want...you shouldn't drink..."

I released her and stepped over to the post, laying my hand on it for the first time in years. I remembered the ridges, knew them intimately.

Sofia reached out to take my hand, the one that held the whip, and walked behind me. When the fingers of her other hand traced the scars on my back, I flinched, tightening every muscle. She stopped moving but didn't pull away. With an exhale, I bowed my head, my hand turning into a fist on the post.

She followed each line, her touch like a feather.

She saw everything. She saw me. And I let her. I stood there, and I let her. And only after she'd acknowledged every scar did she pull away. It was only for a moment, and I remained as I was. When I felt her breath on me, her lips on my back, kissing me softly, kissing scar tissue, I shuddered.

When I turned, she straightened. She stood naked. She'd stripped off the T-shirt. Her nipples tightened in the cool cellar air. I looked at them, at her. And when I took her and turned her so she stood with her back to the post, she let me. Even though her gaze warily skimmed the whip, she let me.

Kissing her, I drew her wrists up over her head and secured them in the shackles.

She made a sound, a breath escaping. It was that sound—that and the look in her eyes—that betrayed her fear. I stood back to take her in, saw how she stood on tiptoe, trying to slide her wrists from the irons. My cock hardened at the sight of her there, bound to the post, naked and mine.

At my mercy.

"Are you afraid of me now?"

She shook her head, but it wasn't convincing. I smiled and cracked the whip at my side. She jumped and let out a small scream.

"I think you are," I said.

"You won't hurt me," she managed, her voice shaky.

"I don't know that you believe that." I walked around the post. She followed me with her eyes. "You're taking a chance, Sofia."

"You want to feel what it's like to whip someone? To hurt someone who is helplessly bound and unable to fight you?"

"Sick, right?"

She didn't reply. I stood in front of her. Her gaze fell briefly to my briefs, to my cock pressing like a steel bar, before she dragged it back to mine.

"You're not like him," she said.

"Isn't this evidence enough of how sick I am?" I asked, gesturing to my erection.

"I don't care. You're not your father, Raphael. Whatever you think, however sick you think you are, you're not. You need to let the past go."

"Maybe I need to feel it first. Feel what it's like." My voice came out tight, and it was hard to swallow. It took a long time before I said the last part. "Maybe I need to hurt someone first."

Her eyes searched mine, and tears like two delicate crystal drops slid down her cheeks.

"Turn around and hug the post, Sofia."

Her teeth began to chatter, and more tears followed. My cock ached. In one step, I was on her, gripping the back of her head, taking a handful of hair, and tugging it back to force her face up. I crushed my mouth over hers. She whimpered, kissing me back, weeping fully now, almost frantically, the kiss desperate as if with her lips alone, she would cling to me.

I slid the whip handle between her legs, and she let out a scream. But when I squeezed her cunt, it was wet, her clit swollen. I looked down at her, exhaling before taking her mouth again.

"You're wet," I groaned, grinding myself against her.

"I want you," she said, leaning her face forward when I pulled back. "Make love to me."

No. Now wasn't the time for lovemaking. And I didn't like her using sex to manipulate me.

I turned her roughly so she faced the pole, then pushed my briefs down and off. She pushed her ass into me.

I groaned with need, burying my face in her hair, imagining her tight pussy around my cock, smelling her scent, her skin so close. "I wasn't the only one," I said like it was a confession, pinching her nipple before gripping that handful of hair again and turning her head, kissing her tearstained cheek, finding her mouth.

"Raphael—"

"He whipped my mother too. I don't know how long he'd been doing it."

She shook her head.

"How long she kept it a secret."

I pressed the whip against Sofia's cunt. I wanted to fuck her. God, I wanted to bury my fucking cock inside her, but I couldn't. Not yet. "If I'd just let him beat me...if I hadn't fought back, maybe he wouldn't have hurt her."

She craned her neck and looked at me, hearing me. And maybe I heard myself for the first time, because to say it out loud, to hear it, fuck. I knew the guilt I felt. It wasn't new. It wasn't something I buried. But to say it out loud? To another human being? To Sofia?

I shook my head, pulling back, gripping the whip hard. "Hug the post, Sofia."

"It's not your fault."

She tugged frantically at her restraints. They'd hold her tight, though. I knew that.

"What he did, Raphael, it's not your fault."

"Hug the fucking post!" I roared, raising the whip.

She screamed and turned, wrapping her forearms and legs around the thing as best she could, and she wept and begged and fuck, God knows what she said. What words she muttered, because I couldn't hear them. Not anymore. All I could do was watch her cling to the post, watch her trembling body as she waited for me to whip her. All I could do was see her.

See myself in her.

See fear.

Feel it.

Feel her terror.

And it reminded me, took me back so many years.

And it made me falter, and I hated that it made me fucking falter.

I couldn't be weak.

I wouldn't.

A sound came from me, something foreign and full, like glass breaking into a thousand shards. Shattering. Damaged beyond repair.

That was me. That was what I was. A wrecked monster. A killer. A hateful, vengeful beast.

Sofia craned her neck, her wet eyes meeting mine, the terror inside them slicing me again. As if that were even possible anymore. There wasn't anything left to hurt.

My throat tight, I went to her, hugging her back, prying her from the post.

"I'm sorry," I said, turning her, holding her. I buried my face in her hair and kept saying it, kept repeating the words, holding her so tight, so fucking tight.

I reached up, my hands fumbling as I undid the restraints. I expected her to pull away. To run from me. It's what she should have done. But instead, her arms wrapped around my neck and, still weeping, her tears salty on my lips, she kissed me, hugging me with all her strength, clinging to me like she had that post when I'd scared the fuck out of her. When I'd been moments from lashing her back, hurting her like I'd been hurt, scarring her like I was scarred.

"I'm sorry," I said again. "I'm so sorry."

"Make love to me," she said against my lips, our bodies never separating, never apart.

I lifted her, using the post at her back as I slid her onto my cock, still fucking hard after all this.

Our eyes locked, our lips touched, and I thrust into her.

She sucked in a breath, and I knew it hurt her. She was too tight. Too small to take me. But I wanted it. I wanted her. Like this. Fuck. I needed it.

"Harder."

For me? Did she know what I needed? Did she need it too?

I did it again, thrusting again, and again, and my cock swelled and her pussy tightened and she gripped me with all her strength, and when her walls squeezed and pulsed around me, I watched her, watched her eyes close, watched her lip disappear between her teeth, and I emptied inside her, buried deep, leaving something behind, some ancient part of me, almost as if it left me physically.

17

SOFIA

I woke up in Raphael's arms. I didn't move and tried to keep my breathing level. What in hell had happened last night? How close had I come to being whipped? I knew he'd needed that scene—that insane scene—to happen. He couldn't tiptoe around the past any longer. Maybe coming back here, maybe subconsciously, he'd sought the confrontation because without it, there could be no relief. I hoped that last night was his victory over the demons that haunted him. I hoped that last night, he'd banished them to the hell in which they belonged.

What kind of childhood had he had?

What kind of guilt did he carry on his shoulders?

He'd told me he'd protected his brothers from his father, and I understood he took whippings to save them. What he'd said last night, though, had his father—once Raphael was too big to beat—had he turned his rage on Raphael's mother?

What a beast. What a monster.

I looked up at my husband's sleeping face. It was the first time I'd seen him like this. The first time I was able to watch him without being watched myself. And for all his hardness, for all those sharp edges, to see him like this, his face quiet, there was a softness to him. An innocence he hid so well in his waking hours.

I knew he was beautiful. That wasn't a question. Thick dark hair and tanned olive skin, and bones a model would kill for. But even without that, even if he were ugly, that innocence inside him, that damaged little boy still buried there, it made me want to shield him, protect him from his monsters.

He slept holding on to me, and his arm weighed a ton on my side. I shifted a little, unable to resist lightly touching the scruff of hair on his jaw. I wondered if Lina was awake. She had to be and was probably waiting for me.

Raphael blinked, a blue that didn't fit with his coloring flashing beneath heavy dark lashes. He rolled over onto his back and stared up at the ceiling.

"What time is it?"

"Almost eleven. I didn't mean to wake you."

"Almost eleven?"

He turned to me, and his face grew grave. It was like watching him remember.

"Are you...okay?"

I smiled and touched his face again. "Yes."

We hadn't showered when we'd come upstairs last night. He hadn't allowed it, wanting to hold me instead. The room smelled of sex.

"I need a shower," I said. "My sister is probably waiting, wondering where I am."

"She probably figured out where you are."

He rolled over on top of me and trapped me with his elbows on either side of my face. He kissed me.

"I like my smell on you."

"Well, I don't know if everyone else will, so I should shower."

"What are you two going to do today?"

"I'm not sure yet." I thought back to yesterday, to seeing my grandfather with that man. "Raphael, that man from the wedding, who is he exactly?"

Hid face grew serious, and he rolled off me. "Vincent Moriarty. A self-proclaimed businessman. A thug, and an extortionist too, to whom my father owed money."

"He's dangerous, isn't he?"

"I told you I wouldn't let him hurt you, Sofia."

It wasn't me I was worried about. "Does he want to hurt you?" I asked.

"He expects me to repay my father's debt."

"I have to tell you something," I said, sitting up.

"If it's about him meeting with your grandfather, I know."

"What? How?"

"Eric mentioned it. He saw them, when you and your sister went to get her phone."

"Oh," I'd forgotten about Eric. Of course he would have seen. "I want to see my grandfather again today. Ask him what it was about. Have him lay all his cards on the table."

Raphael chuckled and climbed out of bed. "You're naive, Sofia."

I followed him. "I'm not naive. Things have changed. You're my husband now, and it's different than it was meant to be."

He stopped and turned. The look on his face made me falter.

"I don't want to lie to you. And I don't want to play games with you," I said.

"That's good, because I don't want to play them with you."

"We're not enemies, right?"

"No, but your grandfather—"

"Needs to go home and accept what's happened. Accept his loss."

He took my face in his hands and drew me to him, then kissed my forehead.

"Naive, but sweet."

He went into the bathroom. I followed him.

"You never answered me when I asked you if there was more to tell me about the consummation. I've been thinking about it, and it doesn't make sense. He doesn't stand to gain by requiring that. There was something else, wasn't there?" I knew there was from the look on his face. "What did you give up for me to have time with my sister?"

"Five percent."

"What?"

"I get forty-five percent now. Not the full fifty."

"For those few days she can be here?"

He nodded and switched on the shower.

"Raphael, you did that for me?" He didn't have to. He hadn't had to do anything for me. I went to him but when he turned, I saw how his face had hardened.

"I told you once; don't make a saint out of me. I'm not that, Sofia."

His words startled me. "What does that mean?"

"It means exactly what I said."

"I want Lina to stay. I want to be her legal guardian," I blurted out before I could chicken out.

"Stay? As in here with us?"

"She'll be eighteen in two years. And she's self-sufficient, not like a child—"

"I'm not worried about that. What makes you think your grandfather will allow that?"

"I'm going to ask him."

"No." He shook his head. "You can't see him again. I forbid it."

"You *forbid* it?"

"He's my enemy, Sofia, which makes him your

enemy. Didn't what you saw with your own eyes prove that yesterday?"

"Exactly why I need to work out for my sister to stay here with me. I don't feel safe sending her back with him."

He shook his head, stepped into the shower, and picked up the shampoo.

"Raphael! I'm talking to you."

"I'm late for a meeting."

"What meeting? What is with all your meetings?"

"I can make some time for a quick fuck in the shower, though."

He grinned, that arrogance I hated back.

I flipped him off and walked out of the bathroom, slipped his T-shirt over my head, and ran for it to my bedroom, not wanting to bump into anyone until I'd showered. It took him all of two minutes to follow me, dripping and naked, down the hallway. At my door, he gripped my arm and pushed me inside, slamming it shut behind us.

"Don't you ever do that to me again, understand?"

"Which part, this?" I gave him the finger again. "Or the walking away?"

He squeezed my arm, his mouth tightening. "You want to play after all?"

I narrowed my eyes, but my heart pounded at the look in his eyes, the tone of his voice. I always seemed to forget my inexperience. Forget his power.

Or maybe I just thought things had shifted between us last night.

"We can play."

He turned me and pushed me over the footboard of the bed.

I made to get up, but he pressed a hand between my shoulder blades and kept me down, then shoved the T-shirt up over my back and spread my legs apart before coming to stand between them. I felt him then, felt his hardness at my ass, and as much as I didn't want to, as much as I wanted to stay angry, my body was responding, like it always did to Raphael.

"You have a great ass, Sofia," he said, then slapped it once.

"Ow!"

"Keep your face on the bed."

He twisted my hair around his hand and leaned over me.

"You're hurting me."

"Seems to be the story of our lives."

He slapped my hip again.

"Stop!"

"You going to keep your head down?"

He squeezed his fist, and I nodded. When he straightened, I stayed as I was. His hands came to my ass and spread me open.

"A very fuckable ass," he said, fingers caressing me, holding me wide.

I made a sound, embarrassed, and buried my face in the bed.

"And your cunt is always dripping for me, isn't it?"

"I hate you," I muttered.

"That's not true."

In the next moment, his tongue was licking the length of me, from my sex to my ass, circling there, then sliding back over the lips of my sex.

"I'm going to fuck every hole, you know that, right?"

I swallowed, more aroused than I liked.

He licked again, this time, pressing his tongue against my ass.

"Stop."

"Don't worry."

He straightened, his cock at the entrance of my pussy.

"Not that one yet."

He dipped his cock inside, and I arched my back, biting my lip.

Fuck. That first moment, when he first entered me...fuck.

"You want to come, don't you?" He moved slowly in and out. "You like being fucked."

I swallowed, gripped the bedcover, and refused

to answer. Too humiliated to let him know how turned on I was.

"Not this morning, though,"

His hand in my hair, he drew me up, held me to him with his cock still buried inside me.

"Consider it your first punishment. A relatively easy one."

He slipped out and turned me around to kiss me once, then pushed me to my knees.

I looked at him, at his cock before me, slick with my juices.

"Open wide, honey. I want to come down your throat. Take care of this hole before I take care of that ass"

I wanted to hate him, wanted to be repelled by him, by his words. He got hard while humiliating me. So why couldn't I hate him? Why did I, instead, open my mouth and lick him, tasting him and myself on him, before opening wide, like he said, and taking him into my mouth? Why did I drip for him?

"Fuck," Raphael groaned, drawing the word out.

I looked up at him as he moved me over himself with his hand in my hair, hurting me a little, still leaving me wanting.

This was fucked up. This wasn't how sex was supposed to go.

And it was even more fucked-up that it made me wet.

When he looked down at me and gave me that lopsided, dirty grin, all I wanted to do was reach between my legs and make myself come.

"I like your virgin mouth, Sofia. I'm going to like coming down your throat, making you choke on me."

He moved me faster along his length, going deeper, not easing up when I struggled for breath.

"And I want you to know that when I say I forbid you something, I expect obedience."

He squeezed my hair, his cock stuffed deep in my mouth, forcing me to look up at him.

"Remember your wedding vows."

He smirked and thrust deeper, his face tightening, his cock thickening.

"Because I didn't take a whip to your back last night doesn't mean I won't take my belt to your ass when you need it. Punishment earned is something else entirely."

The head of his cock hit the back of my throat.

"Understand?"

Tears fell from the corners of my eyes as I pushed against his thighs, struggling to breathe.

He pulled out a little, and moved my head in a nod.

"Good girl."

In that moment, I hated him. I hated his power over me. Hated that it aroused me even now, even through this.

But then he leaned me backward at an angle just this side of painful and fucked my face, really fucked it, and when he stilled and came down my throat, all I could do was take it, take him, and watch his face, his beautiful face as he took his pleasure from me then drew out, releasing me.

I wiped the back of my hand over my mouth, sitting back on my heels.

"That was good for your first time," he said. "But you missed some."

With his toe, he pointed to where some cum had dripped onto the floor.

"Lick it up."

Rage burned hot inside me, starting at my belly, searing my throat as it made itself heard. "Fuck. You." I stood, somehow not stumbling, and faced him. I refused to look away. And when he grinned, I drew my arm back and slapped him.

His body didn't move, only his head snapped to the side. He exhaled, and the side of his mouth curved upward as his hand rose to touch his cheek. Slowly, he turned to look at me.

His gaze slid over me, and I shuddered, holding my breath when he brought his fingers to my belly and slid them up between my breasts, over my chest. His hand then fisted around my throat, and I grabbed his forearm as he leaned over me.

"Don't ever fucking do that again."

He squeezed, and I trembled. He was volatile,

like a land mine that if I didn't tread lightly, I'd set off. He crushed my neck in his hand, and I couldn't speak. I made a sound as he lifted me up on tiptoe. That was when he must have realized what he was doing, because he blinked fast several times, as if seeing me anew. When he released me, I clutched the footboard. It was the only way to keep upright.

He looked around the room, and it took him a minute to face me again.

"Get dressed. Don't force me to punish you."

His warning said, he crossed the floor and left, slamming the door behind him.

I exhaled, rubbing my throat. What the hell had just happened? After last night? How had we devolved to this point? What had I said? What had I asked? I'd flipped him off and walked away. He'd gotten so angry. Too angry.

My legs trembling, I walked into the bathroom and switched on the shower. I hurried to wash and got dressed, pulling my hair into a ponytail as I went to knock on Lina's door. But there was no answer. When I opened the door, her bed was made and the room empty. She'd taken to sleeping with Charlie on her bed, and he too was gone.

I didn't hear Raphael, When I got to the kitchen, I found Maria rolling dough at the counter and Nicola drying and stacking dishes.

"Good morning."

They both smiled and wished me the same.

"Is my sister here?"

Maria said something, but I didn't understand so Nicola translated.

"No. She left with Damon earlier. She said she would be back by dinnertime."

"With Damon?" I guess she'd been waiting for me. "Did she leave me a note or anything?"

"No, sorry. She said to let you sleep."

"Okay. Thanks." Charlie chose that moment to come back into the house, yapping in excitement when he saw me. Eric followed behind him, looking irritated. "Where's Raphael?"

"He left for a meeting," Nicola said.

So I was on my own. Well, on my own with Eric.

"If you want to go anywhere, I'm to take you," Eric said.

"I'm fine. Thanks."

After making myself a cup of coffee, I walked outside. Charlie followed. The fields were quiet, not another person in sight as far as I could see. I walked toward the vineyard with my coffee, enjoying the sun, the quiet all around me, disappointed that Lina had left but glad she had. She only had a few days left, and it was good that Damon was here and he could show her around. But what would I do all day? Staying here, rattling around the house, just made me feel isolated, even more alone. I wondered if I'd ever settle in. Ever call it home.

I drew my phone out of my pocket and dialed

Lina, but it went directly to voice mail. I left her a message and told her to have fun, then tried Damon's phone. His, too, went to voice mail.

I then did something else. Something I knew Raphael would not approve of. But if he was busy with his meetings and expected me to stay here alone all day and just let everything happen around me, well, he had another thing coming. I had to remember that no matter what had happened between us, this man carried a lot of baggage. Physical abuse as a child, most likely accompanied by emotional and mental abuse. Murder—even if it was self-defense. Prison.

No matter what he did, no matter how much I wanted things to be good, no matter how much I needed to believe that demons could be banished, I needed to remember the reality of things. And his hand squeezing my throat this morning, well, that was reality.

I touched my neck, which felt tender. Bruises had already begun to form, and I decided I wouldn't cover them up. He should see what he was capable of. They all should.

Scrolling through my cell phone, I found my grandfather's number. He was the only one who answered on the second ring.

"This is Marcus Guardia," he said formally.

I rolled my eyes. He had to know it was me. He'd see my name on the display. "It's Sofia," I said.

"Good morning, Sofia."

"Good morning, Grandfather."

An awkward moment. "This is a surprise. A pleasant one."

"I..." What was I doing? "I need to see you."

"All right. I'm just getting ready to leave for the winery. Would you care to join me? Have a look at it yourself?"

"The winery?" I had never been to it. Neither had Lina. Over the years, my grandfather had taken trips there, but he'd never brought us along. "Yes."

"I can pick you up in about forty-five minutes, if you like?"

I glanced behind me at the house but didn't see Eric. "Yes, please. I'll be waiting by the gate."

"I'll see you in a little bit. And Sofia," he said just as I was about to disconnect the call. "I'm glad you called."

I didn't have a response apart from a good-bye, and we hung up. I returned to the kitchen, already knowing what I'd tell Eric to ensure he wouldn't follow me. As for Raphael, I risked his rage, but I had no choice. I needed to talk to my grandfather about Lina. About Moriarty. I needed to get things out in the open and be finished with it.

Forty-five minutes later, Charlie and I stood at the gate alone. A sedan came toward us down the dusty road, pulling to a stop at the gates. My grandfather opened the back door and stepped out at the same time as the driver, and I climbed into the car with Charlie on my lap.

"What is that?" he asked, a clear look of distaste on his face.

I scratched behind Charlie's ear and held him on my lap. "It's a puppy, Grandfather. His name is Charlie."

"Does he have to join us?"

"Yes."

He didn't argue with me but gave me a resigned look. The driver closed the door, and we were off.

"No one to wave you off? Where is your sister?"

"Resting," I lied. I knew he wouldn't like knowing Lina was in enemy hands. Although Damon was hardly the enemy. Maybe he was my only ally. Funny how, just a few hours ago, I'd been thinking Raphael was my ally.

"And Raphael?"

"Meetings."

"Does he know you're with me?"

"No."

"Good girl," he said with a smile, shifting his gaze out the window.

"Why haven't you ever brought us to the winery?"

"I wasn't sure you'd be interested. You were both too young."

"It's our history. Of course we'd be interested."

"Well, then forgive me my poor choice."

His voice told me he didn't want to talk anymore about it. And that was fine. Neither did I.

We drove in silence for a little while, Charlie making what could have been a long trip a little less awkward. The winery was located about an hour from Raphael's property. I had no idea it was that close. Why hadn't Raphael mentioned it?

Much like his, it was set off the road with a large house at the top of a hill, surrounded by vineyards in full bloom, the vines thick with lush green leaves. Dark purple-blue grapes grew in abundance. That was so opposite the blackened vines surrounding Raphael's house it was startling.

"We're here, Sir," the driver said.

"Thank you." I reached to open the door, but my grandfather put a hand on my knee to stop me.

"We'll be right out."

"Sir." The driver nodded and left us alone.

"About what you said the other day. I don't hate you," Grandfather said. "And I may have blamed you for your mother's...choices...but I realize that's not quite right. I am trying, Sofia."

I looked at him, his lined gray eyes showing his age. I bit the inside of my mouth and nodded. Too many questions to ask, but this moment, I felt like it was truth. His truth, at least.

But then, I thought about the amendment to the contract. Had Raphael lied about that? Had my grandfather ever asked for the marriage to be consummated? I should have asked, but I couldn't. Instead, I managed a thank-you.

We opened the doors and climbed out. I had Charlie on a leash, and I kept him on it as we walked up the hill toward the house. "It's bigger than I realized it would be."

"About four-hundred acres. And I've put a bid in on a nearby property."

"A bid? We're buying more?"

"You will lose half in three years, Sofia. I want to make sure you have something left once this marriage is dissolved and Amado feels as if he's gotten his just desserts."

I felt the hostility in his voice as if it were a physical thing.

"But how will you keep it from him?"

"It will be in your name. Not Guardia Winery. My agreement with Amado is Guardia Winery shares. Not Sofia Guardia's private property."

I'd never have thought of that. Clever, I supposed. And maybe I was naive, like Raphael liked to say, but I was glad I didn't think of how I could manipulate things to my advantage.

But there was one question. "How will you buy it? With what money? If it's not Guardia—"

He gave me a smile and turned to head into the house. "Don't worry about that. You just keep that little bit of news to yourself."

I followed him inside, appreciating the coolness

of the place compared to the heat outside. Although mornings were nice and the air was relatively dry in the region, the afternoon sun could be stifling.

I found myself in the entryway of what once must have been a grand house. Opposite the beauty of Raphael's house, this was, as I'd told him, used more like a factory than anything else. Gutted and dirty, it stored machinery and had long counters of work space where employees did their jobs as we walked around, surveying it all.

"When your mother was younger, we used to come during the harvest. The bedrooms upstairs are still intact. If you'd like to see them—"

"Yes!" I was so excited, I cut him off. I cleared my throat. "Please."

A man approached us with a pleasant, but urgent smile. My grandfather introduced him as the manager. After shaking my hand, the man mentioned something to my grandfather, and Grandfather turned to me.

"If you don't mind, you'll have to go on your own. I have to take care of something."

"No, that's fine. Thanks."

Even better. I couldn't believe my luck.

"The last room was your mother's."

Leaving them behind, I went up the stairs with Charlie at my side. There were only three bedrooms here. The first was very small, fitting only one single bed and a nightstand inside. There was no mattress on the bed, only the frame, and the walls were bare. The few steps I took inside left my prints in the layer of dust on the floor.

The second bedroom was twice as large. A king-size bed stood against the far wall. This one had its mattress intact, but it was covered over with a dust cloth. A nightstand on either side held lamps without lightbulbs. A dresser stood against one wall. I tried the drawers but found them empty.

On my way to the final bedroom, I passed a bathroom. It looked like it hadn't been updated for some time. As I neared my mother's room, my stomach fluttered with butterflies. I wondered when she'd been here last, how old she'd been.

I reached it, laid my hand on the doorknob, and took a deep breath. I needed to be prepared for nothing. The other bedrooms had no personal touches. Anyone could have lived in those rooms. My mother's might be just as disappointing.

I opened the door and stepped inside, then, after a moment, closed it behind me.

Dust covered the floor here too, and I must have been the first person up here in a long time. The room was slightly smaller than the last, and a double bed was pushed against one corner with a window on each wall. I lifted the dustcover to find the mattress and pillow beneath. My mother had once slept on this bed.

I looked around at the bare walls. Nails had left

holes in them. A vanity stood against the wall nearest the bed. I ran my finger through the dusty surface then pulled the drawer open. I smiled.

Inside, I found an old tube of half-used lipstick in an awful hot pink and a small sample of perfume. I sprayed a little and inhaled and was immediately taken back.

A tidal wave of emotion passed through me.

I didn't have many memories of my parents. I barely remembered what they looked like anymore and had to look at photos of them often. Their voices too I couldn't remember. I hated that. We had a few videos of birthday parties, but most of the footage was of Lina or I. Either my mom or dad were always behind the camera, and although you could hear them, they weren't in the videos. The perfume though, that scent. It was my mother's. I'd forgotten that too.

I sat on the edge of the seat. My heart hurt at the realization.

After setting the tiny bottle down, I ran my finger over the surface of the mirror and picked up the tube of lipstick and looked at the brand. It was a cheap drugstore brand I used to buy when I was a teen and had limited funds.

Taking the lid off, I brought it to my lips and applied some. It was hard and cakey, but I imagined her gliding it across her mouth, and it almost felt like her. It was the closest I would come to my mother physically.

Pocketing both, I closed the drawer and checked the dresser and closet. I found nothing. Not a piece of clothing. Not a forgotten stuffed animal or book or anything.

"Sofia?" My grandfather's voice called from the distance.

Wiping my hand over my nose and eyes, I went to the door, taking one last look around. "I'm coming."

Downstairs, the manager pointed out the new equipment they'd installed, including a new security system. He toured us through the vineyards with Charlie tagging along, playing and running at my feet. As much as I wanted to take him off leash, Grandfather asked that I refrain.

Only when we sat down at a table set for lunch did I have a few minutes to talk to him while the manager left us with glasses of wine and went to take a call.

"This is our wine, obviously," he said to me, gesturing for me to take it.

I hesitated. He'd never allowed it at home. Not even a small taste. I picked up my glass, and he held his aloft. I touched mine to his.

"To better relationships," he said.

"Do you mean it?" I asked after taking a sip, which was delicious.

He nodded.

"Then I want to ask you to give me guardianship of Lina." His face changed instantly but I continued. "I want to have her here with me. I've missed the last four years being away at school, and—"

"That's out of the question."

"Why? It won't interfere with your financial arrangement. You can carry on like you always did."

"No, Sofia."

"I can have the best teachers come to the house. I can—"

"What about your husband? I'm sure he wouldn't want your sister hanging around. He hates us, remember that."

"He doesn't hate *us*."

He bowed his head, his lips tight. "Right. He hates me."

"I miss my sister."

"Then you'll have to convince Amado to let you return to the States for visits."

"Will you at least think about it? Let her stay the summer at least?"

Two women and the manager returned then, carrying plates of food, warm smiles on their faces. Our conversation came to a halt, and I knew it was hopeless. When Grandfather decided, he decided. It was how it always was growing up. He made the rules. We obeyed them.

But we weren't kids anymore. I wouldn't let him

bully me into silence, not with something as important as this.

I sat through lunch not speaking much, frustration mounting in my belly, rebellion at my powerlessness. While Grandfather and the manager talked business, I pushed food around my plate and decided Maria was a much better cook. By the time the plates were cleared, I couldn't hold my tongue any longer.

"What was Vincent Moriarty doing at your hotel yesterday?" It came out harsher than I'd intended.

The lone sound of a fork on a dish, then everything went quiet. The manager cleared his throat and focused on picking tiny crumbs of bread off the table.

"Mr. Moriarty is a business developer in this area. I'm surprised your husband hasn't mentioned him."

"His name is Raphael. Just Raphael. Not Amado. Not 'your husband.' And he has. That's exactly why I'm wondering what you were doing with him."

"Ah."

I raised my eyebrows.

"The property that I am buying *for you*, Moriarty has an interest in it as well."

"Your meeting was over buying a piece of land?"

"What did you think? What sort of business did you expect me to be in? Perhaps I'm not the man *Raphael* has painted me to be, Sofia."

Had Raphael lied to me? Was Moriarty legitimate and not a thug at all, like he'd described him? What was his relationship with Moriarty? And why had the man given me chills?

"I...I didn't know."

"Well, unfortunately, our meeting wasn't as fruitful as Moriarty would have liked. Truthfully, he tried to convince me the property I wanted wouldn't be in my best interests to buy."

"Why?"

"It doesn't matter, really, and neither does he. The bid is in. That's all that matters."

I was grateful then that the women brought dessert out. My grandfather made a show of how it looked too beautiful to be eaten, and the women smiled, blushing a little even. I watched him, this side of him different to the man I knew, charming almost. Not a man capable of doing the things Raphael claimed he did. Certainly not capable of threatening a man's life.

But then again, didn't my presence here, didn't the ring that weighed heavy on my finger, prove otherwise?

Although Grandfather smiled, something cold settled in his eyes, and it chilled me.

I needed to tread very carefully here. Liars came in all shapes and sizes.

So did monsters.

The looks on their faces when they saw me approach their cozy little lunch was priceless. I wished I had a camera. Shock and awe felt about the right words to describe it. At least as far as Sofia went. I had a feeling the old man expected me.

When Eric had called to tell me neither she nor the dog were anywhere to be found, I knew exactly where she would be. Or at least whom she'd be with. She had ignored me completely and done the opposite of what I'd said. Which I guess meant she hadn't ignored me completely. I did always try to see the silver fucking lining.

I'd called the hotel in Siena where her grandfather was staying, and it had taken only a few minutes for me to get them to tell me where their driver was taking him. Guardia Winery.

"Well, well, what a surprise," Marcus said, wiping his mouth with his napkin.

I ignored him, my eyes on my disobedient wife instead. In that moment, I realized I couldn't name the storm of emotions swirling inside me. They were too confused, too strange.

"Nice lunch?" I forced my voice to sound calm, but it didn't. Not by a long shot.

Charlie yapped at her feet, his leash secured under her chair the only thing keeping him from running to me. As if I were his master to greet.

"Yes, it was," she said, taking the napkin off her lap and setting it beside her plate. "We're out of dessert, or I'd offer you some." She rose to her feet, surprising me.

"Are you leaving?" her grandfather asked. "So soon?"

"If Raphael came all this way to get me, I don't want to keep him waiting. He has a lot of meetings. Busy man, you know."

She said good-bye to the men.

"Just a minute, Sofia," her grandfather said.

She stopped. He nodded to the manager, who'd reached into his pocket to produce two keys on a ring. Marcus took them and held them out to her.

"These will open the gate down below when it's locked as well as the house itself."

She looked confused.

"Take it. It's still yours, after all."

She reached out her hand to take the keys. "Thank you."

"You're welcome."

A moment later, she turned to me. "You didn't have to come pick me up. My grandfather would have dropped me off."

I fumed. My fingernails dug into my palm. When I got her home...

"Get your dog, and let's go," I snapped.

"Like I said, you didn't have to come."

Her grandfather watched us, barely able to keep the pleased smile from his face. She picked Charlie up, and I had the feeling she was working very hard to keep from having to meet my eyes.

Once she reached me, I took her arm and tugged her close.

"Let go."

"I should get *you* a leash."

"I bet you'd like that. Jerk."

"Coming here with him was a stupid thing to do."

We reached the car, and I opened the passenger side door to let her in. She sat down and set the pup on her lap. Once I got in and started the car, she spoke.

"It wasn't stupid. Lina was gone with Damon. What was I supposed to do, hang out with Eric?"

"I don't know, play with your dog, swim, read. Take a fucking nap."

"I'm sure many women would envy my position, but you know I needed to talk to him."

I turned to her and glimpsed the bluish marks on her neck. Marks I'd left. I swallowed my rebuke and returned my attention to the road.

"Eric is there to keep you safe, Sofia," I said more calmly ten minutes later.

"My grandfather doesn't pose a threat. Not to me."

"He may not, but his associates do."

"Moriarty isn't an associate."

Raphael glanced at me and chuckled. "Is that so?"

"What does that mean?"

"Did your grandfather tell you that?"

She seemed confused. I knew there couldn't be any truth to it. The old man was a manipulative liar.

"And what about becoming your sister's legal guardian? Did you ask that? And did he readily agree? Putting his grandchildren before himself?"

She shifted in her seat and looked straight ahead. "He refused outright."

I didn't say anything, although I wanted to.

"Go on, Raphael, don't hold back. Don't you want to tell me you told me so?"

"Believe it or not, I wish I were wrong in this case."

She exhaled and shook her head, looking out the side window.

"Did you think for a minute your sister might be safer there than here? At least for now?"

"Safer?"

"I have enemies, your grandfather being one of them. But Moriarty poses a more imminent threat."

"You said—"

"I said I'd keep you safe, and I plan to. But it would be easier if I didn't have to chase you around Tuscany, and your sister physically not being here is better for her. Your grandfather will take care of her."

"He wouldn't hurt me either."

"I know he wouldn't physically hurt you."

Our eyes met, and I saw a thousand and one questions behind them. But she didn't ask even one. She doubted. She doubted her grandfather. She doubted me. And she should. She'd be smart not to trust either of us.

"Can you see how her not being here may be safer for her? Out of reach of Moriarty."

"What do you owe him?"

"I owe him nothing. My father, on the other hand, owed him half a million dollars."

Her mouth fell open. "Half a million dollars?"

I nodded.

"Why?"

"He stole from him. Like the fucking idiot he was."

"Can't you just pay him off?"

"It's half a million dollars, Sofia. Besides, it's not my debt to pay. If I paid this one off, I'd be sending a message. I want it to be known that I will not pay for my father's mistakes. His sins are his. I'm no longer his whipping boy."

"What are all your meetings about?"

"Vineyard. I'm thinking about selling."

"Sell the land?"

"The land. The house. All of it."

"Raphael—"

"I wonder if it wouldn't be better. To walk away from everything. Start fresh."

"But it's home. You said so. It's where you remember your mother. Your brothers. You said it's where you remember being happy. If it were me, and I had something of my parents, I wouldn't give it up, no matter what."

Did she think I took this decision lightly? We sat quietly for ten minutes. "Your neck, Sofia," I finally said.

She wrapped one hand around it.

"I'm sorry. I can get very...angry."

"I noticed."

I turned to her. "I don't want to hurt you."

"Then don't. You have to figure out how to deal with the anger."

"How do you not despise me?"

"How could I? How could I hate you? You're a victim. Maybe more of one than me."

"I don't know that there are degrees or that they matter."

"What do your brothers think about the sale?"

"Doesn't matter. I own it."

"Raphael, you want to—"

"I'm not decided yet," I said honestly. "One way or the other."

"But—"

"Leave it, Sofia. I need to think."

"You'd do this?"

I didn't reply. Instead, I took the turn onto the property. Lina and Damon walked out of the house together to greet us.

Sofia leaped out of the car after Charlie, hugging first her sister, then Damon. He said something to her, but I didn't hear it. From the look on her face, it was a reproach. Good.

Lina took Sofia's hand, and they went into the house. But just before they were out of sight, I noticed the look Lina threw over her shoulder at Damon. There was something strange about it. Something unexpected.

"Where did Damon take you?" Sofia asked.

I didn't hear Lina's response as they disappeared ahead of us, but I did study my brother, saw how his eyes followed them, how they narrowed as they tracked Lina.

"She's a little young, isn't she?" I asked, meaning

it to be a joke but realizing he took it as more of a taunt the moment I saw his face.

"What the hell does that mean?"

"Just that she's young. Sixteen, right?"

"So first you accuse me of being—what was the word you used? Cozy? Yes, cozy with Sofia, and now it's something else with her sister?"

I grinned. "I thought you'd be better at masking your emotions by now, brother."

"Fuck you, Raphael."

"What is happening to the clergy these days?" I said, walking into the house and toward the kitchen, stopping at the door. "Are you coming? You wanted to work on the chapel. I mean, it's why you're here, right? There's no other reason."

Damon's face grew red, and he fisted his hands at his sides. But he kept his mouth shut. We grabbed some bottles of water, left through the back door, and headed to the chapel. We walked over a mile in silence. I didn't care. Didn't give a single fuck. I'd hit a nerve, which with my twin was almost impossible to do.

DAMON and I worked in silence for the first few hours, and the more time that passed, the more I thought about how he'd taken my comment. About how if there were some truth behind it, it would have heavy consequences for my brother.

I glanced over at him. He'd taken off his shirt and was lifting broken blocks of stone to carry outside.

"Damon," I said, wiping my forehead with my discarded shirt. "It's hot. We should take a break."

"You go if you need to. I need to keep working."

"Why? It's been sitting like this for years. Now you're in a rush?"

"I just need to work, Raphael. Go back to the house. I don't need you here."

He didn't look at me once while he worked. I leaned against the wall and drank from my bottle of water, which was warm by now.

"Tell me what happened," I said.

He stopped, his back tensing either from my question or the weight of the stone he carried.

"Nothing," he said with a glance over his shoulder. "I don't know what you're talking about."

He walked out of the church, and I heard the stone crash against the pile we'd already made.

I chuckled. For all his talk, my brother needed help being honest with himself.

"Well, if you don't know what I'm talking about, how can it be nothing?" I asked when he returned, taking another sip of water. "Warm as piss."

He stopped, his eyes darkening. "You're in a church. Watch your mouth."

I held up both hands in mock surrender. "Didn't know you cared that much, considering."

"What the fuck is your problem?" he asked, suddenly in my face.

"Whoa, brother. Who's got to watch his mouth now?"

"If you're trying to goad me into a fight—"

"I'm just asking you a question," I said, leaning into his space. We were equal in height and similar in build. I hadn't fought him since he was a kid. I would if had to. Hell, maybe it'd feel good.

"Well, don't."

"You're my brother. I'm just watching out for you."

He gritted his teeth. "I don't need watching. And I never asked you to protect me. Not once. You just did it. You took it."

"What the fuck are you talking—"

He swung his fist so fast, I almost didn't see it coming. But prison had perfected my fighting skills. I caught his arm, stopping the collision with my face.

"I said watch your mouth. You're in a holy place!"

"Does a holy man have any business looking at a sixteen-year-old girl?"

Damon's hand closed around my throat, and he shoved me hard against the church wall. I chuckled. "Where'd you learn that move? They teach you to fight in that seminary?"

"Stop."

"What, Damon? Am I getting under your skin?"

"I saw your fingerprints around Sofia's throat, brother."

My mouth turned into a hard line, and this time, it was Damon who grinned.

"What is she, half your size? Learn that from dad after all?"

My breathing came tight, my chest heaving with each breath. I guess he knew how to get under my skin too.

"What's the matter? Too much truth for you?" he asked.

Fuck. He sounded like me. Exactly like me.

I shoved his arm off me and knocked my fist into his jaw. Damon stumbled backward, almost tripping into a pew, but righted himself fast and came at me, arm raised to strike me back.

"Yeah, that's better. Hit me. I can take it, and I can give it back. You don't fucking hit someone half your fucking size," he said, his fist colliding with the side of my face.

I shoved him backward, this time smashing him into the wall and grabbing him by the throat. "I don't fucking hit her. I've never fucking hit her. I would never—"

"And those bruises, did she put them there herself?"

I drew my arm back again, so angry, so fucking angry all I saw was red. Damon's eyes moved over my shoulder. I hadn't even heard her come, but all of a sudden, Sofia's hands wrapped around my arm, and she used all her weight to keep me from knocking Damon out.

"Stop!" she cried out. "What are you doing?"

"Tell him I don't hit you."

"What?"

"Fucking tell him."

"Get off him, Raphael!"

"Get away, Sofia!" Damon ordered.

He'd managed to pull my arm off his throat.

"You'll get hurt."

"No," she said pulling me back, forcing me away from my brother.

"Tell him," I said, my gaze still locked on Damon, his on mine.

"He doesn't hit me. He hasn't hit me once, Damon. Not once."

Damon turned to her, his eyes searching her face, maybe trying to make out if she was lying.

"I swear, Damon. Raphael won't hurt me."

She shoved herself between us, standing in front of me as if she would protect me.

"The bruises on your neck," Damon said.

"Something else. I promise, okay?"

Damon looked at the floor, then ran a hand through his hair, shaking his head. His face when he looked at me showed only confusion.

"Let's go back. Maria has dinner almost ready,"

Sofia said, taking my hand in one of hers and reaching out to take his.

Damon shook his head. "You two go." He took another step back, his gaze landing on the altar.

"Sofia," I said, watching him as I spoke. "Wait for me outside. I'll be right there."

She hesitated.

"Go. No more fighting."

She nodded and gave us both a weighted look before walking out of the chapel.

"I'm sorry," I said, stepping toward Damon. "You're right. I was trying to goad you. I don't even know why."

He rubbed his hand over his mouth, his face, and shook his head. "I'm sorry too. I don't know what came over me. I'm not…"

"It's my fault. Just forget it. If you need to talk—"

"I need some time alone."

I nodded and walked toward the door. "You coming for dinner?"

He walked to the front pew and sat down. "Go ahead. I'll be there later."

As much as I wanted to go to him, to force him to talk to me, I made my legs carry me in the other direction and walked over to Sofia, who stood waiting on the church steps, her eyes wide with worry.

"Let's go," I said.

"What happened?"

"Later." I took her hand, and we headed toward the house. I felt grateful nighttime would hide my face, because Damon was right to worry about Sofia. And he didn't even know the whole story. Didn't know what was still to come. And I hated myself a little more for it every day.

Raphael and I walked back to the house in silence. He held my hand, his thumb making circles inside my palm. The air hung heavy around him, his mood dark. I wished he'd tell me what had happened between him and Damon.

"Are you okay?" I finally asked before we went inside.

He turned to me and rubbed my arms, backing me against the wall. His expression looked as though he had a thousand things to say, but instead of saying any of them, he cradled my head with one hand and leaned down to kiss me full on the mouth, his lips soft against mine, the touch intimate and sensual. Different than his other kisses. Not erotic. Not at first. When he pulled back, his eyes almost gleamed.

I touched his face, and he flinched. He'd have a wicked bruise tomorrow.

"My intention when I started this, the whole time I planned it, I never thought about *you*. Not you as in flesh and blood and human. My brother is right to be worried. I keep telling you I won't hurt you, but I do, don't I?"

"Raphael—"

"It's what I do."

He shook his head and touched a finger to my face.

"I could stop. I could call it off. Let you go. Forget about the inheritance. If I were good, I would do that. But I'm not good."

I searched his eyes, confused. He looked solemn, almost sorry, and his words, they sounded so...final. But before I could ask him any questions, the door opened. Maria stepped out with Charlie running around her feet. She looked irritated and then when she saw us, embarrassed. She told us dinner was ready, and if we didn't hurry up, it would be cold soon.

"Come on."

Raphael took my hand and led me inside.

After he had a quick shower, the three of us sat down to dinner. I didn't miss how Lina's eyes roamed to the empty seat where Damon was supposed to sit.

When I'd gotten back to the house that afternoon, she'd seemed...different. Happy, but different than usual. She'd told me about her day with Damon, said he'd gotten to the house early, and they'd had coffee together while waiting for me, but when by ten I still hadn't made an appearance, he'd offered to show her around his favorite village, Pienza. After that, the story had been fairly superficial. Lunch. A tour of the church. Then driving around the countryside. Something had told me not to ask more questions, but to wait for her to tell me.

I wondered how much Damon and Lina's day together had to do with the brothers' fighting. I was dying to ask details of Raphael but couldn't, not with Lina there. Instead, we made small talk, and every little sound had both Raphael and Lina glancing at the door. Damon never turned up, and it was past eleven at night when Lina finally went up to bed, her disappointment hard to miss.

"What was that at the chapel?" I finally asked when we were alone in his bedroom.

"Well—"

He pulled off his T-shirt and tossed it on the floor before facing me.

"Did you notice how he and your sister looked at each other when we got back?"

"I noticed something, but she's sixteen. I mean, she'll be seventeen in a few months, but I thought I was wrong, given the fact he's at seminary and she's, well, young."

"I'm not saying anything happened. Damon's far

too responsible for that. Although today showed me a different side of my brother."

"How did the fighting start?"

"I made some comment about what you just said, Lina being young, and he blew up. Things then rapidly moved on to your favorite topic. My anger issues."

I bit the inside of my cheek, not denying anything.

"And it all just escalated into what you saw. You know, it's maybe just years of anger he has too. I mean, I have no idea where he is in his head with what happened. With mom and, well, with what I did."

"You've never talked about it?"

"We didn't grow up talking about anything, Sofia."

"I think it hurt Lina's feelings when he didn't show up tonight."

"Well, it's probably better off he didn't. Not like anything could ever happen between them."

Him saying that out loud, though, it felt strange, almost as if he were tempting fate. Too caught up in what he said, I didn't respond but stood studying him until he took my hand and led me to bed.

I SHARED the discovery of mom's perfume and lipstick with Lina. She didn't have a connection with the scent I thought of as Mom's, for which I was grateful. I didn't want to give up my find.

She and I spent the next two days together. Eric drove us around to some of the villages during the day, then we'd go back to the house and swim into the evening. Raphael pretty much left us alone, and Damon remained a no-show. Whenever I tried to steer conversation toward him, Lina managed to turn it around. It was clear she didn't want to talk about him.

On the morning she was to fly home, we got up early and took a long walk around the property with Charlie.

"I'm not sure who you're going to miss more, me or him," I teased.

"Both of you. I wish I could stay longer."

"I tried, but Grandfather wouldn't allow it." I left out the part about Raphael thinking it was safer for her to go home anyway.

"Well, maybe I can come back over the Thanks-giving break. We can show Maria what an American holiday is like."

"You mean we cook a turkey? You and me?"

"Nah. We don't want to kill her." She paused, hesitating for a moment before reaching into her pocket. "Do you think when you see Damon again you can give him this?" It was a sealed envelope.

I took it from her hand, studying her, trying to work out how far I could go.

"What happened with you two?"

"Nothing. Not really."

She turned to walk, and I stepped alongside her. She kept her eyes on the ground, but I saw the small smile creep along her lips.

"I don't even know how to describe it." She looked up at me. "I mean, he's twenty-four years old, and he's going to be a priest. It's not like anything *can* happen."

"He and Raphael were fighting at the chapel yesterday. Physically fighting."

"Did Damon give him that shiner?"

"He's got a matching one."

"Ouch. What was it over?"

"What Raphael told me was that he'd made some comment about how you'd looked at each other, and Damon blew up."

"He did?" She searched my face, hopeful, but then hers darkened again.

"It doesn't matter anyway. I'll be on the other side of the ocean."

"And you're sixteen."

"Almost seventeen."

"He'll take vows of celibacy."

"He hasn't yet."

"Lina," I stopped and took her hands to make her look at me. My sister and I were close. I knew Lina.

But I realized then how, over the last four years, we'd been apart more than we'd been together. Lina wasn't just my little sister anymore. She'd grown up. She was almost an adult. This—whatever this was that had happened between her and Damon—it belonged to her and something told me to let it be. To not push.

I suddenly didn't know what to say. She looked at me like she thought I'd lecture her. Maybe that's what she was used to with Grandfather. But that wasn't what I wanted.

"I don't want you to be sad when you go home, that's all," I said, meaning every word.

Tears burst from her eyes, and she fell into my arms.

"I'm already sad. I'm losing you, Sofia. You're not just two hours away. We're not even in the same time zone anymore. There's a whole freaking ocean between us now."

I hugged her back, squeezing tight. "I don't care. We're going to talk every day. We'll Facetime for hours. And I'll come for visits."

"What if he doesn't let you?"

"He will. He has to."

"Sofia," Raphael called out, walking toward us from the house.

We both wiped our faces. I knew he'd seen our tears, but he didn't mention it.

"Time to go."

We nodded.

Things felt different with him for some reason. I wish I knew what else he and Damon had discussed and had fought over.

Lina climbed into the backseat of the sedan with Charlie in her lap. Raphael would drive us to Siena, where Lina would meet Grandfather. They would head to the airport together. I was determined to squeeze out every last minute I could with my sister.

When we reached Siena, Grandfather was already waiting along with their driver beside their sedan. We climbed out, Lina and I with tears in our eyes.

Raphael didn't acknowledge my grandfather. Not with more than a nod of the head. Lina went to Raphael, and he turned to her.

"Take care of my sister." She looked him square in the eyes, my little sister standing taller, all grown-up.

He studied her for a long minute, then nodded. "I will."

I saw the shadow behind his eyes. He was preoccupied, which I understood.

My grandfather gave me an awkward hug, and although Lina and I had promised each other we wouldn't cry, our last hug was tearful. Even Charlie seemed somber when the sedan drove away. Raphael remained silent, waiting and watching with me until their car disappeared.

"Okay?" he asked as we climbed back into our car.

I shrugged a shoulder, unable to look at him. I hated when he saw me cry.

We drove in silence, heading home. Charlie dozed on my lap, and I petted him absently. I wasn't paying attention to our surroundings, and when I did finally look up and saw Raphael gazing too frequently into the rearview mirror, I, too, glanced over my shoulder. A large black SUV drove behind us.

"What is it?" I asked Raphael.

He shook his head, his gaze intent for a moment on the SUV, then on the winding road. These streets weren't very busy, and I wasn't sure if it was Raphael's reaction or what, but something felt wrong. Something about that SUV struck me.

When Raphael accelerated, so did the SUV. And when he slowed, same thing. They seemed to be keeping pace with us. I could make out the shape of two forms inside, although all the windows, including the windshield, were heavily tinted.

That was when I remembered.

Moriarty.

He'd come to the house during the wedding reception in an SUV similar to this one. Was it him?

"Raphael?" I asked. "Are they following us?"

"Hold on," he said, taking a sharp, unexpected turn.

"What are you doing?" I screamed, startled, the sound of screeching brakes scaring the hell out of me.

Raphael didn't answer me. Instead, we both watched as the SUV bounced around the turn, the driving erratic now.

"Goddamn asshole," Raphael said, reaching across to open the glove compartment. That was when I saw the shiny butt of what I knew was a pistol.

"Raphael!"

He was slowing the car, pulling off to the side.

"What are you doing? Why do you have that?"

He came to a full stop and took the weapon into his palm. Charlie must have felt my panic. He started to bark and circle on my lap.

"Keep him quiet!"

"I can't help it! What's happening?" He reached to open his door, but I grabbed his arm to stop him. That was when the SUV's brakes screeched, and they swerved violently around us. I screamed, and Raphael muttered a curse, then turned to me.

"Are you okay?" he asked.

"What was that?"

"Are you okay?" he demanded this time.

"Yes!"

He shoved the pistol back into the glove compartment, put the car into gear, and drove it back around onto the other road heading toward home.

"Moriarty's goons."

"What are they trying to do?"

"Scare us."

"Well, it worked."

"I'm taking you home."

"Where are you going?"

"I'm going to pay him a visit and end this once and for all."

"They're dangerous, Raphael. You can't—"

But the look in his eyes when he turned to me stopped me short.

"I'm dangerous too, Sofia," he said, looking calm, taking a deep breath in.

"The gun," I said. I didn't need to say more.

He didn't respond but kept his gaze on the road. He made two calls, and by the time we pulled in through the gates and parked at the house, I saw Eric and the other two men I'd met when I'd first arrived waiting for us.

Raphael got out of the car but left it running. He said something to Eric that I didn't hear. I let Charlie out and went to Raphael.

"What's happening?" I asked.

Eric nodded and gave some orders to the others. Raphael turned to me.

"Stay here. I'll be back. Understand?"

"You can't go to him."

Raphael gave me a tight smile, his eyes not quite on me. I could feel the anger, the rage, coming off him.

"Raphael?"

"Go inside, Sofia. Swim if you want. Whatever. Don't do anything stupid, am I clear?"

With that, he dismissed me, and I realized I had not one guard but two. Eric's cousins stayed at the house while Raphael and Eric drove off. I watched them go, feeling powerless and afraid.

I went into the house, pacing for a little while, unsure what to do. Charlie lay down in the kitchen for his nap, and Maria and the others were working. I went up to my room and fished out the card Damon had given me and dialed him. He didn't answer his cell phone, so I called the seminary where, after holding for more than ten minutes, Damon came on the line.

"This is Damon," he said.

"It's Sofia."

"Sofia?"

"Raphael just left with Eric. He's going to see Moriarty."

"Moriarty?"

I nodded. "Yes. On our way back from taking Lina to Siena, this SUV started following us. It was pretty scary. Damon, he has a gun."

"Shit."

When I heard the urgency in Damon's tone, I dropped onto the bed, too heavy to stand. "Damon?"

"Sit tight, Sofia. I'm going to meet him, try to intercept him."

Stupidly, I nodded again. "Thank you, Damon. Thank you."

"I'll call you as soon as I can."

He was almost gone when I called out his name. "Damon?"

"Yes?"

"Take care."

"I will. It'll be fine. Don't worry."

I hated those two words. They always meant the opposite of what they said.

My fucking brother wouldn't stop dialing my phone. I guessed Sofia had called him as soon as I left, and I knew he wouldn't stop calling. Finally, after the eighth time, I answered.

"What is it, Damon."

"Where are you, Raphael?"

"I'm guessing you know that."

"On your way to Moriarty's offices?"

"He's gone too far."

"Sofia said you have a gun."

"Do you propose I go without one?"

"I propose you don't go at all. Not until you've calmed down. He's not some two-bit thug we're talking about. He's a legitimate businessman—"

"There's nothing legitimate about him."

"Unless you want to give him ammunition, you can't go into Florence with a fucking gun."

He was right. I knew it. But fuck. "He sent a car after us. *Us*, Damon. Sofia was with me."

"I realize there has to be a meeting. Just not like this, not when you're out of control."

"Aren't I always out of control? That's what you were telling me a few days ago with your fists, wasn't it?"

He sighed. "I need to be there too. This concerns me as much as it does you."

"No, it doesn't."

"The house may belong to you, but it's my past too."

"No."

"Are you still protecting me, brother?"

"Oh, that's right, you didn't want my protection."

"Goddamn it, Raphael. Just fucking wait. I'm on my way. I lost you once. I'm not willing to lose you again."

I paused, as if hearing his words in slow motion. It took me a full minute to respond. "I'll wait. I'll get there in forty-five minutes."

"I'll wait for you, then. I'm closer. I'll be there in twenty."

Damon was right, I knew it. Moriarty may be an asshole, but he was a powerful man. Legitimate enough that I needed to do this right. If I walked into his office brandishing a gun, he'd have me tossed into jail. Considering my past, I'd just be making everything easier for him.

Traffic getting into Florence delayed both of us, but once we arrived, I found Damon at the café at the corner of Moriarty's building, which was an old, three-story property, ancient on the outside, meticulously modern on the inside. I knew because I'd seen pictures in a magazine once.

I told Eric to wait outside the building and went into the coffee shop where, before I could protest, my brother had a waitress bringing me over an espresso.

"Sit."

Although reluctant, I did.

"Drink and breathe."

"If it was just me, that'd be one thing, Damon. But Sofia was there."

"I know. I get it. And agree we need to handle this."

"He wants the property. He's made perfectly clear he'll buy us out—after subtracting the amount our father owed him."

"Generous of him."

"I'd rather see it burn to the ground than give it to him."

"Well, it almost did, didn't it?"

I shook my head, feeling more at ease now that Damon was here too. I didn't realize how much I needed him. And he was right. I was too angry. Moriarty wanted that. He knew having that car chase would scare the fuck out of Sofia, and he knew I'd react.

"Better?"

Damon was reading me. He always did have a knack for that.

"Yeah." I stood, pushed the chair out. "Let's go do this thing."

He nodded and rose to his feet, tossed a few bills on the table, and we walked out. Eric waited just outside the building. Once inside, we bypassed the young blonde receptionist and headed toward the large marble staircase.

"Sir, you can't go—"

I ignored her. We both did. I knew she'd call up to Moriarty anyway.

On the third floor, we were greeted by two men in suits standing outside the large double doors that led to Moriarty's office.

Damon put his hand on my arm as we approached. Moriarty's private secretary cleared her throat.

"Don't let him get to you. He's going to do whatever he can to get under your skin. Don't let him, no matter what you hear, understand?"

I thought what he said sounded strange, and I would have questioned it, but the secretary spoke then.

"Mr. Moriarty is expecting you. You can go in."

"How nice."

The men opened the doors, and Damon and I headed into his office. Inside, two men sat in large armchairs in one corner and two more flanked his large, mahogany desk. Behind it, Moriarty leaned back in his chair, one leg crossed over the other, a stupid grin on his fat face and his fingers steepled.

"What a great pleasure. A visit from not one but two Amado brothers. With matching black eyes. How interesting."

"Six men. Is that special for us, or you need that much security with all your visitors?" I asked.

"You always did think yourself special, Raphael," he said, then turned to his men. "Search them."

Two men patted us down. Moriarty sat forward and rested his elbows on the obnoxiously oversized desk. One of the men announced we were unarmed.

Moriarty nodded and cocked his head to the side. "To what do I owe the pleasure?"

"Your boys tried to run me and my wife off the road."

He feigned shock.

"Let's cut the crap, Moriarty."

"I don't know what you're talking about."

"You're not getting the house."

"Someone tried to run you off the road?"

My jaw tightened, and my hands fisted. When I took a step forward, Damon's hand closed over my shoulder.

"Raphael," he said. "Don't let him get to you."

"Yes, Raphael. Don't let me get to you."

"You don't involve my wife in this, do you understand? She has nothing to do with this."

"Sadly, she does. She did the moment she said the words *"I do."* Ah, young love. I remember those days. Very well, in fact."

"Cut the crap."

"You know, once upon a time, your mother, father, and I were very close."

"Ancient history." I did know that. My father had gone to school with Moriarty when his parents had moved to Italy. He'd met my mother two years after that, and the three of them were once friends. For a short time at least.

"Still." He shrugged a shoulder.

"Wait a minute." I chuckled and looked around the room. I had a feeling the two leather armchairs the men sat on had been moved from the front of his desk so he would keep us standing. "Mind if I sit?" I asked, picking up a smaller, hardback wooden chair and carrying it toward his desk before he could reply. Damon remained standing. "So, is that what all this is about?" I asked. "Is it what it's always been about?"

His eyes narrowed just a little. I would have missed it if I wasn't paying attention. Damon wasn't the only one who could read people.

"My mother?" I continued.

"Raphael," Damon's low voice warned from beside me.

Moriarty picked up a pen, and I saw how his knuckles whitened around it. I was right.

"She chose him over you, didn't she?" I asked.

"Your father met her first. It was never a competition."

"No? You don't think I remember your name being tossed around the house when I was growing up?" What I said was true. It was suddenly all coming together. "Let me ask you a question. Did you love her, or did you just want what my father had?"

"That's enough. Are you here to tell me you have the money you owe me? Because you know if you don't, there's one other way."

"I'm here to tell you it's not my debt to pay."

"But, it is. In my book, at least. And you specifically, Raphael, since you're responsible for your father's death—self-defense or not. Therefore, you inherited that debt."

"That is some interesting logic."

"Once you pay me, I'm off your back. If it wasn't for the astronomical amount, I'd forgive it. Again."

Again? "Bullshit. You forgive nothing."

"You see—"

He rose to his feet and turned so he looked out onto the street as he started to speak. "Your mother tried that too once."

My hands clenched at my sides at the mere mention of her.

Damon cleared his throat. "Let's go, Raphael." He turned to Moriarty, who now faced us. "We'll figure out a way to get you the money, but it won't be the house."

"It's not our debt to pay," I repeated to Damon.

Moriarty watched me, ignoring my brother altogether. The smirk on his face suddenly sickened me.

"You mother's been here once before too. Well, multiple times. Renata loved Florence, after all."

"Don't say her name," I said.

Damon's hand closed over my shoulder.

"That's enough," he told Moriarty. "Raphael. We need to leave. Now."

I glanced at Damon, saw how some of the color had drained from his face.

"See, your father and I had a falling-out a very long time ago. Maybe around the time you two were born. He couldn't wait to put babies in your mother. Thinking it would keep her bound to him."

I stood, my breathing tight now. The men who were sitting in the armchairs also rose to their feet. The two men before Moriarty's desk stepped closer together, letting Damon and me know it would be stupid to launch any sort of physical attack.

"But your father, well, I suppose Renata gave him reason to question. Even your paternity, believe it or not. Right up to the very end. The man didn't even believe in the truth of science."

"What the hell are you talking about?" I asked.

"Raphael. We're leaving. Now."

This time, Damon's command carried a very real sense of urgency.

"Renata, may her soul rest in peace—"

Damon cut him off. "Leave the dead be," he said through gritted teeth.

I looked at Damon, but he didn't seem as upset as me. And the look in his eyes the moment they met mine was one of resignation.

"Damon. Always reasonable," Moriarty started again. "What's Zachariah like? Oh, you don't know. He's missing in action or was he AWOL? I can't remember."

"You're not getting her house," Damon said. "Let's go, Raphael. We need to leave."

Moriarty touched something on his desk, and the doors opened. The two men outside came in. "Get him out," Moriarty said, gesturing to Damon.

"Raphael. Come with me. We need to go. Now."

But I couldn't. All I could do was stare at Moriarty's ugly, fat face. The victory in his flat, dead eyes. No. I couldn't leave. I had to hear.

Damon fought them, and a third man joined in to drag him out the door. Moriarty turned to me.

"Your brother already knows the story. It'd probably bore him anyway."

"Speak your fucking mind, and do it fast."

"As I was saying, your mother, well, she was a whore. She wanted every man who wanted her—"

I didn't know if he had more to say. If he was midword. I stopped hearing the moment he called my mother a whore. I lunged, but they expected the move. His men grabbed me by the arms and held me so that I faced that bastard.

Moriarty looked at me. "See, your mother once sat in that very chair," he said, pointing behind me.

"What the *hell* are you talking about?" I asked.

"The first time she came to me, she wanted me to forgive your father's debt. She knew she'd chosen the wrong man. Knew he was weak."

"My mother—"

"Offered to do anything." He drew out the last word.

I grunted with the effort to free myself, but the men held me tight.

"Anything," he repeated, "See, this is déjà vu, really. But I don't want you to kneel under my desk and suck my dick, Raphael. I prefer women."

Fingers bit into my arms as I battled his guards to get to him. I wanted to wrap my hands around his throat and squeeze until the life had gone out of him.

"I prefer your mother's tight little ass bent over my desk. And I did fuck her in the ass. She needed to be taught a lesson—"

"You're a fucking liar! A goddamned fucking liar!" They held me tight. I heard the click of a gun being cocked and felt the cold steel of it behind my ear.

"I don't want a mess in my office, boys," Moriarty said, calm as could be.

He returned his full attention to me.

"See, I did keep my word. I did forgive his debt. That time. But your father didn't learn. When she came to me again, well, there's just so much a man can do for used-up old pussy, isn't there?"

Rage throbbed inside me, burning hot, pumping my blood with adrenaline. With a roar more animal than human, I tore free from the men who held me and lunged across the desk to fall on top of Moriarty, knocking his chair over, sending him to the floor. I wrapped my hands around his throat and squeezed, his fat flesh too thick to snap his neck. His eyes bulged, his face reddened as he struggled to breathe, but before I could kill him, I was dragged off and tossed against the far wall, a fist landing in my gut, then another, then another until I hunched over, gripping my middle. Someone kicked my legs out from under me, and I dropped to the floor. A shoe closed over my throat and held me down when Moriarty came to stand over me, kicking me hard in the kidneys.

When I looked up, I saw how disheveled he looked, his tie askew, his shirt and suit splattered with what I assumed to be my blood. I laughed as one of his men kicked me again and again until I couldn't see straight.

"Get him out of here," Moriarty finally said. I heard his chair creak under his weight.

"I have a buyer," I said as I was hauled upright. "You're not getting her house, you disgusting prick." I spat blood as I spoke, and I wasn't sure he could even understand my words. "You will never have any part of her. I'll kill you before that happens."

DAMON DROVE ME HOME, and Eric followed in Damon's car. My head was spinning, my body hurt. I think I passed out once or twice. I glanced at Damon, remembering that look in his eyes, that resignation. Remembering his insistence that we leave.

"Are you okay?" Damon asked.

"Is it true?" I ignored his question.

"Does it matter?"

Fuck.

My mother? With him? To pay off my father's debt?

"Did you know?" I asked.

He ignored my question. "She's dead," he said. "He can say whatever he wants, and she can't defend herself."

I pressed the heels of my hands against my eyes.

"He was trying to get a reaction out of you," Damon continued.

No. No fucking way.

"Is it fucking true? Tell me. Say it."

But he didn't have to say anything. All he had to do was look at me.

"God. Fuck." I pounded my fist against the dash, and pain shot up my arm. "You knew?"

Damon returned his gaze to the road. "I found a diary she kept. In the chapel. I shouldn't have read it. I wish I hadn't."

"Why? Why did she—" I choked on the words, swallowing blood.

"She felt like she had no choice. She knew he always resented her for choosing our father. Used that to get him out of debt. Dad didn't deserve her."

"Is that why he beat her? He didn't start with her until later."

"I think so. The timing fits. He must have found out."

"I thought it was because I fought back."

"It doesn't matter anymore, Raphael. They're both gone."

"I'm going to kill him. I'm going to kill the bastard."

"Maybe we have to think about the buyer. We may have no choice. I don't want him to have the property even if it means we have to give it up to someone else."

I couldn't respond. Instead, I opened the visor and flinched at my reflection. "Sofia's going to freak."

"That's why I'm taking you to the seminary first to get you cleaned up. We can't cover up the bruises, but I can at least clean up the blood and get you a change of clothes."

We rode in silence, each of us lost in our thoughts, me trying to make sense of this. Him, well, I didn't know.

"Where's the diary?" I asked him when we reached the seminary.

He studied me.

"Give it some time. If you want to see it after, I'll give it to you. Not yet. Let's deal with this first." He opened the car door. "We'll get you cleaned up and home. Sofia's probably anxious."

Damon didn't quite look at me after that. I suffered through a shower, wondering if they'd broken ribs when they'd kicked me, feeling bruised inside and out. He was right. I was anxious to get back to Sofia. It took all I had to sit still as he treated cuts and bruises before handing me a mirror.

"Fuck. I look good."

"Yeah."

He helped me out to the car. "Don't they wonder what the hell you're up to?" I asked, gesturing to the brothers who stood watching from a distance. "You come home beat up. Then you bring me here beat up."

"Oh yeah. I keep things interesting around here."

Damon drove us home. I knew he'd called Sofia to warn her. When we pulled up to the house later that evening, she was waiting for me at the door. The minute she saw me, she gasped, covering her mouth with her hand, her eyes filling with tears.

"I know, I've looked better." I said, flinching as she tentatively touched me. "I wish I could say you should see the other guy."

"Take him upstairs," Sofia said.

"Bring me some whiskey," I said as I headed to the stairs, offering Maria, who stood with her hands on her cheeks, tears streaking her face, a weak smile.

I let them take care of me for one full week. Damon stayed at the house, and Sofia never left my side. And all the while, all that kept going through my head was my mother, my mother with that man.

I wanted to kill him. I would fucking kill him.

He called her a whore, but if what he said was true, he was a rapist. He extorted those humiliations from her. She was no whore. Her only sin was loving her family.

But just alongside those thoughts, the image of Sofia kept appearing.

Because ultimately, wasn't I doing the same thing to her that Moriarty had done to my mother?

Three weeks went by, and in that time, Raphael healed. I gave Damon my sister's note and watched him when he took it. I don't know if I made up the fact that his eyes seemed to sadden a little when he looked down at her neat little script.

Damon returned to the seminary but came for dinner each night. Neither of them would tell me what happened that day, and Raphael grew more and more distant than ever. We hadn't made love once, not even as he'd healed. And he'd even told me it was more comfortable for him to sleep on his own and sent me to my room.

It was the end of the second week when I overheard Maria sending Eric to fetch Raphael from the chapel for dinner.

"I can go," I said. "I've been sitting around all day

anyway." I knew for sure now that he was avoiding me, so I headed toward the chapel. It was early evening, but the moon was bright. By now, I had a pretty good sense of the lay of the land. I saw a light on in the chapel, and although I wasn't trying to approach it quietly, Raphael seemed so caught up in his own thoughts that he didn't hear me when I came inside.

I watched him for a few minutes. He knelt in the confessional, staining the wood. He had taken off his shirt, and sweat glistened on his tanned skin as he worked. The bruises had mostly healed, only dark spots remaining. I wondered if they were still tender and realized I hadn't touched him in more than a week.

"It's late," I said after clearing my throat to get his attention. "Maria has dinner ready."

Raphael looked up. He checked his watch and capped the can of the wood stain, then stood.

We stared at each other for a few minutes.

"I'm going to have to sell the house," he said. "The land."

"But I thought—"

"I gave the attorney the go-ahead today."

"Oh..." I hadn't even realized he'd been thinking about it this seriously. "Are you okay?"

He scratched his head and went to the front of the church to sit in the pew. I followed and sat by his side, sliding my hand into his.

He bit the inside of his cheek, his eyes on the altar. "My mom loved this place. It was sacred to her."

I watched him.

"I never understood it. She came here a lot, especially the last year. I thought—after finding out my father was beating her—I thought that was why." He scratched his head. "But I don't think it was anymore."

"What happened that day with Moriarty?"

He looked at me, his eyes intense on my face as if he'd draw everything from me.

"I think my father was punishing her for her betrayal."

"Betrayal?"

"His perceived betrayal. She tried to get Moriarty to forgive his debt. Succeeded once."

"I don't understand."

He turned back to the altar, his face resembling stone. "She fucked him. That's how she paid it off."

"What?" Raphael just kept staring straight ahead.

"It makes sense, you know? He had never raised a hand to her before the end. He must have found out."

"Is that what Moriarty told you? Because men like him, they lie, Raphael. They're hateful monsters."

He shook his head. "Damon confirmed it. He'd found a diary of hers."

"Then she had no choice. She couldn't have."

He turned to me again. "I know that. That's not... Don't you get it, Sofia?"

I looked at him, confused, the pain in his eyes making my heart hurt.

"How is what I'm doing to you different?" he asked.

"Raphael." It took me a few minutes to process his words.

He pushed my hand away, stood, and went to the altar, where he set his hand on it, touching the crucifix. Almost caressing it.

"I've made a whore out of you, haven't I?"

He didn't look at me.

"I just keep repeating history, act for act."

That caress suddenly changed, and in one quick, violent tug, he pulled the crucifix from the wall.

"Act for fucking act."

He threw it across the chapel, slamming it into the far wall, where it fell and broke in two, the plaque of inscription, *INRI*, sliding to the far corner.

"Raphael." I stood and took hold of his arm as he gripped the broken tabernacle door and tore it off its hinges. "Stop."

I couldn't stop him. He pulled the other door off, exposing the empty interior where communion would once have been stored.

I pulled harder on his arm. "Look at me."

He wouldn't.

"Look at me, damn it!"

He did, but only when I managed to squeeze myself between him and the altar.

"What that man did to your mother is different. It's not us." I shook him, forcing him to face me. "After all, how can you make a whore out of someone who is willing?"

He studied me, his eyes more defeated than angry. He stepped backward, his shoulders slumping. I shook my head and cupped his face.

"No. You can't do this. The memory of your mother is sacred, Raphael. Don't let that man taint it with his lies."

"They're not lies, though, Sofia. Don't you get it? And you? I've made you my whore."

"Then fuck me."

"Go back to the house, Sofia," he said, shoving me away.

"No. Fuck me. Fuck your whore." I said, growing more and more angry myself.

"I said go."

He took my arm roughly and physically moved me away.

"No. You can't do this! I won't let you!" I yelled, getting back into his space, my hands on either side of his face. I just needed to get him back, to draw him back to this moment, here and now, from what-

ever hell he'd bound himself to. "You think you're
the only one with demons?"

"Go!"

"You think you're the only one who suffers?"

"I said—"

"Fuck what you said. And fuck you! You brought
me here. You married me. And I think you care
about me more than you're willing to admit, but you
won't let yourself have that, will you? You can't do it.
And you don't want me to have it either. Well, fuck
you, Raphael Amado. I'm taking it!"

I pulled his belt apart and undid the top button
of his jeans.

His hands covered mine, but he didn't stop me.

"That's what you want?"

He leaned down, his face an inch from mine.

"You want a good, hard fuck? You miss my cock
inside you?"

He spun me around, bending me forward and
slapping my hands hard on the altar.

"Keep them there. Don't fucking move."

I gasped as he undid my shorts and tore them
and my panties down and off, then shoved my tank
top up and pushed my bra beneath my breast, so
that when he bent me all the way over, the cold
stone of the altar made me shudder.

"Ra—"

But before I could even speak his name, he was
inside me. He leaned over me and thrust in hard.

"You want to be fucked?"

His breath was hot against the side of my face.

"You want my cock in your pussy? You want me to make you come?"

I let out a groan as he thrust.

"Like a whore? Here? Before your God? Here, bent over his holy altar?"

It should have felt wrong. I thought it would. This sacred place, us doing this in this holy place.

But Raphael's hands closed over the backs of mine, and he dragged my arms out to the sides and pinned me to the altar, and nothing had ever felt more right. He needed this. And I needed him close to me. I needed him inside me. It was the only way to reach him, to drag him out of his hell.

"You don't even know the half of it, Sofia."

His voice was hoarse against my ear, and my breath caught when his fingers pinched my clit.

"I don't care," I managed, closing my eyes. Taking him. Letting him take me. Own me. "I don't care. I love you."

He suddenly stilled, his cock buried deep inside me.

I didn't turn around. I didn't need to, because I could imagine his face. I could imagine his shock.

"I love you," I said again, not caring.

Finally, I craned my neck to look back.

"You don't know what I planned to do," he said,

pulling out. He stepped away from me. I turned. He pulled his jeans back up over his erection.

"Raphael?" But he'd gone back into his hell, and there wasn't room for me there.

"Would you still say that if you knew? If you knew the amount of damage I intended to do to you?"

"Stop. Look at me. Just look at me. I'm here. Right here. You don't need to do this."

He stumbled backward. "When I made the deal with your grandfather to let your sister stay, he wanted five percent of what I'd take. I agreed, but maybe he thought it was too easy. That I didn't suffer enough."

He sat down again in the same pew, almost falling into it. I went to him and knelt before him, my hands on his lap, holding his hands. His eyes— even though he was physically here, he was so far away. Too far for me to reach.

"I already know that story," I said quietly, my vision blurred from unshed tears.

"That's when he asked for the sheets to prove we'd consummated. He knew already. He knew you'd become a weakness. My weakness."

Watching him, watching his eyes, I knew there was more. And it wasn't good.

"I didn't do it, though. I burned them. He never saw the sheets."

"You did?"

"I still wonder why he did that. Why he asked for that one thing. And all I could think of was that he didn't believe I'd go through with it. Maybe he hoped you'd say no. Stop me. End this. I don't know." He paused. "But it doesn't matter. I'll say the marriage wasn't consummated. We can have it annulled."

"What?" I asked, stunned.

"What matters is what I decided after that day."

Could he even hear me? I shuddered, suddenly chilled, and hugged my arms around myself.

"My thirst for revenge, my hatred for him, it over-rode all else."

"What did you decide?" I asked, my voice small. I didn't want to know. I didn't.

He finally looked down at me, and with his thumb, he wiped away a tear. I closed my eyes and leaned into his palm, at least for a moment, missing this. Missing how tender he could be, so opposite his violence. His burning rage.

I opened my eyes when he next spoke.

"I wonder if after I tell you, you'll still think you love me."

"Tell me."

He caressed my cheek for a moment more, then drew his hand away. He wouldn't let me hold it again.

"I was going to burn down the Guardia estate. Turn it to ash."

I froze, staring up at him, at this stranger who, day after day, while he made love to me, plotted this destruction? This betrayal? This wouldn't just impact me. It meant my sister's inheritance too. Her birthright. Her future.

"You have no right."

"I considered driving the company into the ground, at least with my half of it. But then he made that deal, and he thought he had me. But I'd rather have destroyed you than allow him to win. His losing was more important to me than you."

I shook my head. "You keep saying was. You're talking like it's past."

"It doesn't matter. Don't you see?"

"Raphael, what you thought then, what you wanted to do then, it doesn't matter. It's all changed. Everything has. What that man did to your mother..." I shook my head. "That's nothing like us. You're not a monster. And I love you."

She thought she loved me.

Moriarty's rage was real. His hatred for me, it was because I was my father's son. He didn't care about the money he felt he was owed. That didn't matter. What he wanted was the decimation of my family. Because that was the only way he could have his revenge. Revenge against my mother for not having chosen him. Revenge against my father for being the one she had loved. The one she had chosen.

He wanted the house, the land, to destroy it.

I knew now he would stop at nothing. My life, it was forfeit. But hers? I couldn't let him destroy her because of me.

I watched Sofia's sweet face, her trusting, innocent, hopeful eyes. She believed she loved me. The thing was, the moment she'd said it, I'd known it too. I'd loved her for a long time now.

And that was exactly why I had to let her go.

I hardened my face and stood.

She remained kneeling at my feet.

"There's just one problem, Sofia. I don't love you." How my voice carried the power it did, I had no idea. And when I saw her face as she processed my words, I had to steel my heart not to reach down and wrap my arms around her, hold her to me, tell her I was lying. That I did love her. Give her that truth I'd promised her she'd always have with me.

Because right now, I was a liar on top of everything else.

"I don't love you," I repeated.

"I don't believe you."

She sat back on her heels, her fingers closing around the clothes still strewn on the chapel floor.

"Well, believe it. I enjoyed taking what I took. I liked playing with you—for a time." I shoved her away with my knee, got up, and walked a few steps to where the pieces of the broken crucifix lay on the floor. Bending, I picked them up, holding the image of Christ in my hand.

"Raphael."

I turned to find her on her feet, buttoning her shorts up.

"You don't mean it. I know you," she said.

I laughed this strange, ugly sound. "You keep

saying that. You really think you can ever know someone? Know what's in their head?"

"I don't care what's in your head. That's the point. I know what's in your stupid heart." Her face was all scrunched up, and her hands fisted at her sides. "You promised me truth, Raphael."

"And I'm giving it to you." I set the cross on the pew I'd abandoned and touched my own ring of thorns. "Tomorrow morning, I'll call the attorney and set things in motion for the annulment." I dragged the ring off my finger, watching blood streak down it as I did so, wanting the pain, needing it. Once it was off, I walked over to the altar and set it on the corner.

"Raphael, please…"

Her eyes were watery as she looked at the bloodied iron band.

"You don't want—"

"I want this done as soon as possible," I said, my voice hard.

She looked at me, flinching, almost startled.

"I want you out as soon as possible. I'll make arrangements." I walked to the door. "Let's go."

"No."

She stayed where she was. She reached out to touch the ring, then pulled her arm back, hugging herself.

I rolled my eyes and sighed as if irritated, even though it broke me a little to do it, to see her like this. To know I was the cause of her pain. Again.

But it was better this way. Better for her. Safer for her.

Maybe when this mess was finished...

No.

No maybes.

No future.

This was finished. It had to be, for her sake.

"Listen, I've got somewhere to be. You go back home. Eat dinner. Go to bed like a good little girl."

"I'm not a little girl."

"Well, you are, actually. And I'm a little tired of the virgin girl act, honestly."

"You don't mean that."

No. I didn't. But she had to think I did.

"It was fun for a while. But it's time for me to move on. To put the past behind me. What was it you said? If I let the past go, maybe it will let me go? I think you were right." I looked around, gesturing big with my hands. "All this is the past. *You're* the past. I'm done with it. I want to live my life, and the only way I can do that is to walk away. Let it go, so it lets me go."

She just stared at me.

"Let's get out of here, Sofia."

"You want this? You want to walk away?"

"Yes." Something in my chest twisted. "And if you really do believe you love me, you'll do as I say and let me go." Fuck. I was a first-class asshole. I didn't deserve to lick the ground she walked on, but I needed to drive the nail into the coffin. "I'm hungry. Let's go."

She shook her head and sat down. "Go."

"You can't find your way back."

"I can find my own way. I don't need you."

I watched the back of her head, saw her draw her knees up on the pew and hug herself.

"Come on."

"Go, Raphael."

"Sofia—"

"Just go! Pull the fucking Band-Aid off, right? Just go."

"Fine. Suit yourself."

I walked out of the chapel and toward the house, hating to leave her there alone, knowing I had to. Because if she hated me, this would be easier.

I don't know how long I sat in the chapel like that, but by the time I got back to the house, a single light was left on over the stove and Raphael's car was gone. Charlie was the only one waiting for me. The moment I opened the door, he nudged his little nose around the corner, and I bent to pick him up and hug him to me.

What had happened in the last three weeks? Had it been in those weeks that Raphael had come to the realization he didn't want this? Didn't want me? Or was this the truth all along? Was I just blind?

I really thought he'd cared about me.

No, more than that.

I thought he loved me.

A sudden chill made me shudder, and I carried Charlie up to my bedroom.

When Raphael had stood like he had, with me

kneeling at his feet, when he'd looked at me, I'd seen something so strange in his eyes. So at odds with what he was saying. At least for one single and very fleeting moment.

Once inside my room, I set Charlie down. He circled my legs twice then looked up at me with his big puppy-dog eyes. I bent to pet him, and he took a finger in his mouth and gently tried to tug me toward the bed.

"You go ahead, sweetie. I can't sleep yet."

He whined, and I swear he knew I was hurting, but when I straightened, he went to the bed and hopped up on his own. He was growing.

I walked into the bathroom and fished Raphael's wedding ring out of my pocket. Studying it, I touched my thumb to the sharp thorns along the inside of the band. I turned on the water and rinsed it, cleaning off the blood before setting it on the edge of the sink. I then slipped mine off my finger and put it down beside his.

Gripping the edge of the sink, I doubled over, feeling like I would vomit, feeling like something deep inside my belly needed to be expelled. Thrown up. But there was nothing. Nothing but tears, thick and heavy. Although I knew no one could hear me, I covered my mouth against my sobs and wept for what seemed like an eternity until finally, I was dried out, nothing left inside me.

He didn't love me.

He didn't want me.

He wanted me to believe this whole thing had been a game to him, but I couldn't. Not when I remembered his face down in the cellar, not when I'd felt his hand on my cheek as he told me he didn't love me. That he was tired of me. What had he said? *Tired of his virgin girl?*

A sudden surge of energy ripped through me and I slapped at the rings, sending them flying to opposite corners. I turned on the water and washed my face before meeting my reflection, my eyes red and puffy.

"All this is the past. You're the past."

My heart ached at the memory of his words. I was angry and humiliated, and I just felt so sad. For him. For me. Because in a way, he was right. And I had been right. He had to let the past go for it to let him go. Maybe he had no choice. But how did I come out as collateral damage? I'd thought it would be different. I'd thought this thing that had started out so ugly had turned into something beautiful. A lasting love.

I gripped the hair on either side of my head and pulled.

I needed to go. To get out of here. I couldn't see him again. I couldn't be in the same house. It was just too painful. I found my phone, and although it was late, I dialed a local taxi service and arranged for someone to pick me up within half an hour. My phone was low on battery, so I plugged it into the charger and began to pack. I'd just take a duffel bag of essentials. My priority right now was getting out of there.

Twenty minutes later, I called Charlie, who raised his head and came when I opened the door. I checked my purse for the key my grandfather had given me. It was right where I'd left it, in the little zipper on the side. As quietly as I could, I went down the stairs. Although Raphael's car was gone, I wasn't sure if Eric was somewhere on site or if he'd come back. But I didn't run into anyone as I made my way blindly through the living room, into the kitchen and out the door, where I walked down the mile-long gravel path toward the front entrance of the property.

When I got there, the taxi was waiting. I opened the back door, and Charlie jumped in ahead of me. After dragging my duffel in behind me, I settled Charlie on my lap and told the driver where I was going. Guardia Winery. Luckily, he knew exactly where it was, because I didn't remember, and within a few minutes, we were out of sight of Raphael's house.

It was Saturday night. No one would be working tomorrow, so I'd have the day to plan what I wanted to do and get things sorted out for myself. I would spend the night in my mother's old bedroom with her ghost for company. We were twenty minutes down the road when I realized I hadn't grabbed my phone off the charger. In my rush, I'd forgotten it.

I sat back in the seat. No way was I going back for it. I wouldn't get lucky not getting caught leaving twice. Although it's wasn't like Raphael wanted me to stay. Hell, he'd probably be pleased I was making this so easy for him. I shook my head, banishing all thoughts of him.

24

RAPHAEL

It was close to midnight by the time I got home. My attorney had worked overtime, getting the paperwork for the sale of the house in order. I'd been ready to sign, but we'd hit a snag. A document the buyer had to provide, and he hadn't. I guessed the holdup was the fact that it was the weekend, and Italians didn't like working weekends. I'd hoped to get everything signed and finished today. The less I had to think about it, the better. And the faster I could do what I'd told Sofia I'd do—let go of the past.

And once I'd signed, I couldn't change my mind.

Selling the house was my last resort. I hated to do it. Damon hated me having to do it. But there was no other way. Moriarty wasn't fucking around. I couldn't take a chance he'd hurt my family over this. It wasn't worth it.

As I walked past her room, I tried hard not to think about her at the chapel. Not to see her face when she'd knelt at my feet, looking up at me when I told her I didn't love her. I just needed to remember I was doing it for her own good.

When I reached my room, I heard her cell phone ring but ignored it. It was probably her sister. It'd only be early evening on the East Coast. I stripped off my clothes once in my room and had a long shower before collapsing into bed.

My old sleeping habits had returned over the last couple of weeks. I was running on three hours a night, and I was exhausted. But part of me didn't want to sleep. It was the only way to keep the nightmares at bay, and the one about Sofia being behind that door—well, I just couldn't handle that anymore.

I don't know if it was the phone ringing in the distance that woke me or something else, but at a quarter to three, I woke hearing it. Maybe it was because the sound was wrong, out of place. A sense of foreboding forced me out of bed. I put on a pair of briefs and went into the hallway. The phone stopped ringing just as I got there, and I almost returned to my own bed, but then it started again.

It came from Sofia's room. And my gut told me something was wrong.

I didn't bother knocking on her door. Instead, I pushed it open and switched on the light.

"Fuck."

She wasn't there, and the bed hadn't been slept in. Charlie wasn't around either, and he was always with her. Her clothes were still in the closet, and her two suitcases were tucked on a shelf. I didn't know what toiletries she had but noticed no toothbrush in the bathroom. On my way back out, I saw the ring on the floor in the corner. Her ring.

I bent to pick it up and slipped it on my little finger, then saw the ring's twin. Mine. It was in the far corner. I left that one where it was. The phone began to ring again. I went into the bedroom to answer it. It sat on her dresser plugged into its charger. I checked the display and saw it was Lina. It'd be nine o'clock her time, but she had to know this was the middle of our night. I swiped the green bar before it went to voice mail.

"Hello? This is Raphael."

"Raphael?"

"Yes. Lina, how are you?"

"Where's my sister?"

"Well, that's a good question. Another good question is do you know what time it is?"

"Yeah. I'm sorry. I just really need to talk to Sofia. I've been trying for the last few hours."

"Is everything okay?"

"I don't know." She sounded anxious. "Where is she? Is she okay? Why are you answering her phone?"

"Because she's not in her room, and the phone

woke me. She's probably just downstairs." I didn't believe she was down there, but I unplugged the phone from the charger and walked through the house, going downstairs to check. Maybe she couldn't sleep. Or she got hungry and went to get a snack. "I'm checking the house now, Lina. Tell me why you're calling so late."

Lina hesitated, and I grew more anxious to find the living room and kitchen in darkness. When I'd arrived home, both the second car and the truck had still been parked outside, so I hadn't thought to look in on her, figuring she didn't want to see me. Taking the easier route myself. Where the hell was she?

I went toward the cellar door.

"Lina?" I asked, opening it, switching on the light when I found it dark. She'd never go down there without turning on the lights, but I walked down anyway, finding it empty. "I can't find your sister, so you'd better tell me what's going on."

"What do you mean, you can't find her?"

"I mean she's not here. Why are you calling so late? Maybe the two things are related."

"She wouldn't go anywhere without her cell phone."

"Okay." I tried to sound calmer than I felt. I didn't want to worry or upset Lina. "Hold on a second. I'm going to check her call log." Pulling the phone away from my ear, I scrolled through her call history and breathed a sigh of relief to know she'd called a taxi around ten o'clock. I guess some part of me thought Moriarty or his men would have come for her. Taken her to get to me.

Hell, maybe they had.

"Lina, she called a taxi around ten o'clock. We had a fight. She's probably fine, but I need to figure out where she is. I'm going to need to hang up to do that."

"Will you call me right back?"

"Yes."

"Thanks."

I'd almost hung up when she called my name.

"Raphael?"

"Yes?"

"Did you sign the papers to sell your property?"

"What?" How in hell did she know about that?

"Just tell me. Did you sign already?"

"No. There was a holdup. A missing document." I heard the relief in her exhale. "Lina, what the hell is going on?"

"Don't sign, okay? Just don't."

"I need more than that, and I really need to go look for Sofia." Silence. "Lina?"

"I think my grandfather is the buyer."

It felt like a trapdoor had opened up underneath me. I stood there holding the phone to my ear, trying to make sense of what she'd just said.

The buyer had a representative, and all the paperwork was being done over wires and faxes—as old-fashioned as the latter sounded. The buyer had been missing one legal document that was necessary for the sale to be acknowledged by Italian law. That holdup was the only reason I hadn't signed over the property today.

I'd tried to find information on the buyer, so had my lawyer, but everything pointed to a company in southern Germany. It hadn't occurred to me once that would be a front. The offer had been above the value of the land. Why in hell would Marcus Guardia want to buy this house? This dead land?

"Are you still there?" Lina asked.

"I need to find your sister. Lina, does your grandfather know you know?"

"No. I overheard something he said, and I snuck into his study when he went out for dinner. I just knew something wasn't right."

"Thank you. I'll deal with that later. Don't tell him that you told me."

"I wasn't going to. Raphael, I found other things too." Her voice quivered.

"All right. I'm going to find Sofia, and we're going to call you together. Sit tight, okay?"

"She's not hurt, is she?"

How did I answer that? "I'm sure she's fine," I lied, not sure of anything at all.

We hung up, and I dialed the taxi service she'd used. They could confirm that a taxi had come to the property at half past ten and delivered a woman and her dog to Guardia Winery.

I thanked them and hung up, quickly texted Lina, and went upstairs to get dressed and go to the winery to pick her up. Her grandfather had given her a key that day at lunch. She must have planned on staying there after our fight today.

The winery was a little over an hour away. I drove fast over deserted, dark roads, having only the moonlight at intervals between the clouds and my headlights to navigate the winding road. I couldn't shake the feeling that something was wrong. That foreboding, it seemed more like a premonition, and images of my recurring dream kept flashing before my eyes.

I hit the accelerator and rolled down the window, feeling nauseous. It was getting so bad, I thought I could smell it even, smell the scent of fire, of flesh burning in fire.

Fuck. I was going crazy. It was a dream. Nothing was wrong. Just a stupid fucking dream.

But as I took the next bend, the clouds cleared, and a plume of smoke rose over the next hill. I recognized that smell. It wasn't the dream. It was ash. It was in the air.

As my brain tried to process what was happening, my hands tightened around the steering wheel and I pushed the gas pedal to the limit. Not more than two miles away, a blaze rose high, the sound of fire, the roar of it still a whisper, a hint.

"No."

I drove like Satan himself was chasing me and fumbled for Sofia's cell phone on the seat beside me, the charger hanging from it like the tail of a mouse. Taking my eyes off the road for a second, I dialed 1-1-2, the smell stronger as I neared Guardia.

This couldn't be happening.

Not again.

It was my fucking nightmare. Not reality.

A voice came through on the line, crackling with bad reception. I turned onto the property, where the gates stood partially open, shoving them wide with the front end of my car. I gave the agent the address. Told her there was a fire. We needed the fire department. We needed help.

I stopped the car halfway to the house.

She asked if anyone was inside. I opened my door and climbed out, ash choking me as I looked over the destroyed land before turning to the house.

I don't think I answered her. Somewhere along the way, I lost Sofia's phone as I ran to the structure, calling out her name, screaming it against the roar of fire. The front door was locked. I tried throwing my shoulder into it, the pain shooting through my side with the impact. It still didn't give. It wouldn't open.

"Sofia!"

All I could hear was the sound of fire. All I could

smell was ash. Fire was burning the back of the house, and I needed to get in there. To get her out.

I backed up, looking up at the windows, seeing one was open at the side closest to the fire. It's where she was. I knew it.

Without thinking, I picked up the nearest stone and hurled it at the window downstairs, smashing it. Not caring that shards of glass tore my clothes and skin, I climbed inside, the distant sound of sirens giving me some hope, even as the scent of gasoline filled my nostrils.

She'd be okay.

I'd find her. I'd be in time.

I wouldn't let her die.

But all I could see were images from the nightmare. Hearing her. Unable to reach her. Opening the door only to find I was too late. Finding charred remains...

"Sofia!"

I tore my shirt off to cover my mouth and nose and ran to the stairs. Thick smoke made it impossible to see.

"Sofia, where are you?"

Nothing. Not from her.

But a bark.

I stood at the top of the stairs and looked down the hall at the last door. The one farthest from me. More barking. It was Charlie.

The hallway seemed to grow longer as I moved,

too slowly even as I charged, battling the nightmare, the demons who kept replaying that reel, over and over and fucking over again.

"Sofia!"

Something crashed behind me, a beam falling, the ceiling opening to the sky. Choking, I went forward, reaching the door. Charlie's barking was continuous now.

"Sofia. I'm here." I touched the door handle. It burned. Wrapping my T-shirt around it, I turned it.

In the nightmare, it was locked. It was always locked, and I had to break the door down. That's what always slowed me down. I could never reach her in the nightmare. Not when it was my mother. Not when it was Sofia. But this time, it turned. I pushed.

The room was filled with smoke, too thick to see through.

"Charlie!"

He barked, and I followed the sound to another door. Another fucking door.

It must have been the bathroom.

This one too opened. My heart pounded.

Charlie sat beside Sofia, who lay unconscious on the floor. He barked and licked her face and wagged his tail briefly and barked at me again, rising to all fours, then sitting again, licking her face again and again.

I dropped to my knees.

Outside, lights flashed, and someone shouted orders.

"Sofia?" I touched her face, slid my hand to her chest to feel her heartbeat. I don't know if it was ash or smoke or what that had my eyes blurry, but I picked her up. Charlie barked at my feet and followed as I covered her mouth and nose with my T-shirt and ran down the hall, fire raging inside the house now. When I got to the stairs, I backed away. Too late. I'd have to find another way. Back to the room where I'd found her, I went to the window and leaned out, breathed in the fresh air. I called out to the men below. Two fire engines and three police cars stood parked below, and in the distance, an ambulance was driving up to the house.

The instant they saw us, they raised a ladder. One of the men climbed up.

Sofia moved in my arms, choking, coughing. I looked down at her and couldn't help smiling just a little.

She was alive. I wasn't too late. She was alive.

"You're here."

A fit of coughing stopped anything more she would have said. When the firefighter reached us, I handed her to him. He hoisted her over his shoulder and descended the stairs. I looked down for Charlie, who'd gone back into the bathroom, backing as far from the approaching fire as possible.

Someone yelled for me to get out, but I ran back

in, grabbed the sheet off the bed, and wrapped him in it, holding him to me. An intense heat had me running back toward the window, and, with Charlie bundled in my arms, I climbed out and down.

They pulled the ladder away from the house and trained their hoses on it, raining water down over it.

I went to Sofia, who was lying on a stretcher in the back of the ambulance with an oxygen mask over her face. Her eyes opened and closed, and she reached a hand toward me. Someone brought a bowl of water for Charlie, and I set him down to drink.

Sofia sat up and pulled the mask off. She looked at the house behind me, then looked to me.

"Raphael?"

That was when everything hit me. All of it. The fire, the timing of it, the destruction of Guardia Winery—because it was destroyed—the loss.

The near loss of *her*.

I stumbled and gripped the door of the ambulance to steady myself.

Was this Moriarty's work? Was this the form his vengeance took?

Was this what I myself had planned to do? Had thought I could do?

"Raphael?"

I turned to see tears streaming down Sofia's face.

I DROVE myself to the hospital two hours later, when the fire was finally under control and no longer threatened the adjoining properties. They'd given Sofia a sedative after checking her out, so she was asleep when I got to her room. She'd be fine. I was in time.

Stepping out of her room, I first called Lina to tell her Sofia would be okay. She already knew about the fire. Of course she would. The manager would have called her grandfather as soon as he heard. After reassuring Lina that Sofia would call her as soon as she was awake, I dialed another number, a man I knew who had ties to the police department, who'd done some investigating for me in the past. I wanted to know if the police ruled it arson. I'd smelled gasoline in the house. That meant someone had intentionally set the fire. I also told him what Lina had told me and asked him to confirm. That Marcus Guardia was the one who'd been this close to buying Villa Bellini. After that, I went into the hospital room to wait for her to wake up.

I sat on the chair beside her bed for the next few hours, watching her sleep, still smelling the fire on her, on myself. I'd almost been too late. If Lina hadn't called, if I hadn't heard Sofia's cell phone and woken up, Sofia would have died up in that bedroom. That thought kept me from sleeping until almost dawn. It had me looking at her, watching the monitors measuring her steady heartbeat, making sure she was really okay.

The feel of her hand on mine was what finally woke me later that morning.

"Hey," she said.

I straightened myself up, rubbed my face, and checked my watch.

"Hey." My voice came out hoarse and groggy, much like hers.

"Thank you."

Why did I think it was a strange thing to say? And what should I say back? Turned out I didn't need to reply. She spoke before I could.

"Charlie?"

"He's fine. Damon picked him up and took him home."

She smiled, then her face grew serious again.

"Is it gone?"

"Yeah." I hated to be the one to tell her. "Everything is pretty much destroyed."

She nodded. "How did you know I was there?" she finally asked.

"You'd forgotten your phone, and your sister kept trying to call you. It woke me up, and when I realized you were gone, I scrolled through your phone and found you'd called a taxi. It didn't take me long to get the address they took you to."

"My sister!"

She tried to sit up but then lay back down again.

"I have to call her."

"I already did. Relax. You can call her later."

"Thank you. Again."

She tried to sit up again, and this time I helped her, adjusting the bed and pillows at her back.

"You shouldn't have left."

"I couldn't stay."

Awkward silence.

"I guess it was all for nothing, huh?" she asked.

"What do you mean?"

"You didn't have to marry me after all. My inheritance is up in smoke."

I studied her pretty caramel eyes, watched them fill up with tears, watched her hold them back.

"Oh, wait," she continued. "Insurance. I guess you'll be paid off with insurance money."

There were a hundred things I could have said. I should have said. Things like "I'm sorry." Or "I didn't mean what I said." Or "I love you." But I didn't say any of those things. Instead, when my cell phone rang, I looked at the display and left the room to answer it.

It was the investigator. "You were right," he said. "Gasoline canisters were found throughout the property. The person who set this fire wasn't hiding the fact that this was arson."

"Which rules out Marcus Guardia." I wouldn't put it past him to destroy the winery, so I wouldn't get my hands on it. So he could cash-out. But he would be careful to hide the evidence.

"And what the girl told you is right. Marcus Guardia is using the German company as a cover. He's the one who put the bid in on your house."

I'd told Moriarty the other day that I had a buyer. That he wouldn't get the property because I'd already sold it. Could Moriarty have known all along that it was Sofia's grandfather? Could this fire have been set to punish the old man?

"Thanks. Keep me updated, will you?"

"I will."

When I opened the door to Sofia's room, I found her sitting on the bed with her phone at her ear, her forehead wrinkled as she listened.

"Lina, are you sure?"

The concern I heard in her voice made me curious. She met my eyes then shifted her gaze away.

"Okay. Okay, I have to go. Let me think about this. I'll call you back."

She hung up and looked at me a bit awkwardly. I wanted to ask what she'd been talking about with her sister. It had obviously upset her. But I didn't feel that I could. A few minutes later, her doctor walked into the room to tell us she'd need to take it easy but that she would fully recover.

"When can I leave?" she asked.

"Later today," the doctor said. "I'll sign off on your paperwork."

"Can I fly?"

The doctor seemed confused, so I stepped in. "You'll stay at the house while you recover, Sofia."

"But—"

"But nothing." I walked out with the doctor to discuss a few things. When I returned, Sofia sat on the bed, her face unreadable.

"I need to ask you something," she said.

"Ask."

"Was it an accident?"

I studied her. Truth. I'd promised her truth. I'd already broken that promise once. I wouldn't do it again.

"No."

She swallowed, blinking several times, and looked away for a moment before returning her gaze to me. Her voice had an edge to it when she next spoke.

"Did you have anything to do with this?"

I snorted, shook my head, and quashed the emotion bubbling in my gut. The hurt at her accusation. "I never wanted you dead, Sofia."

Arson.

Somebody had deliberately set the fire that destroyed Guardia Winery.

Two weeks had passed, and the information Raphael had received from his source was confirmed by the official investigator. My grandfather had arrived the day following the incident. He hadn't brought Lina with him. I hadn't seen him yet, although I would later today. I wasn't sure how I'd be able to look at him, knowing what Lina had told me. What she'd found. Evidence of what Raphael had told me about Grandfather's transfers of money. More than that, more information that would leave the business vulnerable if it ever got out.

I didn't tell Raphael what Lina told me. He took good care of me while I recovered, spending time with me during the day, having dinners in my room sitting beside me on the bed. When he touched me, it was tenderly, but nothing more than that. Not once did we talk about what had happened at the chapel. It felt like the elephant in the room, but neither of us brought it up. As much as I longed for him to tell me what he'd said in the chapel wasn't true, I didn't want to lose the moments I had with him.

Raphael had told me what Lina had told him about my grandfather, that he was the one who'd put a bid on Villa Bellini. That Raphael had almost signed everything over to him.

I didn't understand. Was this the land Grandfather had said he was buying for me? To keep in my name for when I lost everything? Was he going to steal Raphael's home right out from under him just as Raphael had stolen half of Guardia Winery from us?

An eye for an eye, a tooth for a tooth. It all gave me a headache.

Today, Raphael was going to take me to the winery to see the damage for myself. Then, we had a meeting with Grandfather and his attorneys about the state of things.

At the winery, we drove as far as we were allowed to go, which wasn't very far, since the investigation wasn't yet closed. I climbed out of the car with Raphael at my side.

"Oh, my God."

The damage, it was unbelievable. The lands—all

that remained of the bursting, healthy vines were their charred remains. A burned smell still hung in the air, and the house itself was rubble. One wall remained partially standing, and yellow tape cordoned off the area. It was still considered dangerous.

"I remember the smell of our house afterward," Raphael said.

"I can't believe this. What a loss. What an incredible loss."

I shuddered, and I thought for a moment that Raphael raised his arm and hoped he meant to wrap it around me, but then he stuck his hands awkwardly into his pockets.

"Who would do this?" I asked.

"Only one name comes to mind, Sofia."

"Moriarty."

He nodded.

"But why? What sense would that make? Wouldn't he then be better off to set the Amado property on fire?"

"You said your grandfather and Moriarty had some interest in the same property. I wonder if that was my property and Moriarty threatened your grandfather if he didn't pull his bid."

"He said that day we had lunch that Moriarty had told him the property he wanted wasn't in his best interest to buy."

Raphael looked out over the land but didn't answer.

I remembered something then. "Wait a minute." He turned to me. "The manager told my grandfather they'd installed a new security system. Is it possible there would be some video recording of that night? Maybe we could see who did this?"

"The house is destroyed. I can't imagine anything would have survived the fire. If it had, I'm sure the police would have the evidence by now. I'm sorry, Sofia. No matter what, I never wanted this for you."

We returned to the car and drove to Siena to meet with two attorneys and my grandfather. The offices were in the center of the touristic city in a building that dated back hundreds of years. We were quickly ushered in. Once inside, I found my grandfather, still proud but looking a little more tired, sitting at the head of a long table. Two men sat on either side of the table, going over paperwork.

They all looked up when we entered. The look my grandfather gave Raphael chilled me.

"Sofia," he said, standing. "Raphael."

He barely nodded in Raphael's direction. He introduced the two attorneys, one of whom was American, the other Italian. They both turned their business cards on the table.

Once we sat down, one of the attorneys started talking, going over our options now that the crop was a total loss, as well as the details of the insurance policy.

"But since arson is the cause, everything is...tied up," my grandfather said.

"Any suspects?" Raphael asked.

"No. Do you know any?" Grandfather countered.

"Grandfather," I said. Now wasn't the time.

He closed his mouth and let the attorney continue. Basically, we spent an hour going over the fact that we had nothing, not until the insurance company paid out. Even the house in Philadelphia was in question.

I guess I hadn't realized the extent of this loss. It had never occurred to me we'd go from having everything to having nothing. I wondered if that had been what had aged my grandfather, because he did look older, his suit a little wrinkled, his hair not quite perfect.

"Gentlemen, would you step outside for a moment, please?" my grandfather said to the attorneys.

What?

Both men nodded, clearly knowing this was coming. They shuffled out of the room. Raphael cleared his throat, his gaze never leaving my grandfather, the suspicion in them evident.

Once the door had closed, Grandfather picked up his briefcase, which he had had alongside him on the floor, and set it on the table. He opened it and took out a large envelope, set the case aside, then looked at us.

"Raphael, you understand forty-five percent of nothing is nothing."

"The property was insured."

"Yes, however, with the arson investigation, nothing is clear."

"Are you saying they can decide not to pay?" I asked.

"Well, it's a large amount of money, so they're using whatever they can to hold off on paying."

"Because it was intentional," I said, understanding. "They think it was done by someone who would stand to gain by a large insurance payout."

"Guardia Winery has been a profitable company for a very long time. In recent years, sales have been down, but that was turning around."

"What do you mean? Was the winery in trouble?" I asked.

"No, not in trouble, but revenues have been steadily declining over the last few years. That's why I hired the new manager. He has modern ideas."

"But—"

He held up a hand. "And with those modern ideas came the new security system he'd insisted we install." Grandfather opened the folder and drew out a stack of papers along with a smaller envelope.

"What is this?" Raphael asked.

"I have a new contract, Raphael."

"What?" I asked, glancing at Raphael, then back at my grandfather.

"Once the insurance pays out, there is no need to wait until Sofia is twenty-one to collect the funds. As manager of the trust, it will be up to me to pay it out to her, or in this case, to you, sooner."

"But you said the payout is tied up with the investigation," I said, realizing where this was going.

"It won't be forever," Grandfather said, sliding the paperwork toward Raphael. "A payout. A healthy one."

I glanced at the paperwork, blinked twice at the number written there.

"It's potentially more than the shares would have been worth, considering the winery's decline," Grandfather said.

Raphael skimmed the first page, then the second and third before setting it aside and waiting for my grandfather to continue.

"Annul the marriage, and the money is yours as soon as the insurance situation is sorted out."

"What?" I asked, my heart dropping into my belly. I reached a shaking hand under the table to touch Raphael's, which was remarkably, unsettlingly, steady. He didn't pull away but took my hand in his.

"You want to buy her back?" Raphael asked, not once looking at me.

"Don't be crass."

"Crass? Being crass is at about the very bottom of

my list of things I give a shit about right now, old man. What's in the envelope?"

He pointed to the one my grandfather still held.

"A memory card."

"And what's on that memory card?"

"Evidence that it was Moriarty's men who set the fire."

"How?" I asked.

"The front gates had cameras installed. His men didn't realize it. I don't think Moriarty knew, since the security system was so new. Footage from the house would have been destroyed, but I have them coming and going at the time the fire started."

"Why haven't you given it to the police?" I asked.

Raphael sat back in his seat, studying my grandfather.

"Moriarty is very well connected in Italy," Grandfather said.

"But he's not above the law."

"I'm afraid he just might be."

"But you have proof!"

"And I'm going to use it to buy your freedom, Sofia." He turned to Raphael. "Sign the contract, and you'll have the memory card. The man doesn't scare easily, but I have a feeling you'll be able to convince him to wipe out your father's debt and save your property."

I turned to Raphael. This was what he needed. This would free him. This would give him exactly what he said he wanted at the church. To have this, to have the guarantee that Moriarty couldn't hurt him or his family anymore.

Raphael shifted his gaze from my grandfather to me, but his eyes revealed nothing. My hand rested in his. His thumb drew circles in my palm.

The longer he took, the heavier the silence grew, the more tears welled in my eyes.

This was it.

Raphael and I were finished.

My grandfather cleared his throat and rose from his seat. "Five minutes, or the offer expires, and you can take your chances on the payout." He buttoned his jacket. "I'll be outside."

We didn't watch him go, and we didn't speak for an eternity after the door closed.

Raphael stood and went to one of the two windows. "I thought you were dead," he said, his back to me.

"What?" I started, swallowing the lump in my throat.

He faced me but remained where he was. "I have this nightmare—I've had it for six years now—where I keep seeing the fire at the house, keep running inside to save my mother, and keep finding her too late."

A weight heavy as a pile of bricks settled in the room with us.

"Well, it changed over the last few weeks."

He ran both hands through his hair, then tucked them into his pockets and gave me a strange sort of smile.

"It wasn't my mother I kept finding anymore."

He paced to the other window, then seemed to force himself to look at me.

"It became you, Sofia. It was your body I'd find minutes too late."

Warm tears spilled from my eyes, and I opened my mouth to speak, but nothing came, not for what seemed like a very long time. And when it did come, I sounded strange, not like myself.

"Raphael, it's a dream. A nightmare. It's not real."

"The fire was real. You almost died."

It felt like I was hearing his words one at a time, slow to process their meaning. Not wanting to.

"I meant what I said at the church. That I'd let you go. I thought that was the right thing to do." He stopped, took a deep breath in. "I still do."

I opened my mouth to speak, but he held up his hand to stop me.

"But you need to know something first. I lied to you, Sofia. I promised you truth, and I lied to you."

"Raphael—"

"At the church. What you said—when you told me you loved me—it caught me off guard. I didn't realize..."

He drew something out of his pocket. It was my ring, the one I'd left in the bathroom.

"This is ridiculous, isn't it? Fucking ring of thorns."

I had no words.

"But they fit. Being married to me, Sofia, you will always have the thorns, only there is no rose."

I stood, but my knees buckled, and I fell back into my chair, choking on a sob that came from somewhere deep inside me.

I knew what he was doing. And I was right. This was good-bye. He would sign that contract, but he wouldn't be selling back my freedom. He'd be buying it from my grandfather.

And this time, it was so much harder than at the church. This time, it would destroy me. Because telling me he didn't love me, as much as that had hurt, this was worse.

He slipped the ring on his thumb and came to me.

"I love you, Sofia, and almost losing you—" He shook his head, rubbed the scruffy two-days growth on his chin. "I'm fucked up and angry, and I can't keep you."

"No."

He knelt before me and took my face in his hands, wiping away tears with his thumbs.

"No matter how much I want to, I can't keep you. Your grandfather, he's got one thing wrong about Moriarty. He won't stop. He won't care about this piece of evidence. His hate for me, it puts you in too much danger. The other night was evidence of that. No matter what, we would always be looking over our shoulders."

"No. Not with the evidence."

"Even if it weren't for him, Sofia, I should never have brought you here. I should never have started this. Punishing you to punish your grandfather? Look what came of that."

"Don't I get a say in this?"

He rose to stand, bringing me with him, and with my face in his hands, he kissed me. It was a rough kiss. A final one.

"I love you, Sofia."

His gaze bore into mine as if he would memorize every detail of my face.

"I love you too much to do this to you."

Before I could even respond, before I'd even processed his words, he pushed me aside and picked up the pen lying on the table and signed his name to the contract. I watched, stupefied, as he scrawled his signature on the sheet, then set the pen down and placed my ring beside it.

With one more look at me, he reached for the envelope containing the memory card, tucked it into his pocket, turned, and walked out the door.

After Raphael left the office, I stood in the room, staring after him. Staring at the space where he'd just been before falling back into my chair, my legs unable to support me.

I wasn't sure what would be easier, thinking he didn't love me or knowing the truth. Although I guess I knew there was no easy. This would hurt. It would hurt for a very long time.

My grandfather and the attorneys walked back into the room. No one seemed to take notice of me. Grandfather set the ring and pen aside and checked the signature on the contract.

"It's done," he said, handing it to one of the men who slipped it into his briefcase then clicked it closed. No one sat back down. "Gentlemen, thank you. I'll be in touch."

They were shaking hands, almost at the door,

when I spoke. "Why did you want the marriage consummated?"

They all stopped. Someone cleared their throat. My grandfather turned to me, a coldness in his eyes that chilled me, then shifted his attention back to them.

"Forward official copies electronically and in hard copy."

The men left. Grandfather closed the door behind them and faced me but remained where he was.

"What an inappropriate question to ask in front of our attorneys."

"What an inappropriate request to make."

He walked over to me. "I did this for you."

"You also did this *to* me."

"I told you, I was making amends."

"Tell me why you wanted it consummated?"

He studied me. "Because I didn't think he'd go through with it. Because I thought when faced with an *unwilling virgin bride*—"

I flinched at the words.

"His morality would stop him. End this. Hell, maybe I thought you'd cry rape."

My mouth fell open. He was willing to go that far? No. God, no.

He stepped closer and cocked his head to one side, any weakness I'd thought I'd seen when we'd first come into the room vanished.

"But you weren't unwilling, were you, Sofia? You whored yourself out to that man. Just like your mother did to your father."

I breathed in tight breaths and, collecting every ounce of courage, I rose to stand. "Don't you dare call her or me a whore, old man."

He did something then that he'd never done before that moment. For all his coldness, for all his distance, he'd never raised a finger to us. Not until today.

The sound of him slapping my face reverberated off the walls, snapped my head to the side, and sent me stumbling backward.

I touched my cheek. It throbbed, growing hotter under my hand.

"Don't you ever speak to me like that again, understand?"

The door opened just then, and one of the attorneys returned.

"Sorry, I forgot—" He stopped short. "Excuse me."

He made to walk back out, but before he could, I spoke.

"You're a vile old man," I said to my grandfather. "You're a selfish, greedy old man. You never forgave my mother for falling in love with a man you didn't approve of when you never should have had any say at all. You used me like a pawn. You treated me no differently than your enemy. You've been stealing from my sister and me all our lives. It's about time this ends."

I turned to the attorney.

"I want guardianship of my sister. Draw up whatever paperwork I need—"

"And you'll support her how? With what money?" my grandfather asked. "The state will never allow it."

"If you stand against me, I'll go to the authorities with what I know. You'll be investigated. You'll be arrested. You will be imprisoned."

For the first time in all the time I'd known him, my grandfather didn't speak. He stood there, color draining from his face just a little.

"Walk away, and you can keep what you've stolen," I added.

"You don't know what you're talking about," he started, opening his mouth to continue before I stopped him.

"Are you willing to take that chance?" I asked.

My grandfather's cell phone rang just then. I imagined the relief he must have felt, the gratitude for the distraction. He stepped away, taking it out of his pocket. When he did, I scooped up the ring Raphael had left on the table, dropped it into my purse, and walked out.

I didn't know where I was going. Didn't know if my credit card even worked anymore, didn't have any clothes. Luckily, I had my passport. And I needed to get out of there. Get out of that stifling room, that building, before the walls crushed me. I walked out the front doors into the heat and noise of the busy city and lost myself in the crowd, somehow managing not to fall down, not to break into tears as I walked farther and farther away, not knowing where I would go, needing to disappear.

I t had taken all I had to turn my back on Sofia and walk out of that office. I knocked someone's shoulder on my way out but didn't look back, didn't apologize, couldn't stop. I went out the door and into the hallway and flew down the stairs and out the front doors where I stopped, gasping for breath, my hands on my knees, wanting to vomit.

Lying to Sofia on the chapel floor, that had wounded me. But this? Today? Leaving her like that, signing that damned contract and walking out on her, it finished me. I'd promised her truth, and I'd kept my promise, finally. And it destroyed me.

I straightened, wiping sweat off my forehead.

I didn't remember walking through the city to the parking garage. Didn't remember driving home. As soon as I stepped out of the car, though, Charlie came running to me. I stopped and looked down at him. Watched him wait for the passenger side door to open, for Sofia to step out. He barked several times, ran back to me, tail wagging, then returned to sit by her car door to wait.

"She's not there," I told him.

Charlie turned to me, tilting his head to one side as if he didn't understand, then faced the car door again, barked once more, waiting.

"She's not coming back."

I went into the house and to my study. On the way, I told Nicola to pack Sofia's suitcases. I'd send them to her later.

After reviewing the security footage on the memory card, I made several copies, put one in a safety-deposit box, sent one to the seminary for Damon, and took one personally to deliver to Moriarty. This time, though, we'd meet in a public place. I chose the restaurant and made sure I arrived early.

Choosing a booth in the back, I ordered my dinner and waited.

When he finally arrived, I didn't rise to greet him but wiped my mouth and gestured for him to take a seat.

"All healed up, Raphael?"

Although he strove for a casual vibe, his eyes darted around the room. This wasn't one of his regular restaurants, and Moriarty, for all the friends he had in high places, also had enemies.

"All healed up. Thanks for asking."

A waitress came by, and he ordered a glass of water.

"That's not much fun, is it? Water? Order something else. My treat." I turned to the waitress. "A double whiskey." The waitress nodded and left. "You're going to need it."

"My men are right outside. If you need another beating to learn respect—"

"Beatings never worked for me, Moriarty. Didn't my father ever mention how hard he tried? You know where he ended up."

His face didn't change, and when the waitress delivered his drink, he sipped it.

"What's this about?"

"Fire at the Guardia property," I said.

"Shame about that."

"Huge loss." I stared at him. "When did you find out the old man was my buyer?"

"I don't know what you're talking about," he said, taking another sip.

"I guess it doesn't really matter anyway." I ate the last potato on my plate and washed it down with some wine. "Did you know about the new security system they had installed? Top-notch new manager, apparently."

Moriarty shifted in his seat.

"Turns out there were a couple of cameras at the front gates of the property." I ate another bite of my steak, set my knife and fork across my plate and, after wiping my mouth, threw my napkin down on top of it.

"Get to the point, Raphael."

"Happy to," I said, raising my hand for the check. I reached into my pocket to take out the envelope containing photographs of the images from the security footage. "Interesting how sophisticated these things are these days. Amazing, actually."

Moriarty glanced around the restaurant but didn't touch the envelope. The waitress reappeared with my check, and I handed her some bills.

"What is this?" he asked.

"A car coming and leaving the night of the fire. Lights out. A driver and two passengers. Your business logo on the side window—I always did think it was a pretentious one—sticking out like a sore fucking thumb. License plates that confirm the vehicle belongs to you."

He grabbed the envelope, peeked inside, and quickly tucked it into his pocket.

"Where did you get these?"

"Marcus Guardia doesn't play nice, Moriarty. He will cut off his own nose to spite his face." I replaced my smile with something much more sinister. "This is what's going to happen. You're going to stay far, far away from me, from my family, from Sofia and Lina Guardia. You'll stay away from anything having to do with me, my family, Sofia, or Lina. Hell, from anything that you might even *think* may be remotely associated with me, my family, or the Guardia sisters. If you don't, a copy of that memory card as well as the photos you have in your pocket will be delivered to every news outlet throughout Italy, along with every single prosecutor, every judge... Do I need to go on?"

He didn't reply.

I rose to my feet. "Any debt you think I owe you is wiped out. Stay the fuck away from me, or the next time, I will fucking choke the life out of you, you disgusting pig."

He didn't have a chance to speak. When one of his men stepped in my path, I knocked him with my shoulder and kept going. He didn't follow. I walked out of the restaurant and to my car and drove home, finished with Moriarty and his debts, one more step closer to walking away from my past. Only problem was, I knew I'd never give it a chance to let go of me because I knew I couldn't let it go. Not when it meant letting go of Sofia.

28

SOFIA

I left by train from Siena to Venice that evening. Once I checked into a small hotel, I called the attorney who'd overheard my conversation with my grandfather and left him my address, telling him to forward any paperwork to me here. I called Lina and told her I was in Venice, told her what had happened and what I'd done, and told her I needed to be off-line for a few days.

I missed Charlie. I missed cuddling up with him on my lap, missed his unconditional love.

The first twelve days I spent in bed, feeling sorry for myself.

On the thirteenth day, someone knocked on the door. When I told whoever it was to go away, they answered that I had received a package.

Reluctantly, I went to the door, cringing when I caught a glimpse of myself in the mirror. I opened it and took the large white envelope, assuming it was paperwork about Lina's guardianship. I pushed the shutters and window open to let in some fresh air and sunshine. The room smelled stale, and it seemed my sadness had permeated even the walls.

Once seated at the desk, I opened the envelope and withdrew the papers.

And stared.

I checked the return address. It was my attorney, so I'd assumed they were the papers to take over guardianship of Lina. But when I opened them, there was a second envelope inside. This one was from Raphael or his attorney. He must have sent it to my attorney who forwarded it here. This was the document discussing the annulment of our marriage.

"Unbelievable." I flipped through the pages, shaking my head. "Didn't waste any time, did you?"

After everything that had happened, he'd just drawn up the papers and would put things into motion. All that was needed was my signature, and he'd get a nice big payout from my grandfather.

I questioned now what had happened in that office that day. Maybe he hadn't been lying at all in the chapel. Maybe he'd lied after hearing about the payout, knowing he could be rid of me and still get paid in a matter of weeks rather than years. And save his own house and get Moriarty off his back on top of it. Maybe he didn't want me at all. It's not like he was fighting for me.

I shoved the chair back and found a pen in one of the drawers.

Instead of signing the document, I drew an X through the center of it and wrote the words *Fuck You* at the very top in big, bold letters.

Unless I signed, he'd get nothing.

And why should this be easy for him, when it was anything but for me?

I called the front desk and scrawled *Return to Sender* on the envelope, handing it back to the man who'd just delivered it and telling him to send it back. I then went into the bathroom to have a shower and give myself a kick in the ass.

Why in hell was I wallowing in my pain, when he was out drawing up paperwork to be rid of me? To collect money to do just that?

Apart from my father, I'd known two other men. And they'd both betrayed me. They'd used me and then discarded me like I was a piece of trash.

Well, fuck them. I'd had enough.

I left the hotel later that morning and stepped onto a gondola that took me across the canal and spent the day exploring the beautiful old city. I'd always wanted to come here, to see it. I just never thought it'd be alone. But I forced a smile on my face and walked along with other tourists through markets and narrow streets, eating lunch in a tiny café where I ordered by pointing to a dish another diner was eating. I returned to my hotel when it was dark out with a bottle of wine I'd bought, feeling exhausted, the depression I'd been shoving to the side creeping back in as I opened my bedroom door and walked inside. I opened the window, pulled my chair up to it, and watched the water and the people below. I drank the entire bottle of wine and didn't not even bother undressing before I collapsed on top of the sheets, oblivion seeming like a fine idea right then.

***

AT FIRST I thought the pounding was my head.

I'd been drunk once before, at Raphael's house that first night.

That hangover was nothing compared to what was happening now. The sound wouldn't stop, the throbbing wouldn't go away.

"Sofia! Open the door!"

I rolled over onto my side, realizing I still had on my clothes and even one shoe.

"I know you're in there. Don't make me break it down."

I glanced over at the door. The pounding started again, and I heard another door open and someone yell out that it was the middle of the night. I checked the time. It was almost two o'clock in the morning.

"Goddamn it." He started banging again.

Raphael?

I sat up, clutching my head. Was I still drunk, or was this a hangover? Getting up, I unlocked the door and pulled it open to find Raphael standing outside, looking like he was about to ram his shoulder into it.

"Why are you pounding?" I asked, stepping back when he shoved his way in before closing it.

"Because you sleep like the dead. I tried knocking like a normal person, believe me."

He looked at me, furrowed his eyebrows, sniffed, then zeroed in on the empty bottle of wine lying on its side near the window. My gaze followed his, surprised. Had I drunk the whole thing?

"You're drunk," he said.

"No." I shook my head, but it hurt so I stopped. "I *was* drunk. Now I'm hungover."

He grinned, shaking his head.

"No, sweetheart, you're still drunk."

Sweetheart.

Ha.

"How did you find me?" No one knew where I was, not even Lina. Only my lawyer, so I could sign whatever I needed to sign and get Lina away from my grandfather.

"It wasn't easy."

"What do you want?" I asked, blinking hard, forcing my eyes to stay open.

He moved around the room and went over to the

phone, picked it up, and ordered coffee and some bottles of water. The water sounded good.

"Come on, you're having a shower."

He took my arm and started to move me toward the bathroom.

"No, I'm not. I'm going back to bed as soon as I drink that water you ordered. Go away."

"I don't think so."

He lifted me in his arms when I wouldn't go willingly and deposited me in the bathroom.

"Strip."

"Fuck you."

"You already said that on the annulment papers, remember?" A knock came at the door. "Strip, and get in the shower while I get that."

"No."

But he walked away to answer the door, leaving me alone to do as he said. Well, like I said, he could go fuck himself.

I sat down on the edge of the tub and ran a bath instead.

I heard him thank the room-service man. A few minutes later, the bathroom door opened again, and he stepped inside with a bottle of water. I still hadn't undressed, but he seemed pleased I was running the water.

"Here."

He handed me the bottle. I took it and drank almost all of it down while he went back into the other room. He returned with a cup of coffee.

"You shouldn't drink an entire bottle of wine."

"Like you care." I took the coffee from him and drank a long sip. It was good. I felt a little more human.

"I do care. I told you that already. What the hell was with that *Return to Sender* with the big ole *fuck you*, Sofia?"

"You didn't like it?"

"No. You're being immature."

"Well, I am a little girl, right? Isn't that what you said?" I drained the coffee and handed him the empty cup. "Excuse me while I have a bath."

"I'll stay right here." He set the cup on the counter.

"What do you want, Raphael? You want my signature? After everything, you just want to erase this whole thing like it never happened? Well, you can't just do that. It doesn't work that way." I swore at the tears that threatened and shifted my attention to switching off the water.

"You almost got killed because of me."

"No, not because of you. Because of my grandfather."

"I'm giving you back your freedom."

"You're getting paid."

"It's not about the money."

"You sure were quick to sign. *"Five minutes or the offer expires."* You were tripping over yourself to sign."

"Did you hear a word I said to you in that office?"

"The lies, you mean? You told me once not to make a saint out of you. Well, I heard *that*, loud and clear. You're not a saint. Got it. Remembered it. It was just a hell of a lot easier to walk away and tell me you were doing it for me. Admit it, Raphael. Admit it was easier. Then get the hell out of my life."

I felt stronger, like the effects of the wine were wearing off. Maybe it was the water or the coffee, but I had a feeling it was the anger inside me burning away the alcohol more than anything else.

But then he said what he said.

"If you wanted me out of your life, you would have signed the annulment papers."

And I knew it was true. He was right. If I wanted him out, I would have signed and put all this behind me.

"I've changed my mind, anyway. You're not going anywhere, Sofia."

"Not until you have my signature, you mean? Did you bring a clean copy of the paperwork?"

"You're being stupid."

"No, I think the word is naive. You used that once too, didn't you? You had my number all along. I was the fool to fall for it, for your tortured soul act. Get out. I mean it."

"No."

"Get the fuck out."

He cocked his head to the side. "Fine. You want me out? Make me go."

I narrowed my eyes and went toward him. With both my hands on his hard chest, I shoved him backward.

Except he didn't move.

"You're going to have to do better than that."

"Fuck you."

"Is that an offer?"

I shoved again. Again, nothing.

"Get out. I mean it," I said, hands fisted at my sides.

"Like I said, make me."

He gave me a cocky grin. The one I remembered from when I first met him. The one that said he didn't believe I dared.

Well, I fucking dared.

With tears in my eyes, I drew my arm back and slapped him hard across the face. He barely moved. His eyes blinked and his head turned just a little, but his wall of a chest still stood right where it was, not moving, not allowing me to move.

For a moment, I froze. This wasn't the first time I'd slapped him. And I remembered well what had happened the last time.

But Raphael only stood there, waiting for me. Waiting for more?

I could give him more.

"I'd never been slapped before," I said, drawing my arm back again, remembering my grandfather slapping me, readying to strike him again. "It's a really personal thing, isn't it?" I said, swinging. "Humiliating."

He caught my wrist, and when I swung the other one, he caught that one too and shoved my back against the wall, pressing his body into mine, stretching my arms over my head.

"Yeah, it's personal."

He smashed his lips over mine then quickly came up for air.

"It's very fucking personal."

I grunted, trying to free myself, refusing to open my mouth, turning my head. "Fuck you."

He transferred both wrists to one hand and gripped my jaw with the other, forcing me to look at him.

"I told you already, I love you," he said.

"That's why it was so hard to give me up."

He shook his head then kissed me again, grinding against me.

"You stupid, stupid girl."

"Let me go! I mean it, or I'll scream."

"Go ahead and try."

He lifted me off the floor and carried me into the bedroom, where he threw me on the bed.

"I'll do it."

"I said go ahead and try."

He drew his shirt over his head and came at me, one knee on the bed, capturing me as I scurried to the other side. Once he had me, he dragged me toward him. I did as I said I would and opened my mouth to scream, but he closed his hand over it, looming over me with that know-it-all grin, and ripped my dress in two.

"Next time I tell you to strip, you'll learn to strip."

I fought him, but he only laughed at my attempts and tore my bra, exposing my breasts, then dragged my panties down and off.

"I missed seeing you naked," he said, his gaze scanning me. "Missed touching you."

He straddled me with his thighs, keeping his weight off me but trapping me. He leaned down close.

"Do I need to gag you?"

I opened my mouth to scream, but he muffled the sound when his lips found mine.

"I guess that's a yes," he muttered

He mashed his mouth over mine again and held my arms at my sides, pinning me to the bed. After a good, long kiss, he leaned back.

"Now be fucking quiet and listen."

I tried to move, tried to break free, but it was impossible. I stopped fighting and looked at him.

"Did you even bother reading the papers I sent you before scrawling your message to me?"

I hadn't. I hadn't thought there was any need to.

"Did you?"

I shook my head.

"If you had, you would have seen that I opened a bank account in your name. That the money the old man owed me would be transferred right back to you. I don't want the money, Sofia. This has never been about the money. But fuck me. It was never meant to be about love either."

She finally quieted.

Fuck. I hadn't come here to fuck her. I hadn't.

"You still want me to let you go?"

She shook her head.

I released her wrists and flipped her over onto her belly, then straddled her again, trapping her beneath me.

"I love you," I said, reaching over to grab the bottle of hand moisturizer she had on the nightstand. "But you're a pain in my ass." I drew her hips up, so she was on her knees. "Don't get up," I told her when she started to rise. I pushed her knees apart with mine and fisted a handful of her hair, pushing her face down into the bed. "Ass up, face down. Understand?"

"Raphael—"

I slapped her hip—not hard, but enough to get her attention. She cried out and looked back at me from the corner of her eye.

"Understand?"

"Yes."

"Good." I let go of her hair and twisted the lid off the lotion, squeezing about half the tube on her lower back. "Now like I said," I started, unzipping my jeans and pushing them and my briefs down, my cock like steel in anticipation of what was to come. I hadn't had another woman since Sofia, and it had been too long since I'd had her.

I spread her ass cheeks and looked down at her perfect, virgin ass before sliding my cock into her pussy.

She sucked in a breath.

"Like I said." She looked at me. "You're a pain in my ass, so I'm going to be a pain in yours."

Her eyes grew wide as she registered my meaning, and I smiled, pumping slowly in and out of her pussy while smearing lotion all over her tight little asshole.

"You can't," she said, her eyes closing again.

"I told you I'd fuck every hole, didn't I?"

"But—"

"Don't worry, I'll make sure you come, but not until I'm buried deep." I slipped my thumb into her asshole as I said it, and she rounded her back, her muscles tightening at the intrusion. "Relax, let it feel good." It took her a few minutes, but she did, slowly arching her back again, letting me move my finger in and out of her as I slowly pumped my cock in her pussy. I smeared more lotion in and around her asshole, and when she was taking two fingers and moaning, I drew out of her pussy and held her hips.

She stiffened instantly, her eyelids flew open, and she tried to draw her hips away.

"Sofia." I gripped tighter and slapped her hip again to get her attention. "I'm fucking your ass now. Relax. Look at me, okay?"

She nodded.

I brought the head of my cock to her, smearing it in the lotion, rubbing and pushing until her opening stretched to let me in.

"Too big." She tried to pull away again.

"Shh."

She made some sound and I pushed in a little deeper.

"That's it. Relax. Fuck, you're so tight."

"It hurts."

"It'll feel good. I promise." I reached around to take her clit between my fingers and rubbed. Her eyes closed again, and her back arched. I pushed in a little deeper, pumping in and out slowly. "You feel good, Sofia."

"I'm going to come, Raphael."

"Come, baby. Let me feel you come."

She did, as if on demand, moaning with my cock

halfway inside her, my fingers pinching her clit, rubbing, making her come. Her body relaxed, and I pumped deeper. It took all my effort not to thrust harder, wanting to, needing to claim her, all of her. Needing to make her mine.

"You like my cock in your ass?" I asked, pumping a little harder, almost all the way inside her now. "Are you going to take my cum inside your ass?"

"Yes. Fuck, Raphael—"

She closed her eyes, coming again, and this time as she did, I pulled out and drove in harder. She gasped, arching her back, thrusting her hips against me.

"Hard," she managed, her hands flat on the bed, her face buried in the covers. "I want it hard."

I shifted my gaze to her ass, to my thick cock moving in and out of her, glistening with lotion, her cum wet on her thighs and mine. When she cried out a third time, I drove deep inside her and stilled, my cock throbbing, calling out her name as I emptied inside her, holding her hips tight, knowing in that moment what ecstasy felt like.

I LAY HOLDING SOFIA, her back to my front, not wanting to tell her what I had to tell her.

"Are you okay?" I asked.

She nodded. "How is Charlie?"

"He misses you. He sleeps beside the door as if he's waiting for you to walk in."

She turned to me. "Did you really come because you were so pissed off about my *"fuck you"*?"

"That and other things." I wasn't ready to talk about those things yet. "Sofia, you said something earlier. You said you'd never been slapped, which makes me think..." I paused, changing the way I'd ask the question. "What did you mean?"

She snorted, turning her face away again to lean her head on me. "After you left that day in the office, I confronted my grandfather about...well, everything. Long story short, he called me a whore and slapped me."

My face tightened and my hands fisted as anger engulfed me.

"That day at the hospital after the fire, when you walked back into my room, I was talking to Lina. She was very upset, that's why she'd been trying to get ahold of me. Everything you said, Raphael, it was true. Everything and then some. She'd found a notebook, a ledger. My grandfather's personal notes, account numbers. He hasn't only been stealing from us, but investors too. Millions of dollars, Raphael."

I knew that already. Probably in more detail than she realized. And I wasn't the only one. I was glad she had her back to me, not ready to tell her what I'd come to tell her. Not wanting to spoil this moment.

"I told him I wanted guardianship of Lina, or I'd go public with the truth. Turn him in."

"I need to talk to you about that, actually." Moment spoiled.

She sat up, her expression serious.

"Your grandfather was taken into custody yesterday, Sofia. He's being extradited to the States."

"What?"

"That evidence you threatened to turn in, well, someone beat you to it. As soon as he deplanes in Philadelphia, he'll be formally charged."

WE FLEW to Philadelphia the following morning. I had Sofia's suitcases in the car and had already made flight arrangements before coming to Venice.

"You didn't come to Venice because of the annulment papers, did you?" she asked as we pulled through the gates of her family home.

"No."

"What's going to happen now?"

"I don't know. The charges against your grandfather are damning. If he's smart, he'll sign a plea deal, but he will go to prison. And he'll have to pay back what he stole from investors, from you."

She shook her head, forcing a smile on her face as Lina opened the front door and stepped outside.

"I don't care about the money. Not mine, anyway. I need to make sure my sister's okay."

We parked and got out. Lawyers were already waiting for us when we walked inside. Sofia and Lina spent fifteen minutes together before she emerged alone. I'd expected tears, but instead, her face was set. Hard.

"Okay?" I asked her just outside the study doors.

"I'm fine. It's Lina I'm worried about."

"She's not joining us in there?"

"No."

We walked into the study together. Sofia knew one of the attorneys by name, Mr. Adams. He was the one to whom I'd sent the annulment paperwork. He introduced the other two, and we sat down.

"I've arranged for a criminal attorney for Marcus," Adams said. "I'll go see him myself later today, after the bail hearing.

"Will he be released until the trial?"

"It's unlikely, Sofia."

The room fell silent until Adams cleared his throat. He spoke briefly about the charges Marcus would be facing but focused more on winery business.

"All bank accounts have been frozen. Any money will be used to repay investors." He looked around the room. "The house..."

"What about the house?"

"It too will likely be seized."

"But it's been in my family—"

"It's all tied up in the business. If it were in your name, or your sister's—"

"What do you mean, exactly?"

"I mean you will have to move out."

"What? But what about the insurance money? Won't that pay—"

She stopped as Adams shook his head.

"No. And any money that's leftover will go toward your grandfather's court fees. It's all gone, Sofia. I'm sorry."

Sofia sat mute. I stood to shake hands with the men as they cleared out and walked them to the door. When I got back to the study, I found her in exactly the same place.

"What am I going to do? How am I going to take care of Lina? What about her future?"

"You're not alone, Sofia." I stood behind her chair, squeezing her shoulders, then moved around to take her hands. "I won't leave you to do this alone."

"Even the money he promised you..."

"It never was mine to begin with." I paused. "Sofia, your sister... Was she the one who turned over evidence?"

She looked at me, and it took her a long time to answer. "No."

That was the first lie Sofia told me.

The house had never felt like home to me. I didn't want to stay here and wouldn't have if it weren't for Lina. But she'd been closer to our grandfather than I ever had been. And she'd lived here for as long as she could remember.

After the very public scandal, Grandfather took the plea deal he was offered, which meant a reduced prison sentence—they took into consideration his age—in exchange for full disclosure. He'd kept meticulous notes, so much like him. In addition to the notebook Lina had found, there were three others. At least three that were uncovered. I wondered if there were more. If he'd ever tell us. The land in Italy was auctioned off, bought by Vincent Moriarty of all people. And what a deal he got. It was unfair, but it was also finished.

I saw my grandfather during his sentencing. I watched from inside the courtroom. I didn't make physical contact with him. Seeing him like that, up there looking smaller, older, I wondered if there was something wrong with me because after everything he'd done, after all the destruction and pain he'd caused, I felt regret and a sense of loss I didn't expect to feel. Maybe it was for Lina. I didn't know. But when, before they led him away, he turned to me, I didn't smile. I didn't go to him. I only watched him with sad, resigned eyes. Justice was being served, everything coming full circle—almost.

Lina had only started to draw her circle, though, when she'd turned Grandfather in.

I knew she felt that burden deeply, and although we shared everything, she never once spoke about it after that first day, after telling me it was her.

Raphael stayed throughout the proceedings and made no demands of me. We didn't share a bed, and we didn't talk about it. I felt like he grew more and more distant as I spent more and more time with Lina. I needed to be with my sister. She was hurting, and right now, she was what mattered.

Lina went to bed early on our last night at the house. The bank was set to take possession in the morning. Raphael wasn't there. He'd gone out, like he seemed to do most nights. I understood. Being here was probably a downer for him. Hell, it was a downer for me. He had the luxury of leaving. Besides, I still didn't know what would happen with us. Even after Venice, now, now that everything was gone, I wasn't sure he'd want to stay. If I'd feel good letting him, not after everything that had happened to him.

I'd been tossing and turning for hours when, at close to one in the morning, I gave up and decided to go downstairs and make myself a cup of tea. Most of the furnishings were already gone, but the kitchen table with its two chairs remained. I switched on the light over the stove and put the kettle on, listening to the silence, the stillness of an empty house. It was almost eerie, but in a way, I liked it too. I liked the calm, and I liked the dark. I felt safe, like I was hidden from view. As if no one could see me here. Maybe it was because of all the publicity in the last few weeks.

Once the kettle whistled, I reached to switch off the water. That was when I heard the key slide into the door and, startled, I looked up to find Raphael pushing it open.

He gave me a strange smile and walked into the house.

I wanted to ask where he'd been but couldn't bring myself to do so. Instead, I cleared my throat and turned my attention to the tea, unwrapped the bag, and set it in the mug.

Raphael didn't speak. I heard him open a cabinet

and take out a glass then pull out a chair and sit at the small table.

"Déjà vu."

I turned to face him. He pushed the chair across from him out with his foot.

"Sit."

He had a bottle of whiskey and had poured himself some. His cool eyes remained trained on me.

I walked over and sat down. He tipped the whiskey bottle and poured a little into my tea.

"Thanks."

"How are you holding up?" he asked.

I shrugged a shoulder and wrapped my hands around the steaming mug before meeting his gaze. "I'll be okay. Thank you for being here. I'm very grateful. You didn't have to—"

"Of course I did. What did you think, I'd walk away when things got ugly?"

I shifted my gaze back into my cup.

"Do I still make you nervous?" he asked.

When I met his gaze, I saw he had that cocky look in his eyes. "You don't scare me. Not anymore, Raphael."

"Don't I?"

I shook my head.

"Maybe I should try harder."

I wasn't in the mood for laughing. "Where were you? Where do you go at night?"

"Nowhere special."

"What kind of answer is that?"

"What kind did you want?"

"The true kind."

"I didn't lie."

"You also didn't really tell me anything."

"What do you want to know? Exactly?"

He knew what I wanted to know. He just wanted to make me say it. I drank a long swallow of whiskey-tea, squeezing my eyes shut as it burned down my throat.

"Careful. You drink too fast, and I'll have to put you to bed again."

A dirty grin lit up his face.

"Well, I wouldn't want to put you out. You've probably been busy tonight, putting someone else to bed." I didn't mean for it to come out angry like it did.

"Ah." He finished his drink and poured another. "The truth."

"I never lie to you."

"You did once."

"When?"

"You lied to protect your sister."

I felt heat flush my face. How had he known?

"I haven't put anyone to bed but you since we've been together," he said, cockiness gone.

"Oh."

"Did you really think otherwise?"

"I don't know what to think. You don't have to be

married to me anymore. I'm really more of a liability now."

"I think of you as a human being, not a liability."

"But I'm not an asset either."

"Human being. Don't feel sorry for yourself, Sofia. Shit happened to you. You survived it, and you will now move forward. Welcome to life."

"Piss off."

His face changed, hardening a little. "Be careful, sweetheart."

Sweetheart. God, I loved when he called me Sweetheart. "I'm not feeling sorry for myself."

"Then ask the questions you want to ask, and don't hide behind your fear."

"What's going to happen with us?" I blurted out.

"There you go. See, it's not so hard, is it?"

I shook my head and pushed my chair back. "It's so easy to make fun of me, isn't it? Do you just set me up for the heck of it? You just enjoy it that much? I thought you'd tired of it already."

"Sit down, and don't be so fucking dramatic."

"You know what? This *is* a dramatic time in my life. Sorry if it's annoying to you."

"Christ. Sit down, Sofia."

"I'm going to bed." I moved toward the door.

"No, you're not."

His chair scraped across the floor, and just as I reached the door, he caught my arm. He spun me around. I collided with his chest and bounced off and would have fallen if he hadn't had a hold of me.

"You are so good at running away, aren't you? You just up and walk away when it suits you. When things get tough. Let's see, this is the third time now. First, there was your trip to the winery, next was Venice, and now this."

"I wasn't running away from you. Not when it was Venice. And you had made it pretty clear you didn't want me when I went to the winery."

"And didn't I make it pretty clear that you were wrong when I came after you?"

"You never said it, Raphael."

"Don't actions matter to you? Does the fact that I came after you each time not prove anything to you? The fact that I'm here, still, through all of this? It sure as hell does to me."

I stopped fighting and bowed my head, leaning my forehead against his chest.

"Sofia, I love you. How many times can I tell you that before you believe it?"

I looked up at him, his gaze holding me, keeping me, even more powerfully than his hands held me physically.

"How in hell can I make this more obvious?"

He walked us backward until my back hit the wall.

"You know what I want to do most right now?"

He lifted me up, tilting my legs so I wrapped them around him.

"What I want to do most right now—"

He unzipped his jeans, never losing eye contact with me, shoved the nightshirt I wore up to my waist, and slid the crotch of my panties over.

"Is to drive into you against this wall."

As if to make his point, he did just that, thrusting his thick length inside me, making me gasp as he stretched me too fast.

"I want to fuck you so hard, you scream my name and wake the fucking neighborhood."

I dug my fingernails into his shoulders, breathing short and fast as he pumped before carrying me to the table to lay me on it. He tore my panties off and pushed my knees wide. With one hard thrust, he drove into me and planted his hands on either side of my face.

"I want to fuck you so hard it hurts, Sofia. I want you to feel me for days. I want you to know you belong to me. You will always belong to me."

"Raphael."

But he wouldn't let me pull him to me. Instead, he gripped my thighs and pushed them painfully wide.

"No. Feel it. Feel me. You're too fucking stubborn to fuck softly. You need it good and hard, don't you?"

He moved differently now, my pussy so wet, he slid in and out easily.

"Is that right?"

The cocky grin was back on his face.

"You need it hard?"

"Yes."

"That's a good girl," he said. "Truth. Always truth."

He drew out of me.

"No," I whined, looking at his thick cock wet with my arousal.

He grabbed hold of my hair and dragged me down to my knees.

"On your knees, Sofia. Suck my cock. Fucking worship it if you want it inside you again."

He didn't give me a moment to think, to react, not a single second. Instead, with his hand gripping my hair, he slid himself into my willing mouth, thrusting in and out fast and hard. True to his word, he wanted me to feel him, to know he owned me. To know he liked hurting me a little.

"I should come all over your pretty little face."

Instead, though, he drew himself out of my mouth and lifted me to my feet. He claimed my mouth, moaning as he kissed me, his tongue inside, one hand in my hair, the other kneading my ass.

He pulled back and, without ever taking his eyes from mine, ripped my nightshirt off.

"You need to be naked more often."

He looked down at me, leaning forward so he could take one nipple into his mouth, then the other, sucking hard, drawing out each nipple in turn with his teeth.

"I need you inside me," I managed, reaching for him, drawing him to me. "Please."

He straightened, grinning, and bent me over the table. Gripping my hips in either hand, he spread me open and slid his cock into my pussy and his finger into my ass.

"Fuck me, Raphael. Hard. Make me come."

He did. No more words, just fucking. Just taking and owning and hurting me a little, making it feel so damn good. He swelled inside me, and when he wrapped one hand around the back of my neck and squeezed, I came. I came so hard that when I closed my eyes, I saw stars, and when he squeezed harder, I thought I'd die, I'd stop breathing, that I'd never be able to catch my breath again.

We slid to the floor together, Raphael cradling me in his arms, holding me to him, my head resting against his chest. Our breathing slowed down in time, but when I tried to move, he wouldn't let me. He just held me to him, and I clung tight, closed my eyes, and turned my face into his chest.

"Was that clear enough that I want you?" he asked eventually.

"Was it clear enough that I want you?" I asked in turn.

He carried me upstairs and into my old bedroom, where he'd been sleeping. There, he laid me on the bed and lay down beside me, holding me to him like he had the first night we'd slept together, just slept together after I'd found him in that cellar. He held me like he couldn't let me go, and I knew I would never be able to let him go.

EPILOGUE

Spring, One Year Later

She never did sign those annulment papers. My stubborn, beautiful wife.

I stood drinking coffee at the kitchen window, watching Sofia talk to one of the workers. Charlie, full grown and weighing eighty pounds, never left her side.

We'd come back to Tuscany a few days after the bank took possession of the house in Philadelphia. Lina had come with us and would be starting her final year at a school in Florence geared toward gifted musicians.

Thanks to their grandfather's greed, Sofia and

Lina had lost everything. Guardia Winery no longer existed, except as an example of corruption and destruction.

Lina never spoke about any of it. She rarely mentioned her grandfather at all. Sofia worried, but Italy was a good move for her. It got her away from everything, the past, the publicity, gave her anonymity again, and hopefully would give her a fresh start.

I finished my coffee and set the mug in the sink before walking outside. Sofia waved when she saw me approach.

We'd replanted the vineyard. The ground was rich after the fire, and although it would take a few years before the vines yielded grapes for wine, they would come. We'd reestablish the Villa Bellini Winery as it was before my mother's time. I'd already ordered and hung the new sign over the gates, and, for the first time in a very long time, felt excited. Felt like I had something to look forward to. A future.

Sofia met me halfway, Charlie on her heels.

"You snuck out of bed early," I said, drawing her in for a hug and kissing her. That was another thing. I could sleep again. And it felt like I was making up for lost years.

"It's you who sleeps like the dead these days."

"It's Saturday. I thought we could spend the morning in bed."

"You want to spend every morning in bed."

"That's your fault, sweetheart," I said, grabbing her ass.

We walked toward the chapel, Sofia growing a little quieter.

"You okay?" I had a feeling I knew what was coming.

"Lina's decided to go back to the States after graduation, but she wants to take a year off before continuing her education."

"That's fine. She's young. And she probably needs the space, honestly."

"She's not even going to the audition, Raphael."

I knew that. She'd told me before she'd told Sofia, knowing her sister would be disappointed.

"She'll get another one." With a recommendation from her piano teacher, she'd secured an audition at a prestigious music school.

"She's going to miss her opportunity. This is a full scholarship."

"Give her space. She'll be fine."

She stopped as we neared the chapel. "You knew, didn't you?"

I looked at her. Truth. Always truth. I wouldn't lie to her ever again. "Yes."

She dropped my hand and walked away, shaking her head.

"Sofia." I followed her inside.

"She trusts you more than me."

I caught up with her and turned her to face me. "No. She's just using me as a sounding board before coming to you."

I followed her gaze around the chapel, which Damon and I had almost completely restored. Damon. That was another thing. He'd grown more distant in the last year.

"Am I that bad?" she asked, sitting down in the last pew.

"You're that good. She loves you and doesn't want to hurt you, but this is her life, and you need to let her go. Remember what you said to me once."

"*If you let the past go, maybe it will let you go.* Will those words ever stop haunting me?"

"Maybe that's what she needs now. Her guilt at turning over evidence—"

"She shouldn't feel guilty. Grandfather is the only one who should have any remorse."

"Well, life isn't fair, is it? I thought you got that by now."

She shrugged a shoulder.

"I have something for you." I reached into my pocket and pulled out a small box.

She looked at it, then reached out to touch it tentatively. "What is it?"

Her eyes were already misty when she met mine. She knew.

"Our wedding, although beautiful, it wasn't right."

She blinked and lowered her lashes momentarily.

"And you're too stubborn to sign those annulment papers."

"I want to be married to you, stupid."

I opened the box, glanced inside, and, smiling, turned it toward her.

She gasped, her hand moving to her mouth.

"No more ring of thorns." Inside was a beautiful platinum band with a diamond solitaire set in the center.

She threw her arms around me, her tears wet on my face as she hugged me.

"It's beautiful. It's so beautiful."

"I want to do it right," I said, holding her, drawing her back to wipe her tears away. "Here. We'll do it here. Just family. We'll speak our vows properly and make it right." I took the ring out of the box and looked at her.

She extended her left hand, and I slid the original wedding band off and replaced it with the new one.

This was it. This was my blank slate, my starting over. Our starting over. The black iron ring replaced with bright, shining platinum. From dark to light. Sofia and I together had somehow moved from darkness into light.

"Will you marry me again, sweetheart?" I asked, my vision blurred when I looked up at her.

"I will. I'd marry you again a hundred times."

The End

Keep Reading for a sample from Corruptible, Damon Amado's story!

"Take it off."

I pointed to the bathroom, wanting her to wash the makeup off her face, unsure why I felt so angry, so fucking possessive. But it's like when it came to her, I lost all control.

She looked like she wanted to say something, maybe ask me what the fuck was wrong with me, but instead, she obeyed. Sliding off her coat, she handed it to me, then went into the bathroom and closed the door behind her. I watched that closed door, standing like an idiot holding her coat, still wearing mine, listening to the water run.

Shaking myself out of it, I set her coat over the back of a chair and put mine on top.

I went into the kitchen and grabbed the bottle of whiskey and two glasses before returning to the living area. I poured us each a drink and took my glass to the window, where I gazed out onto the street at the few people strolling outside, not seeing anything at all. I swallowed the contents of my glass and set it down on the side table.

Absently, I rolled up my shirt sleeves before pouring myself a second drink and sitting on the couch to wait for her, knowing exactly what I wanted to do.

Knowing how wrong it would be.

Lina emerged a few minutes later, her hair out of its bun and in one long braid over her shoulder. She stood there, not moving, letting me take her in, in her dress and four-inch heels, only that fine silk standing between us, keeping me from seeing.

And I wanted to see.

I wanted more badly than anything to see.

"I poured you a drink." My voice sounded foreign to my ears.

She looked to where I gestured, opened her mouth, but closed it again. She crossed the room while I watched her and picked up the glass, then forced it down all at once, squeezing her eyes shut as it burned her throat.

I watched her. Couldn't take my eyes off her. And I liked that the whiskey burned. I wanted to punish her.

"You lied to me," I said.

She blinked, having the grace to look away momentarily, not denying what I said. We remained silent, studying each other.

"Take off your dress, Lina." I took a sip of my whiskey and leaned back, crossing one leg over the other.

"My dress?"

"Take it off."

I saw her nipples pebble beneath the silk as her throat worked to swallow. The air in the room suddenly seemed charged with electricity, alive and sparking and ready to electrocute us both.

Lina moved slowly, reaching her hands to either strap and, with her eyes locked on mine, she pulled the dress down to her waist and paused there, letting me look at her, at her small, high breasts with their dark, pebbled nipples.

I swallowed another sip of my whiskey and nodded for her to go on ignoring the voice that was asking me what the fuck I thought I was doing.

Hooking her thumbs into either side of the dress, she pushed it over her hips and let it fall to the floor. She stepped out of it, shoving it aside as if it were a scrap of nothing. She stood with her arms at her sides wearing black lace panties, thigh-high stockings, and high heels.

I let my gaze travel over her, hovering at the slit of her shaved sex visible beneath the lace. I then dragged it back up over her flat belly, pelvic bones jutting out—too skinny—and up over breasts I wanted to take whole into my mouth and suck on until she called out my name. Until she begged me for more.

I forced my gaze to hers.

"Do you do this for him?" I had to ask. I had no choice.

Wide green eyes stared back at me. She knew exactly what I meant. Who I meant.

She didn't open her mouth to speak. Didn't try to explain anything. But she shook her head once.

No.

And I couldn't put words to the relief I felt at that knowledge.

My cock pressed hard against my trousers. I uncrossed my legs and set my glass aside.

"Come here."

She obeyed, moving slowly.

I leaned forward, and once she was close enough, I took her hands and drew her to stand between my knees. Close up, I could smell her sex. Her arousal. A musky, light scent. I kept hold of her tattooed arm and traced the flowers with the fingers of my other hand.

I wanted to punish her. To hurt her for lying to me. To hurt her for that man having touched her. For wearing that dress. For showing herself to them, to all those men and women in that club who watched her with lust in their eyes. Who wanted her.

I wanted to hurt her for all of it.

The hairs on her arms stood on end, and her breathing came short, choppy. She had to feel what I was feeling. Had to know what was coming.

Keeping hold of her wrist, I drew her to the side and pulled her down across my lap. With one hand on the base of her skull, I pushed her face into the seat of the couch and looked at her there, over my lap, naked, or almost so. I studied her tattoo for a long time. She didn't move.

Her back tightened with my first touch, but then she relaxed again.

I took my time caressing every inch of her, every tiny bud inked into her skin, finding a small bird—a robin—I hadn't noticed before. I was suddenly, irrationally jealous of the man or woman who'd held the needle to mark her, jealous of anyone else who had ever touched her. Who had ever looked at her or at these flowers. All these fucking flowers.

My cock throbbed. I needed release. I could jerk off right now, come all over her, mark her as mine. I could come just looking at her like this.

I adjusted my legs, shifting my gaze to her ass now lifted higher than the rest of her. Did she know what I intended? Taking hold of the top of her lace panties, I dragged them down to bare her ass.

Lina shifted slightly, made a small sound, but remained bent over my lap. She didn't move to cover herself.

I took her in, her pale, pristine ass, the shadow of her sex between her cheeks, the scent of her.

I knew that if I touched her now, she'd be wet.

She'd be dripping.

I knew it. I could see it.

Hell, I could smell it.

But I couldn't think about that. Not yet. Not if I didn't want to blow right in my pants.

My fingers caressed her thigh, slowly rising to her hip, circling her ass.

"You are so fucking beautiful." My voice came out hoarse, like it had caught in my throat. "And so fucking bad for me."

She shifted, and when I glanced at her, I found her resting her cheek on the couch, watching me. She arched her back then, offering herself to me. Offering her ass for punishment.

"Don't look at me," I said. I had to. I couldn't have her see me. Not now. Not right now.

She turned her face away but kept her body prone, her ass tilted upward. Anxiety rolled off her, but also something else. Desire. Want. Need.

We both wanted this.

Maybe we both needed it.

Gripping her waist to keep her steady, I raised my hand, all the while warnings sounded in my head, warnings I would not heed. It was out of my control. Tonight, this, me, Lina...it was all out of my fucking control.

I struck.

One-click Corruptible Now!

THANK YOU

Thanks for reading *Dishonorable!* I hope you enjoyed Raphael and Sofia's story and would consider leaving a review at the store where you purchased this book.

Click here to sign up for my newsletter to receive new release news and updates!

Like my FB Author Page to keep updated on news and giveaways!

I have a FB Fan Group where I share exclusive teasers, giveaways and just fun stuff. Probably TMI :) It's called The Knight Spot. I'd love for you to join us! Just click here!

Benedetti Mafia World

Salvatore: a Dark Mafia Romance

Dominic: a Dark Mafia Romance

Sergio: a Dark Mafia Romance

The Benedetti Brothers Box Set (Contains Salvatore, Dominic and Sergio)

Killian: a Dark Mafia Romance

Giovanni: a Dark Mafia Romance

The Amado Brothers

Dishonorable

Corruptible

Unhinged

Standalone Dark Romance

Descent

Deviant

Beautiful Liar

Retribution

Theirs To Take

Captive, Mine

Alpha

Given to the Savage

Taken by the Beast

Claimed by the Beast

Captive's Desire

Protective Custody

Amy's Strict Doctor

Taming Emma

Taming Megan

Taming Naia

Reclaiming Sophie

The Firefighter's Girl

Dangerous Defiance

Her Rogue Knight

Taught To Kneel

Tamed: the Roark Brothers Trilogy

ACKNOWLEDGMENTS

Cover Design by CT Cover Creations

Cover Photography By Wander Aguiar

ABOUT THE AUTHOR

USA Today bestselling author of contemporary romance, Natasha Knight specializes in dark, tortured heroes. Happily-Ever-Afters are guaranteed, but she likes to put her characters through hell to get them there. She's evil like that.

www.natasha-knight.com
natasha-knight@outlook.com